SILENT DEPTHS

REILY GARRETT

Acknowledgments

To Siobhan Caughey, for reading through my rough drafts. Your perceptions are spot on and always appreciated in delving into a character's mind. First drafts are always the roughest, but is also where changes in a character's direction take root.

To Rosie Amber for an in-depth assessment of character and plot, thank you for all your help. You can find her blog and services at rosieamber.wordpress.com/beta-reading-service.

To RE Hargrave, for editing. Thank you for spotting the loopholes and answering endless grammar questions.

To my readers, each one of you who selects and reads one of my books, thank you for the opportunity to share my work. If you've enjoyed it, please consider leaving a review. They are the best way to help your author share her work.

Chapter One

Life made sense when reduced to numbers. Equations followed rules and remained constant. Mathematics didn't shoot bullets or tear through flesh like the sharp edge of a blade. It also didn't confuse her like the strange metaphors often spewed by her adviser.

Callie's world dissolved into chaos with the turn of a key. A mind for facts and logic hampered her ability to balance the current pandemonium as snow-laden whirlwinds hindered her view of freedom on the other side of the chain-link fence.

An impressive storm whirled its frozen burden in quarter-sized flakes, the misty veil a soft and frigid camouflage for escape. Sharp-edged holly leaves further crippled her scrutiny of the facility's front.

Concentration on the standard model of particle physics in Langrangian form didn't settle the acid roiling in her stomach. It inspired mental chalkboards splattered with blood.

"Okay, Callie, we follow the plan. Twenty seconds to cross the courtyard then navigate the breach in the fence. Through the woods and we're home free. Sebastian's waiting with the car running," Jake's whispered instructions wiped away any hesitation.

"Freedom..." Her dream of independence was so close yet threatened to melt like the fat icy crystals liquefying on her cheeks.

"No more schedules, no more timed activities, no one telling you what to do and when to do it. We'll write our own ending to this fairytale, Cinderella." Jake's optimism lacked his usual flare. He'd jettisoned his easygoing veneer in favor of his Special Forces persona.

She swallowed hard.

"What's a fairytale, and who's Cinderella?" For the umpteenth time, two realities clashed. Her structured existence contrasted Jake's life of wonder and danger, excitement and apprehension, highs and lows she'd never imagined existed.

A sad smile accompanied his, "Later, kiddo."

They'd planned down to the smallest detail—until fate reared its head. An unexpected storm upgraded to blizzard status and a surprise visit from the administrator conspired to keep her prisoner.

Each setback necessitated a fluid plan, accommodated on the fly.

Timing remained key to survival while the erratic, pounding pulse in her ears rivaled a snare drum's buzz roll, an executioner's beat. Before the adrenaline in her blood circulated again, she'd be free or dead, depending on which card destiny threw her way.

Crouched between Jake on the left and Franklin on the right, she took a deep breath and waited for the signal. Both men risked their lives to set her free yet asked for nothing in return.

"Whatever happens, don't look back and don't hesitate, regardless of what you see or hear," Franklin issued orders per routine. Years in the military merged certain traits with his basic character. A glance at his watch then around the corner, he assessed the building's front.

Wind shrieked through specimen trees dotting the courtyard and offered the illusion of cover. Neither would stop a bullet.

A shimmer of perspiration glazed Jake's forehead. Steel in his gaze matched the resolve of his harsh whispers.

Jake gave her shoulder a gentle squeeze. "We're in this together, Callie. This is our best shot. Let's go. It's time to set you free."

Omission of *flaxen-haired warbler* attested to his degree of concentration. No quips, no banter, just streamlined focus.

Her mind defaulted to calculating estimated distances while factoring in wind resistance, depth of snow, and the time needed to reach the tree line beyond the fence.

The perimeter guard pulled up his collar against the frigid wind in passing. She wondered if he knew exactly who, and what, he secured.

Anxiety innervated and stimulated her senses, twisted higher by the potential for failure. Unable to distinguish between the urge to run or freeze, she was caught in a limbo of her biological making.

Static squelch of the second perimeter guard's radio faded with distance. Each circuit of the border yielded a like check-in. Stereo came from the electrical channel noise of a tower watchman's walkie-talkie above.

Yet something felt— *off*.

The facility's floodlights defined the unmistakable profile of the rooftop sentry with light glinting off the barrel of his automatic rifle.

She'd never made friends with any of the guards and now understood the reason for the no-contact rule with most of the facility's employees. Killing a friend was different from shooting a stranger.

With Franklin's tug on her hand, she bolted across the pristine courtyard bordering the institution. Fear urged her to go faster.

Islands of evergreen shrubbery rose in stark relief against the thickening snow. Mother Nature's tempest blanketed the earth with its slippery covering to define every step.

Even if the alarm sounded, Jake assured her a collaborator would rise to their defense. Ground-level perimeter guards were the only wildcards.

Seconds into her nightmare bid for freedom, an earsplitting siren blasted the silence.

Jake rushed forward with a stronger grip on her upper arm. Additional pressure compelled her to tap into unrealized energy reserves.

Her life changed in ten strides.

Wind droning through tree limbs didn't swallow low, intermittent thwacks nearby—like snapping rubber bands stretched tight. Franklin stumbled into her path then sidestepped.

Jake's harsh lateral jerk generated a brief shuffle-step that almost toppled them all. A small strop of light flashed over the harsh set of his jaw and grim determination as he met her gaze.

"You okay, Franklin?" The wind's howl consumed Jake's harsh whisper.

"Keep going, Callie. Don't stop. I'm okay." Franklin's strained voice galvanized her determination even as he tugged harder.

Multiple floodlights dissected the yard into a legion of smaller constructs. Mutating, amorphous shapes cavorted as the brilliant blazes cut swaths back and forth in their search for live prey.

Rats running through a shifting maze flashed through her thoughts.

A stuttering burst of automatic weapon fire brought the lights' search to a quick death. More shots sounded as Jake released her to pull back the cut section of fence.

Franklin's grip on her other arm convulsed before sliding to her wrist, then releasing. "Go, Jake. Get her out of here. I'll hold them off as long as I can."

Howling winds tangled her long braid on jagged edges of metal as Jake thrust her through the small opening. Razor-sharp edges tore at her coat sleeve and dug a furrow in her right shoulder even as she struggled to the other side.

Franklin's wound brought a new terror and a dose of confusion to choke her sob. "Franklin?" With her mind shutting down, her body progressed in robotic fashion, higher neural networks preventing support.

In the weak light, dark maroon blooming on Franklin's side widened under applied pressure as he slumped against the fence. Several harsh gasps ended in a choking sound.

"Go, Callie. The perimeter guards will be on us any second." Jake's solid yank on her shirttail freed it from the heavy mesh wire holding her prisoner.

"C'mon, Franklin. We're in this together." She couldn't leave him behind.

Fumbling attempts at helping Jake through the manhole-sized diameter met with a slippery grip on his upper sleeve. His face twisted in pain as he briefly closed his eyes. "Go, Callie, go. I'm right behind you. Sebastian's in the car—through the woods. Straight ahead, there's a deer path. Take this pen light."

Sticky wetness encompassed the cold metal to make her recoil in the waking nightmare. The scent of pennies triggered her imagination before a gust of wind ripped her scream away. This wasn't the planned scenario.

"How bad is Franklin hurt? We have to help him." Mid-December Minnesota wind snatched her words back.

Jake had already turned to his partner.

The slight beam of her light exposed Franklin's clenched jaw. "No. Damn it. No time. Get Callie out of here." Franklin's torso twisted as he pushed Jake's hands away. "Go. Don't let this be in vain. Call my wife. Tell her—Plan B." From beneath his jacket, Franklin withdrew a gun. It shook in his hand.

Tears streamed down Callie's cheeks to merge with snowflakes. She'd never seen death, a concept as foreign as standing outside the fence's perimeter.

Shouting from the left foreshadowed their immediate threat. Partial obscurity of approaching guards transformed them into phantoms, their progress tempered by driving wind and snow. The loyal rooftop sentry who'd shot out the spotlights was no longer visible and unable to help.

Her worst nightmare rose like a golem from one of Jake's favorite stories.

Franklin raised his gun and fired into the veiled night.

She screamed.

"Callie. We move. Now!" The intensity in Jake's voice struck a new chord in her mind. The fact he feared for their lives rocketed another surge of energy through her quaking limbs.

Without hesitation, she clutched his hand, blood-soaked fingers a reminder of the devastation her existence wrought. Aided by providence, they raced in a crouched bid for wooded protection.

Behind her, Franklin's pistol barked one more time.

Neither Jake nor Franklin had included her in the planning stages of the escape, claiming they didn't want her responsible. They wanted her new life built on a clean slate.

I just condemned Franklin to death.

The route from her quarters to the fence line had involved four men, one already dead. She shuddered at the fate of others if not able to slip away.

Chapter Two

Three days of grueling travel pushed Sebastian's limits to the point of gnawing on his tenderized cheek. They'd all sacrificed to set the genius free. At least he wasn't buried deep in the woods.

The fourth member of their team remained unreachable, whether through intent or death was undetermined.

"How far east are we going, Jake? Not that I'm sad about leaving Minnesota behind." Sebastian wondered what great contributions Callie would make to society, and if they could wipe away the façade of guilt smothering her aura.

"Not quite to the end of the map. I won't drop us in the Atlantic."

Cryptic as ever, for our own protection.

"The ocean? I've never seen it. Can we go, Jake?"

From the back seat, Callie looked up at Jake with such hope Sebastian had to turn his gaze from the rearview mirror. So many *normal* things she'd never experienced.

"Absolutely. Come spring, we'll spend a whole week collecting seashells, building sand castles, and eating Thrasher's French fries."

Limitless questions about life equaled a painful reminder of her innocence and unique upbringing. Each day she soaked up more of Jake's colorful language and euphemisms, but remained far beyond the learning curve.

"Can you teach me to swim? Do you think Ray would look for us along the coast?"

"Sure, an introduction to Flipper might prove as entertaining as it would be fun."

"Who's Flipper? It that one of your old teammates?"

"No, hon. it's just an old movie reference. We can watch it when we're settled. And don't worry, we'll be fine. We've put a thousand miles between us so far and still have a way to go. Right now, I think we could all use a diversion. How about it, Sebastian? I think it's time to give our little warbler another driving lesson. The sun will be up soon and it's light enough to see. Plus, we've seen no traffic for over an hour."

Thick woods straddled the narrow, paved road. They'd traveled secondary and tertiary routes, favoring seclusion over small towns and highways with traffic cams.

"Really? Yes, absolutely. Thank you. This is better than learning to rollerblade."

"Why not? The average teen learns to drive at sixteen, and she's well passed that." Sebastian grinned while pulling over and cutting the engine. Discrepancy between childlike wonder and computer-like genius kept them all on the brink of discovery. They had much to learn about Callie as she discovered her new world.

He and Jake both anticipated the discovery of something extraordinary in the young woman. They recognized it in the way she'd suddenly pause in the middle of speech, her mind whirring away at incredible speeds as she nodded then continued at a different pace.

Reality brought her down to earth each time she realized how far behind the eight ball she stood. The most explosive find equaled the internet. Her thirst for knowledge surpassed any force they'd ever witnessed.

Jake took the front seat beside her as Sebastian slid into the back and looked through the search history of their laptop. Curiosity overrode exhaustion.

"Okay. Seat belt, mirror, and seat adjustment, check." She cranked the engine and slowly accelerated while calculating the vehicle's speed.

"Ya know, I see wood burning. Jake chuckled.

"Fire? You see a fire?" Callie slammed on the brakes, the force throwing them all forward. "Where? I don't see it?"

"No, no. It's a metaphor. Tell ya what. From now on, I'll warn you before I use one. Okay? You're calculating our speed but you *could* just look at the speedometer." Jake pointed to the dash, knowing how her mind worked.

Callie nodded. "Will you let me fly a plane?" she asked, her focus on the road ahead as she again accelerated.

"Um, we'll talk about that in a few months." Jake grinned and shrugged a shoulder. "Though, I don't see why not."

"Callie, I see you've added to your file on Ray." In the back seat, Sebastian opened new windows to study her research into the Think Tank."

"Yes, thanks to the starting point you gave me. I think he believes he's safe titling vehicles and property under shell corporations and offshore accounts. I hacked his vehicle's computer system and can pinpoint it at any time. I'd like to steer him off a cliff. Still, the bulk of what I wanted is locked in that damn standalone we never accessed."

"Time for that later. Everyone has a flaw, and we'll find his. Though I didn't realize he was originally from Maryland." Jake turned the vehicle's heat up. "Might actually make him easier to nail down, the sleazy bastard."

Callie settled into silence after navigating a tight S-turn, then slammed on the brakes again. Tires squealed and the vehicle skidded sideways.

Sebastian's laptop skid to the floor and his soda spilled as he set it in the cup holder. "What now? I don't—" Despite the distance traveled, the night carried an ominous noir feel.

A small doe just missed the front fender as it trailed another bounding across the road.

From the corner of his eye, Sebastian saw a large buck—its collision course with his door assured. Raising his arms in reflex, he waited for the ten-point rack to crash through the window and into his chest.

Impact didn't occur.

When he opened his eyes and gazed left, the belly of the buck sailed down the other side to land and stumble-step into the woods. "How?"

Callie shoved the gear in park and pivoted in her seat. "Wow! He hopped right over us. Guess adrenaline does the same thing for animals as humans." Thin trails of blood dripped from her nose until she grabbed a tissue and wiped it. "Damn. I hit my face on the steering wheel."

"We're in an SUV. No deer could clear us like that," Sebastian countered. "Even if he had super strength, he was too close and would've had to make a straight vertical hop."

The animal's momentum should've carried it through the glass to impale me.

"Well, that one did. He must've had the advantage of leaping from the bank." Callie pulled onto the road and accelerated quickly. "Jake, you said we could talk about the other girls."

Sebastian swiveled in his seat. The bank wasn't steep. Its grade was gentle and wide, not to mention he could've touched fur had his window been open.

Jake's frown preceded a long indrawn breath. "I know you want to free the others, but we need to set priorities. First, we need to settle into new identities. Second, we have a lot of research to do. Your skill with computers will shorten that step."

"Okay. I know. Patience. It's just that—I want to help them."

Sebastian stared at the road behind them but lacked sufficient light to estimate the height of the bank. Rounding another bend in the road closed the debate.

* * * *

Callie pulled in a deep breath. Life wasn't as simple as it seemed. She'd almost hit a deer.

The small herd's abrupt appearance hadn't given her time to stop. The last of the trio's hooves brushed the top of their vehicle. Each new learning experience came with unseen responsibilities, the likes of which she hadn't imagined.

"Callie. You all right?" Jake asked.

When she glanced over, he offered his handkerchief.

"Pull over. I'll drive."

Taking the cloth, she applied pressure. "I'm fine. I smacked my nose on the wheel when I hit the brake so hard. Lesson learned. You did tell me not to drive with my knees in my chest." To reinforce her point, she pulled the tissue away to reveal no fresh blood. "See? No more."

"Yeah, okay. We'll be stopping just ahead for a few hours' sleep, if you're sure you don't want to swap now."

His eyes told a different story. He had to suspect she held secrets. To date, he'd never pushed and never asked direct questions. She wasn't ready to discuss something she couldn't explain.

Those days would soon end. She'd have to extend full trust to the men who'd rescued her or strike out on her own to keep them safe. They'd risked their lives, but it didn't give her the right to continue putting them in danger.

If they understood the extent of her freakish nature, would they abandon her or take her back to Ray?

"Callie, there's a narrow dirt road about two miles ahead. You'll take a right. We're almost there." Jake pointed to a spot on his burner phone's navigation screen.

"So, who set up the safe house? You've not had the time..." In the back seat, Sebastian wiped his sticky hands on a towel as her words trailed off.

"An old friend. We'll sleep a few hours this, then push off and meet up with Nate and the rest of the old team tonight."

"I've never heard you mention Nate. College friend?" Sebastian asked.

"Military, like you Sebastian. Before you came aboard. You know the old adage. Keep one favor in reserve. He used to be a ball buster, but if you want a job done right, well, he's your man."

"A favor no one else knows about," Sebastian added. "Good planning."

"Callie, I know you don't understand what Christmas is all about, but I had a special present delivered here for you late last night."

"Really?" But, I don't have anything for you or Sebastian." She'd do anything to avoid disappointing her mentors.

"How could you?" Jake reached over and lightly squeezed her knee. "I want you to enjoy all the wonders life has to offer, and this one is very special."

The concepts of faith and religion didn't make sense to her, but the excitement zinging through her nerves wiped away the possibility of sleep in the coming hours. "Can we put Christmas decorations up? Like the lights on houses we've passed?"

"As soon as we get settled. This will be your first Christmas, and I'm setting a new precedent, a new tradition."

"I wouldn't mind driving again." Callie ducked her head and scrunched her nose.

"We'll see. You may change your mind." Jake's cryptic smile held secrets of his own. "We've avoided cities and large towns. You have no idea how bad traffic can be. I want you fresh and well-rested when we reach our destination." He patted her shoulder in a friendly gesture.

"I'm going to sing tonight?"

"Yep. Your first gig. It'll provide distraction for you and an opportunity for me to connect with old friends." Jake hooked a thumb over his shoulder. "There'll be two vehicles waiting for us at this house ahead. Sebastian, you'll take Callie to Ambrosia tonight while I tie off some loose ends."

"Callie and I'll wait for you in appropriate gear."

"Um, Sebastian, keep in mind her inexperience with society. We're stretching things a bit thin what with meeting Nate at his nightclub, but I didn't want to take any chances, and he said he'd keep things very low key with just a few select members present. Ray would never think to look for us there."

"Do the least expected as always. And don't worry. I'll take care of her, Jake."

Callie yawned, the adrenaline of her near-accident and hours searching the internet wearing off.

"We make quite a team, don't we?" Jake swiveled in his seat to address Sebastian.

The younger man chuckled. "Yup. Always have, always will."

Improvisation of stealing the old SUV had proven an inspiration for the last leg of their journey. The concept of theft was as foreign as causing harm to another. She understood Jake's reasoning for keeping her in the dark, but the time had come to take equal risk in their quest.

She was stronger than anyone suspected.

Chapter Three

Nate's evening deteriorated in exponential fashion with the addition of the yipping German shepherd pup in his office. Dogs weren't the problem. He loved them, even helped his brother train them.

Dogs in his club entailed a different matter. He'd broken his own rules in hiring an unknown to sing and prayed the evening didn't devolve into chaos. Always a sucker for an old Army buddy.

Early arriving couples mingled near the bar, deep in conversation. Snippets include excitement over the invite for a *special* evening. Members of his old team stood on stage with their heads together in conversation. The image spelled trouble, like a team meeting prior to an op. Jake's head full of short wavy hair appeared in the middle as he made his way to the stage exit.

Damn.

Some vagary of fate forewarned he was about to play chicken with a deadly enemy.

A dog in his office and an ex-teammate drawing him into the middle of an op? He'd left Jake and the military in his rearview five years prior and hadn't looked back.

Confidence radiated from every pore with Jake's approach, his smile concealing thoughts of a complicated mind at work. His gaze scanned the room even as he nodded to Nate.

"Long time, no see. Thanks for arranging this for us."

"You said this matter is dire and concerns national security. Why come to me? Why not someone on active duty? And why gather the old team?"

"You'll see soon enough." Jake tilted his head to the side and shrugged.

"A band? Really? Never imagined Blade with a musical instrument. That's like giving a high-end calculator to a toddler and expecting answers in advanced trigonometry." Nate's anxiety ratcheted up the longer his friend remained quiet.

"Seemed like a good idea at the time." Jake's contemplative silence and crumpled brow boded ill.

"For the record, I didn't have time to purchase ear plugs in bulk. I hope your *singer* doesn't throw a fit when her mic malfunctions. We erased torture from our evening's entertainment years ago."

Jake's grin boded ill. "Right to the point as usual. I respect that, and thank you for all this."

"How could I refuse when you spouted national security issues, weapons of mass destruction, and a radical arm of the government?"

"Oh, my friend. I'm going to fry your concept of life in a heartbeat." Jake laughed until wiping the corners of his eyes.

The man always knew how to hold back vital intel and rarely showed emotion. The unexpected outburst didn't sit well.

"Tonight's visit is just a precaution, and a forewarning. I'll explain in a bit. First, I want you to meet Callie. To say she's special is like calling our team... adequate. You'll see. Do you have the Rubik's cubes I requested?"

"Yeah, puzzle cubes with the colors scrambled. Is this some sort of trick?" Nate searched his old teammate's face for signs indicating a practical joke. "Why so many?"

Since arrival at the club, Nate hadn't had the opportunity to talk with his old teammates. Scheduling issues had kept him busy in Conner's office defending the necessity of the crated, noisy pup in the next room. He looked forward to catching up and finding out what new trouble they'd found.

"Ah, my friend, you'll have answers soon. You're about to witness one of nature's miracles. Naïve and sheltered, yes—but talented in ways I suspect she's never let anyone witness. I hope to soon discover what she's holding back."

Hair on the back of Nate's neck rose. He surveyed the room, wondering just how his life would venture off the rails. Instinct told him it would be fast and furious.

"Thanks for putting on this spread." Jake snagged a cinnamon confection from the large banquet and murmured his pleasure.

"When you said this was a quick stop, I figured you wouldn't have taken much time to eat. Can't have your debut singer passing out from low blood sugar."

Scented candles on each table furthered the intimate atmosphere. The unexpected—a glint of light reflecting off the cache of colorful, six-faced cubes sitting conspicuously beside a bowl of chips.

"I don't remember you showing such holiday spirit." Jake nodded to the woodland scene theme including the Christmas tree and fresh swags between wall sconces. Colorful mini-lights completed the festive atmosphere.

"Conner's idea." Nate's eldest brother proved to be a force of nature when set on a path.

Small sofas and intimate seating areas lined the long walls of the club and surrounded dozens of small tables in the center. He and his brothers had built to particular specifications with less concern for finances than comfort. The result provided a relaxing sanctuary for couples wanting a night to unwind.

"Callie has such a long road to enlightenment. I needed this. We both do."

Tonight's audition included a simple meet-and-greet with mellow music, good food, and a few trusted friends.

If his ex-girlfriend's memory didn't linger, Nate could find respite in the familiar and join in the festivities. Meanwhile, he'd promised to assist Jake in any way possible, as long as he didn't end up on a protection detail.

"Please tell me she won't sing Christmas carols all night. I don't think I could handle it."

"No. She doesn't understand Christmas yet."

Nate's thoughts stuttered in turning to his old friend. "What?"

"I'll explain in due time."

Within the next quarter hour, a few dozen people would mingle, dance, and discuss whatever fancied them at that moment. New bonds would form along with the strengthening of old.

And I hired an unvetted singer to perform. His three brothers would lynch him before midnight.

"How does a cognizant adult not know about Christmas?"

A strangled gasp from behind alerted him to imminent disaster.

"What—*Oomph*." Nate's agile reflexes weren't swift enough to pivot. Air whooshed from Nate's lungs after decidedly soft and feminine body parts collided against his flank. A forgotten warmth stirred in his soul.

The episode unfolded at a snail's pace and demonstrated an awkwardness not experienced in years. The force of impact and tangle of long limbs with his own dictated balance and grace devolve into a klutzy and painful plummet to the hardwood floor.

Instead of wind milling his arms to restore equilibrium, he reached for the shapely torso intent on laying him low, to steady her position. A heavy mass of blonde curls disguised the curve of her waist as his grip tightened.

A flash of insight reasoned he couldn't right either of their positions. Instinct bound him to twist his body and take the brunt of the fall. He drew her snug against him to avoid an elbow to the solar plexus.

Descent existed as a split-second in time, enough for his mind to register the extra weight against his body. He'd participated in complex missions around the globe, but an elfin creature covered in blonde waves would lay him low.

As if in slow motion, and instead of gravity pulling them toward the floor, some inexplicable force drew them vertical.

In briefly closing his eyes, the scent hit him, sandalwood and tropical flowers. Golden strands of silken locks sliding across his face enticed him to breathe deep.

The body against him stiffened, her soft mounds of flesh pressed against the walls of his chest didn't move, indicating she held her breath.

Speechless, as if someone knocked the wind out of him, he glanced from the unusual assailant to those surrounding them, intent on defining what happened.

"Ah, crap. Sorry, mister. First few times on roller blades are a learning experience."

"*Hm*, the calamity on wheels has a voice." Of their own volition, his fingers conformed to the shape of her waist. Athletic, thin with little padding, clad in material so soft he could feel the contours of each rib.

With a screech and clatter, band members on stage ceased their warm-up. All eyes focused on the mysterious mixture of curls and exotic delicacy.

Nate received glares from every direction. "What? It wasn't my fault."

Thick tresses failed to find a semblance of order with her frantic swipes. He could only guess at her features since her soft curves plastered against his harder frame derailed every thought.

Those locks held him in thrall as they'd brushed against the back of his hands. Soft and lustrous, they blunted his confusion at standing upright when he should be flat on the floor.

How'd that happen?

Nothing could've stopped him from lowering his face to the satiny mane and inhaling deep. One whiff and he was toast.

If he could bottle the scent, he'd become an overnight millionaire. "If you say you're here to create havoc, I'd call you an instant success."

"Did you just sniff me?" The crystal pure voice bore more shock than indignation.

"She's not a dog, Nate. No sniffing required. A simple hello would do." Jake's irritated grumble blamed him for the encounter.

"Sorry... allergies." Standing erect and in front of her, Nate still couldn't discern her features. With great hesitation, he helped corral the wild mass of wavy mane to glimpse the mystery underneath.

Never before had he found a match between beauty and brains. His preference leaned toward companions who could hold their own in a conversation. Packaging didn't matter.

Yet for some reason, now it did. If she proved as empty-headed as a bag of bricks, he'd be crushed.

"My voice. It's why I'm here." In exasperation, the enigma blew out a heavy breath creating a small wave in the silken fall.

For reasons unknown, reverence stayed his hand in helping her sweep the heavy locks aside. In that twinkling of time, in his reality, nothing could match his imagination. He couldn't bring himself to ruining the moment with anything less than perfection.

She must have felt it, too. Her hand stopped midair, frozen, not spoiling the moment of faultless purity.

When time resumed, allowing her to reach up and open a window to her soul, the first glimpse almost drove him to his knees.

"You're here to make apologies for running over people?" Not since puberty had his voice cracked. "Perhaps you should have some type of license for those things."

His nod to her blades demonstrated a monumental lack of judgment. Attached to those blades for heaven or hell—he hadn't decided which—were long, toned legs with smooth, supple skin.

His gaze traveled north along the well-shaped, gentle curves not upstaged by the outlandish garment covering delicate portions of her thighs. No stockings marred the perfection of the phenomenal anatomic vista.

A saw-tooth hem left long swags of white silk to dangle helplessly between and around her loins.

Jesus. Is she wearing a G-string?

On closer inspection, she didn't dress in an attempt to garner attention. The seraph before him garbed her thin build in a way natural to her angelic genealogy.

"You talk as if I'm subhuman. I'm not. I'm the singer in the band." The intonation equated to a parent schooling an obstinate child.

His gaze traveled the length of her well-toned, bare upper arm to her delicately boned finger which pointed to the stage. Yeah, he had kinda noticed the stage, somewhere off in the distance.

"And you're looking for backup singers in the audience?"

Hard glares from the band brought a mix of chagrin and solidity to his thoughts. The threat blazing from their collective stares might have intimidated had he not known each one.

"No, I'm doing sound checks."

Friends would question his sanity for again glancing at her face when he couldn't think straight. "Hell, your nose is bleeding."

Withdrawing his handkerchief, he held it to her face. "Damn. Sorry about that."

"I got it. I got it. Note to self. Don't run into brick walls." She took the cloth and dabbed the area above her lip. The bleeding had already stopped.

Before he could question the surreal circumstance of their collision, the sum and substance of his existence hurtled his mind back to the present, accompanied by the not-so-discreet clearing of his friend's throat.

"Um, well now. I did want you two to meet, perhaps not quite so informally, though." Astute with people and situations, Jake would recognize and analyze instant chemistry.

"I'm Callie." The flush on her cheeks deepened as she glided back a step and held out her hand.

"Nate." Trembling fingers in his grip attested to her inner turmoil.

"Yes, well, now that we've got introductions out of the way... sound checks, Callie?" A possessive arch to Jake's brow broadcast the nature of their relationship, or at least his intent.

With a smooth pivot glide and a backward glance over her shoulder, the enigma skated off. Even the grace of her strides commanded attention from others.

"Would you like some lanolin?" Jake scrubbed a hand over his jaw. Light jesting belied the tension in his shoulders.

Not again, not in Nate's lifetime. Ignoring the sarcasm, he zeroed in to validate his suspicions. "So, you didn't say over the phone you'd be bringing your girlfriend. You've done well, you old dog."

To travel great distances for the small favor of his girlfriend singing at the club didn't fit with safe house set-ups and arrangement for vehicle disposal. Formidable trouble must've trailed them.

Nate had no excuse for his behavior. Encroaching on another man's territory wasn't his style.

"She's not my girlfriend exactly. Though, I hope to change that, soon, along with her marital status."

Disbelief coiled and writhed in his chest until reality dawned. "You're going to marry her? Wonderful. Congratulations!" He'd always expected Jake to enter his golden years as a bachelor.

"Well, I'm going to ask her tonight. At the end of her last set." From the pocket of his leather jacket, Jake withdrew a small velvet box. The kind to hold a delicate ring fit for an angel.

The reality of his words penetrated the fog clogging his thoughts. "You're going to marry her *before* getting to know her. Are you nuts?" Again, confusion mushroomed in his mind then slithered like a snake throughout his chest. This time it seemed to settle in the area of his heart as well.

"I'm going to propose a sensible solution to her problem."

"Marriage as a solution to a problem doesn't sound reasonable. Does she love you?" A sweet smile did not equal a love-smitten invitation, the former bestowed on Jake before she turned to leave.

In contrast, her confusion after their run-in left her breathless and bewildered. Maybe in part due to the fact they should've both crashed to the floor.

"I don't think her mind understands love. She processes things on different levels, but she'll see the logic in it, which is what I'm banking on." Jake rubbed the back of his neck as if the weight of the world rested on his shoulders.

"Are you sure, Jake? A lifetime together can be agony if feelings aren't mutual."

Uncertainty would cloud judgment and degrade any relationship with time.

The third part of the trio, Sebastian, joined them. His gaze following Callie to the sound check carried a mix of devilment and unease. Did he know something about Jake's enigma?

"Extenuating circumstances which I'll explain, my friend, but before I show you how incredibly special she is, I have a favor to ask and some details to impart."

"I'm listening."

Sounds coming from the stage indicated the band had picked up their instruments and resumed their warm-up, with intermittent glares directed at Nate.

Seconds later, a few chords from the steel guitarist and then—dear God, that voice. He'd never heard anything so sweet and pure. The soft yet strong quality mesmerized the small crowd even before the words ensnared.

"Are you?"

Yes. Nate shook his head to clear it. "Am I what?"

"Listening?"

Again, his attention snapped back to Jake. "Of course. Sorry." A fleeting look at the singer as she skated to another corner confirmed what she'd said.

Yep, sound checks.

The attention of the band remained divided as two gazes followed her and the other two visually dissected him.

"Nice voice. Where'd you find her?"

"Yes, very nice. Now, Nate, focus. Both you and she are the reason we're here tonight."

Oh, no. That interpretation had to result from a cross in Nate's wiring. "Excuse me?"

"She is more special than you could ever imagine."

You underestimate my imagination.

"Remember when you left the unit? I told you I had a sweet gig waiting for me when I got out?"

"Yeah, that was five years, not decades ago. I remember you

wouldn't tell me what you were getting into. Figured it was a type of government testing or something equally clandestine."

"You've got it half right. It's certainly secret and funded by an offshoot of the military. At least, that's what I suspect. Soon as I uncovered what they were doing in the bowels of that Think Tank, I almost left and blew the whistle.

"I realized in doing so, they'd move her, not free her. It took me this long to work my way up the ladder and get the particulars to complete my plan."

"Free her? Like—as in prisoner?"

"Exactly like. She's been raised in an underground superstructure most of her life. An hour of outdoor exercise each day with a whopping two hours on Sunday."

In the miasmic corners of Nate's soul, lethal fury walled off from corrupting his thoughts erupted to close his throat and tighten his chest. Bile from his stomach made a valiant effort to spring free. He swallowed hard. No one had the right to imprison another without just cause.

"Gee, she doesn't look much like a terrorist in need of black site seclusion." In keeping the conversation light, he managed to put a stranglehold on his anger.

"Nate, I guarantee she is the most unique individual you'll ever meet. I've known her for five years and have yet to detect a mean or deceitful bone in her body. I don't think she even knows how to lie.

"Maybe because she's not known another way of life, she lacks the resentment and cynicism you'd expect to find in someone whose movements have been so restricted."

"That's the way I figure it."

"And you're going to marry her?" Nate narrowed his eyes, gauging his old friend's intentions. It took all his will power not to reassess Sebastian's demeanor and get a line on how Jake's second viewed the situation.

"I know what you're thinking. She's about twenty-two as best I can figure. Other than that, I'd be guessing."

"And you want to marry her?" Again, anger toward his old friend made Nate's jaw clench. His old teammate intended to take advantage of Callie's innocence.

"Nate. She needs all the protection she can get. A marriage license will document her attachment in a legal way. I want to create a paper trail anyone can follow, starting tonight."

"With your name... you'll have new ID for her?" Distasteful as the plan was, it did make a twisted kind of sense. Still, there had to be another way.

"Exactly."

"Sacrilege." Shame at his previous thoughts directed his anger in force at Jake.

"Nate. Look at her. In the two seconds you've known her, you're so distracted a herd of elephants would trample you before you became aware of their presence. She will belong with somebody. Better to be someone who will not only protect her but also look out for *her* best interests."

"Protect her from what? People like the brain trust bastards who employ you?"

The soft pellucid tones of Callie's love song transported his attention back to see her settling on a stool beside Spirit, the lead guitarist. Not much between heaven and hell could distract Nate once locked onto a line of focus, until this unearthly creature pulverized his concentration.

"Yeah, exactly like those bastards at the Think Tank. Only I no longer work for them. No doubt, they terminated my services three days ago when they killed Franklin during our escape. Not sure about the other man who aided us, but I still breathe."

"Hell. I'm sorry. Franklin was a good man. Why come all the way to Maryland?"

"I don't have all the details, Franklin swore to protect his source, but from what I've gathered, Ray was hired in Maryland and sent to head up the facility in Minnesota. There may be other facilities like it, I'm not sure."

"Again, you'd come here because...?"

"Several reasons. One, I wanted distance between Callie and the Think Tank. Second, I wanted to see if you could do some digging and find out who's leading the circus. Since you're not associated with the outfit in any way, they won't make the connection to Callie."

Which is why you'd bring her to a place like this. I know how careful you are, but—"

"Always the quick study. And yes, I'm sure we weren't tracked. If they had any means of catching us, they'd have done it already."

"Meaning? I hear a slider coming."

"They implanted a microchip long ago, in case she ever got *lost*."

"Like a dog? That explains the subhuman comment. Damn. Why haven't you taken it out?"

"I scrambled the data so they couldn't track her. She's dealing with a lot. I wanted to break *that* bit of news when things settled."

"Don't know how much help I can be on that count. My training only includes basic first aid."

"No. I'll deal with that. I've got supplies in our next safe house."

"And the favor you wanted to ask?" *Please don't ask me to protect her.*

"Simple. If they catch up to me, take her. Take her and run like hell. I thought about contacting Kenson, but I'd rather avoid that route unless necessary. There's a rumor floating around—some foreign pricks want her at any cost. If that's true, Kenson might be the only refuge."

"Which you haven't done because you wanted to ensure a backup plan first, namely me."

"Yes, that and I needed time to regroup after a minor injury. After her first set, I want you to witness a fraction of the unprecedented potential within Callie's mind."

Jake's slight hand gesture caught the attention of the drummer and conveyed his intent. If the self-proclaimed protector was accurate about Callie's ability, hell would certainly follow.

Patience and careful evaluation of unique situations helped determine the best approach to solving a puzzle. In addition, anything suspected of being too good to be true hid a type of darkness, something Nate had a talent for uncovering. He wondered what dark truths Callie concealed.

Chapter Four

Speaking in front of laser-focused groups never bothered Callie. Knowledge existed for the benefit of others. Tonight, music held the same power. Jake's assurance there wouldn't be many couples present mitigated the minor bout of anxiety.

His tension after her run-in with his friend hadn't dissipated. His brows remained pinched in a perpetual frown.

The night's objective included meeting his former team. Perhaps Nate denied the requested favor or didn't like Faith waiting in his office. If the club owner objected to her pup's presence, she'd pick the dog over his company any day.

Her gaze slid around the stage as she prepared for her next song. She'd gotten the hang of the rollerblades without injuring herself or arriving guests, a bonus after colliding with Jake's arrogant teammate.

"Ready, Callie?" Spirit asked.

"Absolutely. Thanks." In the short time they'd talked, the man proved to be a rock, in both a physical and emotional sense. Self-assurance answered her tentative smile.

"No problem. Jake said you loved rollerblading, but it was your first time performing. A little distraction," Spirit pointed to her feet, "goes a long way. Still, we can't have our star breaking her leg on her big night."

"Oh, I'm not nervous about singing. It's just performing outside of... where I lived. Plus, I'm anxious to be on our way, and Faith is all by herself in the office." Callie pointed toward the hallway from which soft yips echoed.

Gentle understanding graced the Native American's expression. "That place where you lived was *never* and *will* never be your home. Keep that in mind. As for Faith, don't worry about her. Virus might as well be half-canine himself, loves dogs and will make frequent checks."

"I know. It's just that everything is so new and different. Exciting sometimes, terrifying when you least expect it. I never knew life had such dark corners."

"That's true, but we find light in the most unexpected places and times. Remember that." Spirit's moniker suited his demeanor. Tall and broad-shouldered, he bore his heritage with pride and strength, lacking the excessive energy of Whisper and Virus, two other members of the band.

"Jake doesn't look happy. What's got him so tense?" Callie adjusted her position in front of the mic. After she got the first set under her belt, she wanted to mingle with the guests. Other than the band, no one knew her past. What would these people be like? Would they accept her, talk to her, be friendly?

"Ah, don't worry. He always looks a little constipated during a mission. Once we get you three settled somewhere, he'll be fine." Nerd finished adjusting the cords and offered an encouraging smile. "Anytime you're ready to start, Callie, flip the switch on the mic."

She nodded her thanks. "This place is bigger than I expected."

"Don't worry, young'in. Not that many people here. Besides, they'll be drinking, dancing, and carousing." Perched on his drummer's throne, Whisper twirled a drumstick in his right hand. Of medium height with short curly hair, he smiled before executing a perfect drum roll.

From the back wall where he stood beside Nate, Jake smiled. His encouragement filled her with the excitement of discoveries yet to come. He'd promised her a computer of her own if it didn't devour her time. The difficulty came with so many new experiences and the wealth of information on the internet.

Too many questions strafed her thoughts to organize, likened to snatching a single electron from its orbit barehanded.

Jake had remained mute about their next moves except to say she'd be safe, free, and her studies could venture in any direction she chose. She owed him everything.

"You all have been so kind. When Jake said his former team would help us tonight, I had no idea what to expect."

"He told us you were a quick study but a little naïve." Spirit picked up his guitar and strummed a few cords. "Ready?"

"A quick question. The man with Jake now, Nate. He was part of your unit?" Callie dropped her gaze, confusion flooding her mind. When she'd slammed into him, they should've ended in a tangle of arms and legs on the floor. If anyone else had seen the odd occurrence, no one mentioned it.

She understood the basics of what happened but couldn't fathom the linear procession of the steps needed to recreate the action. It defied mathematical structure, and she didn't believe in the supernatural. Intuition was a beast she couldn't decipher.

After their collision, shock prevented her from speaking until he'd referenced her as subhuman and in need of a license.

She'd never interacted that way with anyone before. The combination of anger and humiliation had swept a wave of panic through her chest. What if most men were like him?

How long would it take to circumvent such entanglements.

"Nate's one of us. Though he did tread on the wilder side of life when we were a unit, always pushing the envelope, even for us." Whisper added another short drum roll. "I think that comes from having like-minded brothers."

"Regardless of first impressions, you can trust him, Callie." Spirit strummed a few chord progressions on his bass before adding, "When it comes to strategy and being cool under fire, he's a must-have for the team."

"Besides, he won't join us unless we hit a snag. Should've covered that during our meet-and-greet earlier." Nerd's dramatic notes on the electric keyboard reflected the same dexterity he'd shown on his computer during their first meeting. They had a lot in common.

Intuition dictated she never reference her emerging new skills and what she might accomplish. The implications were dark and far-reaching. Possible discovery inspired new nightmares concerning dissection on a cold steel table.

Logic ruled her world.

What she was learning to do defied scientific explanation.

A sense of trepidation inched along her spine to create doubt with that decision. Keeping this type of secret while accepting Jake's help wasn't fair to anyone who could get caught in the crossfire. Risking his life entitled him to a certain amount of trust. Uncertainty kept her mouth closed.

Like Jake, Spirit seemed to read her emotions as soon as they rose, as if absorbing the energy she radiated. Yet, in sitting down with the group today, he'd put her at ease. He had no design on her future work or emotions, a true ally.

* * * *

All gazes turned toward the raised platform as the soft, lilting voice filled the room. Even the servers, accustomed to excellent performers, paused in their stride.

One song after another held the audience spellbound. The few murmured conversations earned a *"Shh"* from surrounding guests.

With the end of the last velvety note, the room exploded in applause. From a distance, Nate detected the crimson climbing Callie's cheeks before she ducked her head to let the waterfall of blonde curls cover her face.

If she were his, he'd make sure she never felt the need to hide. Such remarkable talent should not create embarrassment.

Every creature had flaws, occurring as a fact of nature. Nate detected none. He wondered what that said about his state of mind.

On stage, Spirit handed Callie a pair of flat-soled shoes, then took her rollerblades and set them aside.

Just as before, appreciative gazes followed her movements, this time down the steps toward Jake.

If exposure of her unique gift created greater awkwardness, Jake deserved a black eye for not preparing the young enigma.

This time, he locked down his emotions with her approach. Something in this mix spelled trouble and death. In their line of work, distractions proved fatal. He wouldn't be caught flat-footed again.

Jake's account of the desperate rescue and Franklin's death bore closer resemblance to a goat fuck, which had never been his style of handling missions. Maybe he was blinded by her uniqueness.

"You should have called us earlier, before leaving the institution. We could've helped."

"No. I needed tonight to start a clean slate. No one other than myself knew the whole plan. Hell, even I don't know how Franklin got us the codes and access information. Said it was someone from this neck of the woods." With Jake's nod to the band, he retrieved the tray of colored puzzles. "Shall we go to your office? The ceiling there should be high enough."

"High enough for what? So—our old unit?"

"You'll see. And the guys have agreed to stay long enough to either see us out of the country or go public and attach ourselves to, well, possibly the military." Jake followed Nate down the short hallway to his office.

"What?"

"With her unique abilities, they'd assign a detachment for full-time protection, which might be the better option now that I've thought more about it. Once her potential is known, the colonel wouldn't risk her falling into foreign hands."

"That could go either way, depending on how she views the military."

"From the chatter I've heard, foreign agents have ramped up their bidding, which changed my timetable and screwed everything. I couldn't take any chances. Even with their extensive connections, my employers couldn't find the mole."

"You want help protecting her?" On the fringes of an op was not a place Nate ever endured.

"No. You're my backup. Since we've had no contact in years, and only a handful knew your identity back then, no one will knock on your door looking for her. I just want her to know she can come to you for help if I fail."

"You? Fail? Nonsense. I remember—"

"What's up, Jake? You wanted to see me?" Uncertainty tinged the soft voice. Callie's mouth firmed to a straight line when stepping into the office and seeing the cubes.

Gesturing to her, Jake set the tray back on Jake's desk. Her hesitant steps signaled knowledge of that to come.

In her crate, Faith sent up a vocal ruckus. Callie glanced at the tray but crouched down to reassure the pup, crooning softly and petting the silky fur through the metal bars.

Nate closed the door behind them.

Her sigh and downward gaze spoke volumes as she stood. "Jake? Is this really necessary? I could just hop on the computer—"

"No need. This will give Nate a basic understanding in the shortest amount of time."

"Oh, snail poop. I hate the blasted cubes."

Nate curled his lips inward on a smile. "Odd choice of expletives."

A sheepish grin crossed her face. "Jake's teaching me."

"Snails—because they hide in their shells?" Understanding the enigma and his old friend's motives would take time they didn't have.

"Because they sleep on their poop. I can't hide, and I can't escape this stigma."

"Then leave the shell behind, embrace who and what you are. You'll find peace." Nate had no right to offer advice. He barely knew the young woman.

Whatever secrets Callie held in reserve, they must contain formidable potential.

Without warning, Jake pivoted at the desk and lobbed the first cube toward her, underhanded. The warm smile curving his lips betrayed a new charismatic Jake, one softened by wonder and awe.

"C'mon, Callie. You know this boggles my mind. 'Sides, Nate here's our backup and needs to know a little of what you can do. Think of this as a pre-emptive strike. He'll never try to out-think you."

With an impressive dexterity, she diverted the block's forward momentum upward five feet after giving it a slight twist, its multicolored sides reflecting light in soft hues.

An odd hush settled heavy in the air, different from other silences, filled with a calm reverence, peaceful yet even more exciting for the expectation of something strange and wonderful to come.

From the moment her misstep precipitated their collision, Nate's concentration derailed while the suspected phenomenal workings of her mind captivated and enthralled him. He now understood his friend's childlike wonder.

Jake's suspicion of her abilities being more than what he could demonstrate added a new level of intrigue. On the other hand, what darkness hid beneath the beautiful shell?

A genius of her suspected status could do anything, wreak havoc on entire civilizations without warning. He couldn't reconcile that understanding with signs of hidden darkness.

No sooner had the block begun its midair descent, Callie caught another cube. This one, she sent a little higher before catching the first and giving it another twist. Its return airborne trip preceded Jake lobbing two more, one at a time.

Nate had watched speed-cubers before, knew one who could solve two in short order, one at a time. This demonstration blew the lid off anything he'd ever imagined. Within a minute, she juggled all the cubes.

Each time she caught one, she'd turn one side to change the color combination before resuming its cycle.

Sucking in a quick breath, Nate realized his jaw had gone slack when Jake stepped closer and with a finger under his chin, closed his mouth.

"Yeah, Nate. This is nothing compared to what I *suspect* she can do." Quiet words meant only for Nate.

Still, Callie cycled the cubes again and again after giving each a slight adjustment. Through their continued movement, he began to see each pattern emerge.

Multicolored sides mutated and transformed to a uniform color. He stood transfixed, unaware of time and space—for the extreme focus in her gaze rivaled nothing he'd ever witnessed.

All too soon, she deflected the first cube back toward Jake. Kudos to the man, he caught it with a smirk. When placed on the tray, each side held a single color, solved *on the fly*.

The final cube landed in his hands with decidedly more force than the previous three, judging by the thud. A glance at Callie and understanding dawned.

Vulnerability in her expression conveyed a crushed spirit. Though she bent her head so her hair fell forward, he'd discerned the single tear escaping the corner of her eye.

Fate drew him closer. With a whisper-soft touch, he reached behind the wall of locks, lifting the evidence of her breached positive attitude. How could a tear be so soft?

"You're not an aberration, sweetheart. You need to get that thought out of your head right now."

His firm tone snapped her gaze up in the next instant. Fragile hope mixed with distrust finally settled with uncertainty as she conveyed her turbulent emotions through changing expressions.

"Yeah? How many people have you seen put on a freak show like that? I may have been raised in a bubble, but I see the distinction between myself and others, the way people look at me when I do things like that."

As if no one else existed, he closed the few inches between them. Crowding her stepped on his friend's toes but couldn't be helped. No one should feel so insecure for having such a rare gift.

"To be honest, I've never met anyone as talented. I'm equally sure I never will again. I consider this a great honor. You don't seem to understand the difference between being a geek or nerd and being a freak. Anyone with a grain of sense will respect geeks and nerds. Freaks... not so much." He'd let the reverence in his gaze guide her in discerning the difference.

When he raised his hand to cup her chin, her widened eyes exposed significant white around the beautiful crystal blue depths holding him captive. Since her guardian had coerced her into the stunt for Nate's benefit, it fell in his duties as host to ease her tension.

On the other hand, with her pulse beating wildly at the base of her neck and her quiet, puffy breaths warm on his cheek, he wasn't doing her any favors.

Again, the clearing of Jake's throat brought him back to reality.

A step back didn't clear Nate's head.

His friend asked him to be second-string defense and now likely thought it the worst idea ever hatched.

"Callie, you can go back now, hon. We'll talk after a bit. Okay?" A new gruffness entered Jake's tone.

Several quick blinks and the little blonde enigma stepped back with a longing look toward the pup. With grace born of the most angelic creature, she pivoted to make her way to the stage.

Again, Jake cleared his throat.

"Sorry, man. I couldn't let her feel bad for displaying such—"

"Don't sweat it, Nate. She is an angel, and most assuredly a keeper. Mine, though. Got it?"

"Yeah, loud and clear, buddy. You know I'd never—"

"I know, I know. We're good."

"Good move getting her the pup. She'll form a connection with the dog that's different than with people."

"Her instincts bend more toward nurturing than I anticipated. Her responses have been to seek kinship with anything related to nature."

"So, your little genius. You know the military will exploit her given the chance."

"I think with the right group, she could be a great help to society, and with someone determined to look out for her, she'll be fine. Win-win situation. Better than waiting for someone to snatch her by force. Someone this special couldn't hide for long."

"Point taken. Tell me, what did the Think Tank bastards want her to do?"

"Weapons of mass destruction. They envision a bomb like no other, undetectable by the usual means, from silicon nanowires to neutron activation and mechanical scent detection. And yeah, buddy, she could do it. Hell, for all I know, she's already figured it out, but she keeps most of her work in her head."

"Damn, she doesn't look like an evil super genius."

"It's not the way she's oriented. No. She doesn't have an evil or sadistic streak that I've ever seen. And what the hell does a genius look like?"

"Not like an angel, that's for certain. Hm, just how is she oriented? Looks like they raised her in a vacuum." During close proximity, confusion had warred with surprise, exposing a type of innocence Nate rarely encountered.

"A very selective vacuum. They handpicked everything she saw, vetted anyone she came into contact with, and directed everything she studied. Regardless of her narrow fields of focus, never discount her intellect. Her emotional equivalent is spotty, but she's not as lacking as you might expect. I think with time—"

Holding his index finger up, Jake unclipped his cell and frowned at the screen. "Franklin, his contact here in Maryland, and Sebastian were the only ones given this number. I'll be back in a sec." Dysrhythmic thuds of Jake's boots attested to his distraction as he raised the phone to his ear.

Chapter Five

The fact her unique mind defied Nate's best attempt to define or categorize her in any way didn't diminish his admiration of the packaging. Realizing he'd capitulated to a jaundiced eye and now envied Jake the divine bundle didn't clarify his thoughts.

Unless she's as good at hiding intentions as her intellect might suggest.

Maybe Jake wasn't as sure of himself as he appeared. Could anyone have an objective opinion after witnessing such an event? Outside the window, increasing winds and heavier clouds played hide-and-seek with the moon to mimic the current situation. One thing remained consistent through every aspect of his life. Circumstances never existed as initially presented.

Back at the entrance to the main room, Nate studied his old unit using a band as cover. He'd trust each with his life, despite the passage of time.

So enthralled with the complexities of his friend's situation, he failed to register Jake's return until the grip on his shoulder made him turn to note the puzzled frown.

"What's up?"

"Well, certainly an interesting conversation. The young woman said her name was Penny. Claimed to be a long-time friend of Callie's."

"And?"

"Callie hasn't had contact with anyone outside the institution other than Franklin, Sebastian, and myself. And I don't know anyone named Penny."

"What'd she want?"

"Said she has information on a group closing ranks on us. Didn't want to talk over the phone but agreed to meet me. She balked when I gave her the location but said she'd be there. Must be from around here, said she knew the spot." A nervous tic over his left eye betrayed irritation when he continued.

"So—let's go check it out."

"No, listen. She'll bolt if she sees or senses anyone else present. I'll talk to Sebastian before I leave. I told him earlier to touch base with Conner and sketch the highlights of what we're doing. If I'm not back in two hours, *you* take her and run."

"Don't trust Sebastian?"

"With my life, but if they've drawn a bead on me, they'd have Sebastian in their sights, too. Callie needs a clean start."

"Hold on. I'll back you up." Nate couldn't override the plan. It wasn't his mission. However, he could supplement it.

"No. First, you're the backup plan, and I don't want your identity compromised. Second, if the bastards find me, I don't want them linked to our old team." Nodding toward the door, he added, "Not many knew your given name when we worked together. Hence, they can't track you before you have time to disappear. There's no one else I trust to look after her."

"Damn. Only the major and a handful of people including Colonel Kenson knew my identity. I couldn't attend the major's funeral three years ago." Few things in Nate's life elicited such regret or hedged the realm of disrespect, but if the work they'd done came to light, lives would still be at risk.

"See you back here by ten. And Nate?" He took a deep breath before continuing. "Don't wait for me. If I'm not back, you take her and go. Trust. No one. No one outside our team. Well, your brothers were team also."

"Yeah, Conner's over at the bar, talking with his flavor of the month. He's been scratching his jaw all evening, wondering what's going on."

"Huh, he never liked being on the outside of a circle. I'll say hi before I leave."

"Stay safe, man."

"Will do. I'd better chat with Callie and the guys, too."

Jake's strides toward the stage held none of the newfound light-hearted charisma witnessed moments prior. Here was the soldier bent on success before an op.

At the end of their current song, Virus, their team's computer expert turned soundman, hunched down at the edge of the platform to speak with his former shadow operative. Seconds later, Jake made his way toward the front exit.

The rest of the band gathered in conversation. Several shook their heads. Seconds later, Virus caught Nate's eye and flashed a hand signal, reminiscent of old times.

Nate answered in kind.

Jake's absence left ultimate responsibility of the operation with Nate. He'd run it like any other mission. He'd not sent a man without backup.

After a nod to his teammates, Virus hopped off the stage and set out to trail Jake. If his friend had a problem with the order, he could bitch about it later.

"Hey. Nate?"

For the second time that night, someone took him by surprise. Sebastian held his hand out in formal greeting.

A wiry build spoke of routine exercise and commanded respect. The firm handshake and strong posture was straightforward, referencing confidence.

"What's up?"

Within their group's skillset, a restless gaze wasn't unusual, yet Nate observed a subtle discontent, not surprising after Jake's mysterious phone call and exit.

A combination of experience and instincts trained them to form opinions and react on the fly. Nate returned the smile as he considered the younger man, trying to determine what factor prodded his unease.

Nothing warranted a red flag—slightly tense stance, casual clothes, and jump boots visible under boot-cut jeans. All seemed appropriate to the circumstances.

Sebastian's easy smile faltered when settling on Callie. Curious that Jake hadn't made his colleagues privy to the entire plan. Were the Think Tank bastards so well-connected to warrant such secrecy?

Absolute transparency numbered one on the essential building blocks of trust. Jake trusted Sebastian to help free Callie and as such, deserved the benefit of the doubt.

"She's something, isn't she? Wasn't sure how she'd take to the old unit, but it seems any concerns were misplaced." Sebastian nodded toward the stage.

Smooth strains of Callie's song filtered through the cavernous room. Like before, a hush fell over the small crowd.

"Never met anyone like her." Nate was damn sure he never would again.

"You're ex-military, too? I should've figured. When were you assigned with Jake?"

Something prodded Nate to learn more about the inquisitive ex-soldier. He shrugged. "A lifetime ago, it seems."

The team accepted Jake's secrecy without hesitation. Considering their prior history, mutual trust came as little surprise, but working with unknown variables never set well. If Nate were part of their team, full disclosure would be priority.

"I'd met him before he joined the unit. How about you?" In the guise of comradery, Nate tossed out the snippet, however far from the line of truth.

"The man saved my life." The slight twitch above Sebastian's left eye belied the smooth tone of his voice.

"So, you worked together at the Think Tank. That must've been a strange situation."

"Yep, we were there together. Have to say, I was a bit shocked to find out about Callie. Thank God, we got her out of there. Lord knows what type of hell she'd cook up under their direction. A slight downward turn of his mouth accompanied the disapproving tone. "Those are the creepiest bastards I've ever met—not to mention well-connected."

"Are there others like Callie still there?"

"Dunno. We intend to find out as soon as we're all clear. Where's Jake heading? We're supposed to leave in another hour." Lack of time traded tact for Sebastian's direct approach. An unnatural disquiet matured the edges of his obvious anxiety. A slight rocking back on his heels accompanied a long, deep breath.

"Said he needed to run an errand. Something Callie might need. He'll be back in a bit." The timing and nature of Jake's call didn't sit well. Overall, coincidences occurred few and far between. Franklin's death and Jake's phone call matured momentary quiet into something dark and ominous.

"Oh." The low disgruntled mutter spoke volumes.

"Jake broke the wonderful news. He's planning to marry her." Prodding at the younger man came by force of habit.

"He mentioned it. And I do see the logic, the need for a paper trail." Tension in Sebastian's shoulders increased before he tilted his head to the side, an audible crack breaking the silence.

"Just wanted to make sure we're all on the same page." *And see your reaction.* Evaluating team members helped determine future responses.

"We should give her time to mingle with guests tonight. She's never experienced normal society in situ." Sebastian's gaze took in the few guests. "Funny. I expected a bigger case of nerves, but she's taking everything in stride, and definitely over the top with that pup."

"From what little I've been told, this is a lot to throw at anyone, much less a sheltered young woman."

"Nonsense. You've gotten a glimpse of her intelligence. She can compartmentalize and analyze better than anyone I've ever met. This thing tonight," Sebastian swept his hand to include the few dozen guests, "is a stopover, a safe place to catch our breath. She's a fast learner. Let her learn."

"Her world's been turned inside out. She watched Franklin die. How about allowing her time to assimilate a sense of freedom? Genius status doesn't preclude human behavior. Besides, excessive undue attention won't endear her to Jake or his plan. Sounds like something he should do on a gradual basis."

"Can't—due to time constraints. They're only performing a couple sets. That'll give her a little bit to observe and interact with guests in between."

"As long as one of us stays with her." Nate contemplated giving Jake a lobotomy on return.

An insolent shrug of Sebastian's shoulder preceded his amble back toward Nate's oldest brother, Conner.

Damn if either man had an appropriate attitude. What was Jake thinking?

"So much for tonight's meet-and-greet." Conner never could disguise the beginning of inquisitor mode.

"Nice voice though."

"What the hell is going on, Nate? And for the record, I sense this scheme is FUBAR from the beginning. I want answers."

"I've seen worse fuck-ups. At least we don't have to distribute ear plugs."

"Nate. There is a *puppy* in your office. Care to explain?"

"Short version, early Christmas present."

On stage, Callie sat and watched the band dismantle their

equipment, jumping with the rattle of Whisper's snare drum thumping on the floor.

Off to the left side of the stage, a local DJ setup for the rest of the evening's entertainment.

"Why's your team so twitchy?" Conner leveled a stare first at Nate, then at the band. "Hell, I barely know 'em and I can feel their tension."

"Something's off. I haven't defined it. Maybe it's Callie. I have to admit, I've never dealt with anyone like her before. According to Sebastian, Jake wanted her to experience a breather before mainstream society. I'm not sure either one is clear-headed when it comes to her."

"Tell me more about why we're turning our club inside out for this, limited to exclusive guests."

"We've done it before."

"Not like this, Nate. Not like this."

"If you'd seen the earlier demonstration, you wouldn't ask. I don't have all the details, but her IQ is in the upper stratosphere, which elevates her to national treasure status. Jake's giving her a fresh start after rescuing her from a Think Tank. I'm second-string safety net."

Conner's low whistle betrayed admiration. "The singer? Jake told me earlier she's embarking on a new career and wanted to get her start here."

"Conner, how much time did you spend talking with Sebastian? I never heard Jake mention him, never met him before tonight. Then again, I didn't keep in touch with the guys, either."

Nate watched as the team surrounded Callie at the side of the stage with Whisper's intermittent gestures alternating between capitulation and frustration. His hand signals during missions included frequent stuttering.

"Not much."

After filling in a few details, Nate added, "I don't like taking this with a new team member. It's too disjointed."

"Anything specific about Sebastian you don't like?" Conner studied his younger brother.

"Not that I can put my finger on." A pause and Nate gestured toward the stage. "The guys are gonna stow their equipment while Sebastian keeps an eye on Callie. I need to make a few calls."

"You worry too much. Go ahead, then collect your little bundle of nerves and have a seat. Talk to her and find out more. I'll be in my office sorting out a problem with the last shipment of liquor. Looks like she could use a calm word or two from a friendly face." With a cryptic smile, he added, "Or a calming touch. You've barely taken your eyes off her since she arrived."

"Funny, jackass. Jake's gonna marry her."

"Ouch. What a shame. Sorry, bro."

Nate watched Callie approach. There existed too much grace, beauty, and brains in the unusual package for Jake to risk clandestine meetings and foolish endeavors. If he wanted to acclimate her to society, there were many subtle introductions possible, all beginning with conversations, which hadn't yet occurred as far as he could tell.

On the other hand, Jake suspected she withheld information and might've used tonight as a tactical diversion. He'd always been a clever bastard.

"Nate? The drummer, Whisper, said you'd explain what's going on. Where's Jake?" Hesitancy overlaying a sliver of determination lowered her brows and firmed the line of her lips. "Jake said the band consisted of his old team, so why don't they know what's going on?

"He had an errand to run. Why don't we have a seat and talk?" Engaging in mundane conversation might help him wrap his mind around Jake's plan. Phone calls could wait.

He led her to one of the sofas lining the room and waited until she perched before sitting beside her. Her gaze flitted toward the short hall and the offices.

"Don't worry. Your pup's fine. I checked on her a few minutes ago."

A spontaneous smile slid into place. "Never dreamed I'd have a dog. Isn't she sweet?"

He nodded at the childlike innocence contrasting the room filled with couples who'd seen and witnessed some of the best and most horrific situations life offered. They filled the dance floor, swaying to the DJ's soft music.

"Where's Sebastian?" Callie's gaze scanned the room.

"He was talking with my oldest brother a few minutes ago." More words failed to form. He sat beside a complete novice lost in a sea of varied intentions with no idea where to start.

"When will Jake return? He said at the safe house we'd stay together.

This isn't part of the plan."

Clearly, she felt adrift.

"Said he'd be back within two hours. Would you like some tea?" At her nod, he gestured to a server and placed the order.

Callie kept her hands in her lap, her fingers intertwined.

"Has Jake told you where you all are headed?" Not knowing where to begin, he needed to assess her general understanding of their circumstances.

"No, but I trust him. I usually have a good sense about people." Her smile warmed when speaking of her rescuer.

"I..." Nate paused to address the frantic server who bustled over from the foyer, out of breath and eyes wide.

"Mr. Crofton. One of the customers said there's a disturbance outside, a fight." A glance over her shoulder indicated the front door.

"All right. I'll see to it." Touching Callie's hand proved a mistake.

She startled before taking a deep breath.

"Callie, sit tight. I'll make sure Sebastian keeps an eye on you until I get back."

* * * *

Sit tight? Keep an eye on me? Again with the subhuman attitude.

That line of thought encompassed the entire sum and substance of her life. She'd spent her entire existence in a controlled environment and didn't understand social etiquette. The only way to learn was to mingle and figure it out. They all had two arms, two legs, and individual thoughts, just like her. It was time to take control and explore.

As soon as Nate stepped out of sight, she hopped up and scanned the cavernous room. Need for understanding—everything—outweighed Nate's directive to remain idle.

It didn't spring to mind until alone that she needed to pay for simple things. She had no money, no job, even the drink in her hand would be out of reach without funds. There was so much she wanted to experience, to do. Success in her newfound independence relied on her learning curve.

Couples swayed gently to the music, their synced movements sensual and instilling a strange longing. What would it feel like to hold someone that close?

Not just someone—the right someone.

Before she'd gotten ten feet, a handsome man in jeans and a leather jacket stepped in front of her, holding out his hand in greeting.

"Hi, I'm Daniel. Haven't seen you around."

His handshake was solid and gaze direct. A smile flirted at the corners of his mouth, increasing the dimple in his chin. He was quite handsome.

"Can I refresh your drink?"

Not giving her time to respond, He took her tea and swirled its contents, nodding toward the glass before returning it to her. "You are old enough, yes?"

"Obviously. I drink every day." *What an odd question.* She held out her hand expectantly, glad when he handed the glass back to her. She took a long drink to sort through the confusing conversation.

The man before her was like none she'd ever met, though she couldn't pinpoint to a specific reason. A cunningness flashed in his eyes, instigating an oily sensation slithering across her shoulders. His gaze dropped to her chest.

Perhaps he numbered among the *strange* people per Jake's warning.

His mouth opened on a quick inhale before a frown slipped in place. "Okay. What's your pleasure?"

"What? I enjoy a lot of activities, reading, exercise, playing with my pup..." If this contorted conversation equaled an example of the norm, maybe she didn't want to mingle.

"Excuse me. The young lady is otherwise occupied." Sebastian's appearance ended the younger man's inquisitiveness. He held up both hands in surrender and backed away with a smile.

Callie accepted Sebastian's hand guiding her around the perimeter of the dance floor, his gaze scanning the crowd. "You have to be careful, Callie. People—men in particular—will take advantage of you.

"How? It's not like I'm going to sit at a table and build a bomb."

"Well, you'll encounter a lot of strange situations as you experience life. Just stay on your toes until you're more familiar with how things work."

"Stay on my toes. So I can run faster? I'd rather fight. Jake said he'd teach me self-defense."

Sebastian's face blurred against the shadowy backdrop created by soft perimeter lighting and tabletop candles. She palmed her forehead and stumbled into the wall.

"What's wrong, kiddo?"

"Not sure. I'm a little nauseous, and my head feels weird. I need to use the restroom."

"Okay. It's just off the hallway ahead. I'll escort you to the door and find one of the wait staff to help you. You've had a lot of upheaval this week, a lot to take in."

"Yeah, things are definitely not what I expected."

A short hall continued black marble flooring and offered three exits. Solid oak doors on opposite sides opened to restrooms. At least they were labeled and without a riddle.

An exit sign at the hall's end led outside.

"You okay?" Sebastian murmured distractedly as his gaze scanned behind them.

She nodded and pushed on the heavy oak portal. "I'm fine. I just need to rest a minute and absorb all that's happening."

Each step felt clumsier than the last. Music and conversations muddled with the door's closing, but she still felt the throbbing beat in her chest. Granite tile walls helped cool her skin when she leaned back and shut her eyes.

Sudden increase in dizziness snapped them open.

Rare were the occasions her body succumbed to illness. Lack of exposure to normal childhood disease would make her more susceptible to many viruses, another disadvantage of life in a gilded cage. It'd only been three days since they escaped, and her mind catalogued myriad viruses and their gestation times. Nothing accounted for the suddenness of her symptoms onset.

Six large stalls stood opposite the expansive counter with an equal number of light gray sinks. Her drink sloshed over the side in setting it down with her swaying movement. A quick grab for the fixture maintained her upright status. At the far end, a cozy sitting area with two wing chairs and a small table between them provided a space for guests to sit. *Perfect.*

Both chairs waivered out of focus. Acid roiled in her stomach and threatened to erupt with each step.

Something's wrong. This isn't emotional.

Deep breaths failed to clear her vision or the cobwebs from her mind. She couldn't recite any reasons for her legs feeling like jelly or her mind to lose focus.

The chair's cushion was thick and deep, the arm rests well-padded as she dropped into its comfort. Leaning against the high back created a sense of stability. Again, she tried closing her eyes and taking slow deep breaths.

A rush of warmer air from the door's opening snapped her gaze up.

Medium height and stocky with a buzz cut and mocha skin, Daniel smiled. "Ready for a little trip?"

She recognized the man but not the accent. "You didn't talk like that a minute ago. What do you want?"

"I'm here to escort you to your new life."

The click of the door behind him defined the ill intent in rheumy gray eyes and brighter-than-white grin. His prowl forward stopped inches from where she sat.

She couldn't focus on his hand as he bent over and tucked a lock of hair behind her ear. "So this is what a super genius looks like, huh?"

"You're an asshole." The word Sebastian used to describe most employees of the Think Tank seemed appropriate.

"And you're a slave. Looks like the drug is taking effect quicker than I thought. I was worried you didn't drink enough. Shall we go, lightweight?"

It didn't' take a genius to know offering resistance against a stronger adversary would end in failure. He gripped her upper arms and pulled her to stand, compensating for her going limp until she stood face-to-face.

"I'm not the pansy you're expecting."

"Really?" He maintained eye contact and shook her. He declared superiority with a sneer and punishing grip.

Of the few maneuvers Jake had demonstrated, they all included using an enemy's weakness against him.

Before he could counter, she rammed the heel of her palm into his nose then jammed her knee into his groin.

"Game on, shitwit." *Maybe that wasn't the right word?*

A satisfying crunch and low groan filled her ears.

It wasn't until witnessing Franklin's death she realized the extent of her sequestered existence. Who knew cross-country travel could be so educational?

Chapter Six

Nate contemplated Callie's situation in striding through the rows of parked cars. Per Jake, she'd never enjoyed the freedom of making her own choices. Everything from friendships, basic activities, even the clothes she wore were all new and different.

It'd be interesting to see how she reacted to the club's clientele. Those who'd witnessed her incredible voice would rush to make her acquaintance. Sebastian had better keep his eye on her.

Club security's shouted command rose above frantic murmurs of those surrounding the night's disruption. Protocol dictated employees advise him or his brothers before leaving their post except in emergencies.

Understanding came on a wash of frigid air sweeping his shirt open. The first stinging needles of sleet plastered his hair to his scalp after descending the broad steps.

Both members of the security team struggled to separate a free-for-all in the remote corner of the lot. Initial assessment made it unclear who or how many combatants were involved.

From somewhere in the melee, a voice yelled, *"Knife!"*

They'd not incurred a serious fight in the four years since opening the club. An occasional tipsy guest requiring a cab ride home topped their list of problems. Upscale décor and entertainment drew select clientele while discouraging trouble.

Nate grabbed the closest non-employee and yanked him back to tumble on his ass. The raised fist stalled after witnessing Nate's expression.

"Go. Now. Leave the property and don't come back."

Employees pulled two others apart, leaving one man wielding a knife, weaving it back and forth in a figure-eight pattern.

Nate approached but stayed outside arm's reach. "Awful lot of anger you're carrying. No one here wants to get hurt." Shrugging off his light jacket and wrapping it around his left forearm provided a small barrier to protect his skin. It wasn't much but would have to do.

Fighting against a knife never ended well. Someone ended up with stitches at the very least. It was a fact of nature. From the corner of his eye, Nate saw the door attendant start to circle. Good intentions would get him killed.

"I got this, Jared. Get those three to the office and tell Conner to call the police. We'll let them sort this out." Inserting himself between the aggressor and those retreating to the club redirected his opponent's attention.

The adversary appeared mid-thirties and lacked obvious skill with the weapon. Unlike trained killers who'd reveal less than an inch of steel in this position, four inches of blade remained visible after repositioning to a forward thrust stance.

Thank God, he's an amateur. "Why don't you leave now and call it quits?"

"Ah, one of the Crofton brothers. I heard you'd be a worthy opponent. I'm surprised. They didn't tell me you were a coward."

"Who hired you?"

"No one you'll live to meet."

"What's worth dying over?" Nate arched his torso to avoid the first swipe aimed at his abdomen. His adversary was fast and direct.

"I'm the one with the knife, moron."

"And I'm the one who's gonna cause you permanent damage if you don't drop it."

No sliver of uncertainty entered the stockier man's gaze. Instead, he brought his blade up, pointed at Nate's torso, and plunged forward.

In a time-tested move, Nate thrust his right hand against the outside of his opponent's wrist. At the same time, he punched the inner wrist with his left.

Flexion under extreme pressure caused clenched fingers to whip open and send the knife flying. It skidded over the slick pavement and halted at the grassy edge.

Nate pieced together various events. There were no such things as coincidences, not like this, not in real life. This display equaled a diversion. If he backed away, the next attack, better planned, might take Jake or Sebastian by surprise.

"How high's the bounty?" Nate sidestepped to place himself between his opponent and the blade on the ground.

"Enough to buy a remote island and retire." As the assailant talked, a Virginia backwoods accent flavored his speech.

They stood at a crossroads. The next few heartbeats would

determine the mercenary's fate, where determination steeled his gaze. Instead of charging, he reached behind his back. "It's okay. I've got another."

At the same time, Nate back stepped and retrieved the fallen knife. A man's weapon said a lot about its owner. In his hand, Nate held a well-balanced blade.

His opponent held a duplicate.

The next attack was faster, slicing through the side of Nate's jacket and into his forearm.

Nate used his left wrist against his opponent's forearm to counter the back swipe of the blade. At the same time, he rotated his hips and stepped close. Keeping his elbow tucked tight, he thrust the blade into his enemy's right armpit and the nerve controlling the limb's movement.

In a continuous motion, he tracked down the flank to the inside of the right hip and through the quadriceps with speed born of experience.

The older man dropped to the ground, disarmed and disabled with a low groan and muttered curse. Blood splattered his flank and dripped onto the pavement.

This distraction covered the real threat, a coordinated effort, which meant Callie was in danger.

"On your right." Barely controlled rage twined through the approaching voice from behind.

"Late to the party, Marc." Nate dropped the knife and bent over with hands on his knees to avoid the stinging sleet. It didn't matter he'd fought against a knife before, his hands shook, something his brother would point out in the weeks and months to come.

"Damn, bro. A little excessive maybe?" Marc knelt to the injured man and cut pieces of his bloodied shirt for makeshift bandages.

"Him or me."

"What started it?" Marc asked while visually inspecting his brother. "You okay?"

"Planned attack. This is about Callie. They've been sent to acquire her." Unwrapping the sliced jacket, Nate inspected his wound. "Minor. I can take care of it with steri-strips. Later."

"Shit. I got this. Find your young friend and get her the hell out of here. I'll claim the damage done." Marc ripped the assailant's jacket and placed the cloth in the injured man's hand, then over the worst of the damage. "I doubt he's gonna argue."

Crimson drops diluted to light rouge with the addition of sleet and flowed toward the edge of t he lot.

"Thanks. I'll collect her and meet Jake on the road." Nate understood his ex-teammate's thorough and methodical nature. He wouldn't have made a rookie mistake and led an enemy to the club. *Then how'd they know to come here?*

Even Sebastian hadn't known the entire plan, which inspired thoughts of electronic bugging or small drone surveillance. Either was possible, and with such a prize, there'd be no limit to resources.

Freezing rain spiked his head and shoulders as he raced into the building. The door attendant shoved a towel in his direction with an inquiry. "Everything okay out there, boss?"

"Yeah, Jared, Listen. 911 is en route and will want to talk to you and the others about *my brother's* fight." He paused to let the words sink in.

"Of course. Marc's still out there. Does he need help?" Jared nodded understanding of the unvoiced message.

Any formal investigation involving Nate would expose Callie, hence, Marc took point.

"Na, he's got it covered, waiting for the ambulance. About our special guest tonight, our singer. I need to find her. You didn't happen to see our cute but dowdy little *brunette* wearing a gaudy turquoise necklace, did you?"

Jared smiled. "*Hm*, I did see her, stood about yay high. Terrible voice by the way. I'd think the club could afford better," Jared held his hand out, chest high. "A little on the heavy side with a pixie haircut. That the one you mean?"

"Yeah, the one wearing dark slacks and a red silk shirt."

Nate nodded then pivoted on his heel. As long as Sebastian stayed by Callie's side, no one would attack her in the public venue.

His youngest brother Julien stopped him at the end of the vestibule and pointed to Nate's torso. "Whose?"

"Not mine. Organized attack. Where's Callie?"

"The singer you've been visually undressing all evening? I saw her a few minutes ago with the guy who brought her here. I think he was keeping her moving to avoid being overwhelmed. There's not a man in this joint who doesn't want to take her home tonight."

"Damn it. I told her to stay put."

"Maybe she was nervous. What's her story anyway?"

"Genius in hiding is the Cliff Notes version. Supposed to leave with Sebastian and Jake as soon as he returns. Taking the old team as protection."

"I guess you're altering the strategy?"

"Yeah. I'll take her to my cabin. Call you from there."

"Damn. They have a leak. From what little I remember of your talk about Jake, he was better than that. Who else knew the plan?"

"No one I'm aware of, not even Sebastian," Nate grumbled. "Tell Conner I'll be in my office in ten. I need to finish a conversation if I'm gonna be second-string defense."

Lights were dim, and the dance floor was covered with couples swaying to a soft melody.

First visual pass over the crowd failed to reveal the slim enigma destined for who knew what. He wondered about Callie's insight into her new world, given her unique upbringing.

A deep foreboding settled in his gut. Timing of the fight, arrival of a protected witness, and a mysterious call to his teammate spelled trouble. He'd never been one to believe in happenstance.

Callie's safety was top priority. Past the long bar and around the stage, he failed to catch a glimpse of her golden hair or sunny smile.

Uncertainty grew to unease during the second half of his visual rounds. Adrenaline overload from the knife fight left him on edge, something experienced many times during his stint in the military but not since. He ignored the questioning glances or those wanting to inquire about his bloody shirt.

Once reaching the hallway, he changed tack, broadening his search to check in with the team. Near the side exit, Nerd entered and held the door for Whisper to carry out the last of their equipment.

"Nerd. Where's Callie?" Another electronics specialist, the southern man paused in toting a digital keyboard.

Surprise etched Nerd's face. He paused. "With Sebastian while the rest of us stow equipment. Why?"

"Just broke up a fight out front. A diversion. I don't know who *they* are, but they want Callie, and they're organized. I don't see her." Panic twisted Nate's gut.

"Couldn't have gotten out the back. We're parked there and would've seen anyone passing." Nerd's keyboard case thumped on the floor.

"I'll check the ladies' restroom." It was the only place he hadn't checked. Nate pivoted before finishing his sentence, feeling his teammate's presence in the continued search. Bits of the phone conversation signaled a call for the rest of the squad to help.

Pointing to the closest server, Nate gestured to the ladies' room. "Sarah, slip in there and see if our singer is perhaps hiding from the world, please." Near the end of the short hallway, he held the door open for her to pass.

Five minutes. He'd left Callie alone and Sebastian in charge for five minutes. Not a good start to her quest for freedom.

Blade shifted foot to foot by the door. "I'll wait here and brief the team."

A muffled request from the server altered the plan. After a deep breath, his loud thump on the door announced Nate's entrance.

Nothing could prepare him for the sight.

Sitting against the opposite wall with legs splayed straight out, Callie moved her head side to side in uncoordinated motions. Long hair shifted across her face. Her eyes never focused in any particular direction.

Stall doors to the right were all open, except the one closest to her. A wing chair lay toppled on its side with the round wrought-iron table upside down. Blood smeared the lip of the tabletop and against the tile floor.

Two jean-clad legs protruding from under the stall door sent a chill down his spine. The size of the black sneakers indicated male. There was no movement.

"Callie? What happened? Is that Sebastian?" Thinking back, the younger man had worn boots and dark-washed jeans.

"I've never been kissed." Callie giggled.

He'd face a man with a knife any day. A woman who'd obviously been drugged—not so much.

"Sarah, go tell Julien I found Callie and could use some help."

Nate snatched back the hand he'd reached out to steady Callie's slide to a horizontal position—until he noted the small trail of blood under her nose when her hair shifted.

"Callie? Did he hit you? Did he knock your head against the wall?"

"Hmm?"

With careful assistance, he righted her with one hand on her left shoulder and snatched his handkerchief to wipe her nose. "Callie. Tell me what happened here. Who is that man?"

"In—tru—der alert." The hand she tried to cover her mouth with slipped across her face before landing on his own, still holding her shoulder.

"Did you hit your head?" Gingerly, he probed her scalp for lumps or bleeding. "I don't feel any signs of injury."

"Nic Nac Nate. That's—that's what I'm gonna call you. Why do you consider me subhuman?"

"What? I don't think that. That's nonsense. Do you hurt anywhere?"

An inrush of air with the door opening preceded a muttered curse. "What the hell'd you do to her?" Blade, a younger member of their team, crouched next to Callie then nodded to the protruding legs. "Who's that?"

"Don't know. Take a look while I see if she's injured."

Behind them, Whisper and Spirit entered, followed by two women.

Blade shoved at the stall door. It didn't budge. "Who the hell's in there? Somebody's gotta crawl under."

"Nate, are you a virgin?" Callie asked.

The curious tone, as much as the words, sent Nate off balance and back to land on his ass.

"Graceful, man. Very graceful. But don't you think it's a little soon and not your place to have *the talk*?" Spirit's calm if emphatic disapproval coincided with a hand held out.

Repositioning himself, Nate nodded toward the protruding legs. "Help Blade with that guy. Don't know how he locked himself inside *then* got rendered unconscious."

Blade opened the door after crawling under. The rustle of material signaled his search through the unconscious man's pockets.

Attention focused on Callie again revealed her head starting to bob, whether from exhaustion or trauma, he didn't know. Checking her pulse, Nate breathed a sigh of relief. "Steady and strong. Her pupils aren't dilated."

"Who in hell drugged her, this guy? If so, why's he unconscious when she clearly couldn't fight off a foam noodle? Where's Sebastian?" Blade made a low noise in his throat. "No ID."

As if hearing his name, Sebastian entered with a quick inhale of breath. "What're you all doing? Callie? What's happened?"

Low groans from the downed man echoed in the confines of the first stall.

"He's clean." Spirit accepted and opened a wallet to reveal it empty except for a few bills and a small Polaroid.

"I did it. I finally figured it out." Callie sing-songed as she flitted her hands through the air like a conductor keeping time for a grand orchestra.

"You knocked him out? How? This doesn't make sense. How'd the door get locked from the inside?" Nate turned Callie's face to lock gazes, except hers didn't focus.

"You're so cute. Do the girls call you hunkalicious?"

Behind Nate, snickers filled the room.

"Nate, look. This guy's clean except for this." Spirit held the door open, flipping the photo over to reveal a head shot of Callie, taken against a white block background.

Blade hefted the assailant onto his shoulder. "What do you want me to do with this one?"

"Take him to Conner's office and tell him we have another problem. He's gonna shit a brick."

"Do you know how man-y muscles that would tear? Very painful I bet." Callie giggled again and waved to Spirit. "You are quite possibly the biggest man I've ever met. What do you put in the pipe you smoke?"

Spirit shook his head, mumbling about incomplete intel during assignments.

"Callie, look at me, little one." Nate watched her eyelids close then pop open again.

"Do you have a harem?"

Behind Nate, Blade tapped him on the shoulder. "Looks like she has your number. Try to add her and we'll skewer you alive, old friend."

Nate snorted. "I don't do innocents. You should remember that much about me. Let's get her to my office." With arms under her knees and behind her shoulders, he lifted and cradled her as if carrying a most precious cargo.

"Sebastian, you've got some explaining to do." Nate eyed the drink on the counter. "Spirit, take that to Conner too, have him send it to the lab."

"I left her in the restroom to grab a glass of water and get a server to check in on her."

Soft murmurs followed them around the main hall. Several guests inquired if Callie needed a doctor. Starting a public record of this nature was the last thing she needed.

"Callie, I know you're feeling a bit off right now, but you're gonna need to talk to us, sweetheart."

The nonverbal response equaled tucking chin tight to chest and curving her body tighter into his frame. She didn't appear frightened as much as determined, with her lips nipped between her teeth. She had a lot more spine than Jake suspected.

In his office, he sat on the sofa and settled her next to him the way he would a small child. At least his team didn't grumble behind him.

Very gently, he slid his finger under her chin to bring her gaze up. "Sweetheart—"

Her eyes widened as the cell phone on his hip vibrated. "Hold on a sec."

Checking the message gave him a minute to collect his thoughts. This wouldn't have happened if he'd kept her in sight. Technically, when Jake left the building, responsibility for her had fallen on his shoulders.

His mouth went slack as he read the abbreviated text from Virus.

Oh, hell.

Chapter Seven

"S'up, boss? Was that Virus?" Nerd made himself at home on the corner of Nate's desk. Perfect dexterity rolled the quarter over one knuckle then the next before disappearing under his fingers to reappear between thumb and index finger. His gaze flicked between Nate and Callie slumped against his shoulder.

The evening morphed from bad to worse with little time for explanations. Dread coiled around Nate's spine to send a chill from one vertebra to the next. Little did he suspect after waking this morning he'd be dropped into a shit storm without warning or the resources to deal with the fallout.

"We're taking Callie and hitting the road. Wheels up in ten."

"What?" Nerd pocketed his coin and stood. "Where's Jake. Where's Virus?"

"Don't know about Jake. Virus is gonna meet us... away from here."

Lifting her head to survey the room, Callie asked, "Where're we going, *schmoopie*?" Callie's designated nickname earned muffled guffaws.

Though her thoughts remained uncensored, her eyes focused on him with concern. Not wanting to lie, Nate opted for a half-truth.

"Someplace quiet where you can sleep off the mickey. Who gave you the drink tonight?" Nate eyed Sebastian, who held his hands up, palms out.

"Hey. The bartender sent her an iced tea via your server. I've had eyes on her all night, except in the head."

Nate returned his ire with a dose of his own. "If no one knew you were coming here—"

"We do not have a leak. Moreover, I trust *my* team. Are you saying no one would try to snatch a blonde-haired, blue-eyed beauty for her looks and voice alone? This club," Sebastian extended his arm, "and all those within, are your responsibility. While we're at it, why is your shirt bloody?"

Sebastian's logic slid a wedge of uncertainty in the mix, until Nate rewound the flashback to the point the knifeman declared his intent.

"The fight outside was staged." He needn't say more, nor could he spare the time.

"It's an organized set up," Spirit confirmed, taking a closer look at Nate's arm.

"No longer bleeding. I'll tend to it when there's time. I've got another jacket. Listen, when we leave, I want you and Nerd to get supplies from my house. I'll give you the address and code. Enter from the southeast window, second story, or you'll encounter a whole lot of unpleasantness."

"The usual supplies?" Spirit checked his watch then nodded.

"Yep. Some things don't' change. And can you get her a *can* of soda?" Nate directed his inquiry to Blade.

"I didn't drink a lot. The tea tasted funny." Callie closed her eyes and shook her head, then groaned. "Not that I've drank much other than water and milk."

"You've never had alcohol before." Sebastian studied Callie and hummed low in his throat. "Could your barman have misinterpreted and given her a Long Island iced tea?" Turning to Callie, he added, "It has vodka, rum, gin, and tequila. Must not have drank much. You already have a little color back in your cheeks, lightweight."

"This spiral with lack of coordination didn't come from what little amount she'd consumed. I saw her glass on the counter by the sink. Plus, who's the guy with the broken nose? How'd he get locked in a stall... unconscious?"

"Okay, this means someone *inside* your club is working against you." Sebastian raked his fingers through his hair.

"Let's revisit the last part of that, the assailant unconscious three feet away, locked in a stall? Ideas anyone?" Spirit finished and stood to face Sebastian, a critical assessment underway.

"That's a mystery to solve later. We'll let Conner deal with both as he sees fit. For now, she's safe. We need to keep her that way without carting trouble with us." Nate held Callie's chin between thumb and forefinger, tilting her face up.

"Prick said his name was Daniel. He called me a slave." Callie held up one fist. "I gave him a good dose of hell just like Jake showed me. What an odd name to call someone. Prick." Surprise lowered her voice to a whisper as she stared at her fist. "It worked."

"Nate, we got here clean. No one followed us. You may not know me, but you know Jake. *He* hasn't grown sloppy in five years. Trust me." Sebastian surveyed the room, his gaze not landing on anyone for more than a heartbeat.

The sly insinuation wasn't lost on the grumbling men.

"Jake told me to leave if he wasn't back in two hours. We start fresh, here and now." Nate mouthed the words *bug out* when Callie gave a long blink. Each team member gave an answering nod.

His old friend had dumped her into a situation—antithesis to her nature, like dropping a guppy in a tank full of sharks. He prayed her unique packaging covered a strong enough personality to adapt. He was about to rip her away from the only security she'd known.

"Where are we go—ing?" Callie slurred then held her hands out to receive the pup Blade placed in her lap. "Hey, Faith. When you get bigger, you have my permission to bite any idiot you come across." Her glare pinpointed Nate.

"Okay, guys, I'll explain on the road. Time is crucial." Nate wanted to detail his intentions and soothe her fears, but survival came first. "You feeling a little better?"

"Kinda, but the ground is still shifting under me, not as much now, at least not literally."

"Everybody, check your gear again. Nothing else from here goes with us." After each nodded, he addressed Spirit, "Get her go bag from Conner's office. Check it. Tell him we're leaving. Can you get her some crackers, too? Anything heavier might make a return trip. We'll stop along the way for something more substantial."

Callie's widened eyes and quick intake of breath reoriented him to her current frame of mind.

Nothing like panic to clear one's head.

"On it." Despite his size, the Native American's movements were quiet and sure.

Accustomed to working as a unit, each man moved with the confidence and precision of long-term practice.

Sebastian remained stationary, expectant.

In addressing the least known member, Nate didn't have time to evaluate his loyalties or specific abilities. "Check in with Marc. See what he's found out from tonight's hired muscle."

Nate stood and nudged Sebastian out the door then locked him out, leaving the other man bitching in the hallway.

The next step with Callie presented a dicey predicament. She was an innocent raised in a bubble and traumatized by witnessing the death of a friend. Those circumstances didn't indicate how she'd react to this situation.

A deep breath blew out his uncertainty. They didn't have time to dawdle. His next instructions would walk the line between gaining cooperation and instilling confidence versus instigating a suspected wide rebellious streak.

Damn.

He had no more idea what he was dealing with than Callie.

That left him to explain their status to the bundle of nerves who surfed her way up through a drugged fog and cuddling a pup like it held all the answers to her problems.

"Callie, the text from Virus said we've got trouble. Jake told you if anything happened, I would take you away and meet up with him later, right?"

A small nod and an even smaller, "Yes," let him know she stood on the verge of a breaking point.

Outside the door, Sebastian's tone signaled spiraling aggression. "What's the plan, Nate?" I don't like being kept in the dark."

"We'll be out in a minute." Nate kept his tone even, listening to the argument Sebastian started with Blade. Thirty seconds along, it stopped with a growl from the instigator.

As if she hadn't suffered enough by the death of Franklin before Jake thrust her into a new and foreign world, Callie would now have his welfare on her conscience. From what little he understood, nothing else had tested her mental stamina.

Trial by fire is not a good way to find out.

"Callie." Silence cocooned them. If she balked and chose to go with Sebastian, the chances of her survival dropped to nil. If Jake had been compromised, Sebastian was too. Even in her present state, she'd deduct that much.

Callie's enemies had a pipeline to Jake's plan and knew the owners of Ambrosia by sight. Did they think the club was just a stop off, or suspect a connection between Jake and one of the Crofton brothers?

Rock, meet hard place.

Without a clear head, familiarity would trump logic in Callie's thoughts. His charge might elect the familiar over the unknown.

"Callie, time to change your clothes. You can't go dressed like that." There wasn't time to explain about covert tracking devices hidden in garments. Items obtained by the team would be part of her fresh start.

"But my shoes. Jake just bought these for me. Said they were all the rage."

"We'll get you new ones."

"Why would someone get angry at their shoes?"

Nate paused, replaying the conversation in his mind. "Um, no. That was just a turn of phrase, manner of speaking. No one's mad at your shoes."

After tucking Faith in her crate and urging Callie to her feet, he dropped her bag on the desk and unzipped it. A glance at her face revealed tears trailing her cheeks and large violet eyes holding a fear she shouldn't know.

When he opened his arms, she stepped into his embrace without hesitation. Why life threw so much crap at the innocent would forever remain a mystery. He didn't have any nieces or nephews, but now understood how it might feel to have kids.

Chronologically, she's only a few years younger. Life experience put miles between them.

Earlier suspicion she might not be as naïve as Jake suspected evaporated in the face of the honesty in her expression. With such intelligence, she could play any number of games. However, what he witnessed now emerged from pure, raw ignorance and lack of awareness—the opposite being stupidity, the *inability* to understand.

Time stood still as the last remnants of her shudders faded. Again, recognition of her uncertainty sidelined his resolve, ensnaring the time essential for planning.

When he stepped back, gone was the sentimental sap in favor of the hardened guardian she needed.

"We have to leave, now. These clothes here should fit you. Put them on. Do you need help?" He let his tone carry the urgency of the moment.

"No!" The response was immediate and emphatic. Callie backed up as if slapped.

Nate held up his hands. "Okay, okay. Didn't mean anything by it. It's just that your coordination is a bit off. I don't know who drugged you or what you ingested. It's my job to keep you safe. Understand?"

"The man in the bathroom..." Callie began with a frown. "Said he was going to take me to my new life."

"Yes. He's been secured in Conner's office. Did you know him? Ever see him at the Think Tank?"

"No. I'd remember him. I've never had anyone look at me that way before, either."

"How'd he end up unconscious behind a locked stall door?"

"I don't know. I remember he came at me. I let him pull me to my feet, and then I rammed my palm into his nose. He fell backward—and I don't remember anything else."

"Did anyone else come in?"

"Not sure. I think I fell against the wall and hit my head. I'd like another stab at him when the confusion clears."

"I like your attitude, but right now, that's a problem Conner can handle."

Nate pondered the strengthening of Callie's demeanor. By action and speech, she'd appeared drugged in the ladies' room. Time had already begun to clear the haze in her mind.

Altered coordination wouldn't prevent the wheels in her mind from turning. News of Jake's delay sobered her speech and reanimated her resolve. She was weighing her options, smart enough to reason her way to an appropriate course of action.

The question foremost in his mind—who sent the bounty hunter and arranged for the altercation out front? That type of teamwork detailed a level of professionalism and took time to set up. Neither of the men had worn ear mics.

More important, who intervened in the bathroom on her behalf? Why remain in the background? According to Jake, she didn't know anyone outside of the Think Tank.

The unconscious man carried an extra hundred pounds, lots of muscle, and probably ten years' experience. She was drugged, uncoordinated, and didn't see who'd helped take him down.

His thoughts flashed back to their first meeting, the collision. She'd slammed into him, hard enough to knock him off balance. He'd known he was going to fall, yet never hit the floor. The strange sensation of being lifted still clung to the corners of his mind.

Chapter Eight

Strength in Nate's embrace fortified Callie's flagging reserves—until it registered, she'd have to change her clothes with him less than three feet away. "*Desperate times and unusual circumstances…*" was one of Jake's newest adages. Jake had been the only person to hug her, yet Nate felt just as safe.

"Why do I have to change? What's wrong with what I'm wearing? I have a jacket and we'll be in a car."

His snort of impatience wouldn't subdue her. Never in her life had nightmares taken physical form. Jake had assured her his team, though military, would never turn her over to an agency like the Think Tank. Though part of the plan, Nate kept his agenda to himself.

"Someone knew you were here, Callie. Think about it. How's that possible?" He gestured toward her shoes. "It would be quite simple to install a tracking device in the heel. Since I don't have the answers and we don't have time to examine every piece of your outfit, we leave everything behind."

"Are the others doing the same? You didn't tell Sebastian. Does he know?"

"Everyone's following protocol." Nate pointed to the bag with a *hurry up* motion to get her moving.

Her brows rose when peering inside at the garments.

Members of the team had been cordial, respectful, and sometimes reverent. Nothing new or unusual there. Of note, she felt a connection with Spirit, more serene and less electrifying than sensations provoked by Nate.

"Fine. Thanks for explaining." Sarcasm was a new addition to her viewpoint, instigated by Jake. It came natural around Nate.

"Okay, enough talk, either change your clothes while my back is turned, or I'll dress you myself." A sudden pivot allowed him to rifle through papers on his desk.

Jake had never been a tyrant, even during their tragic and desperate escape from the institution.

Alone with a dictator, she latched onto the zipper of her outfit, fury claiming a large chunk of her emotional reserve. A metal purr of disengaging teeth reinforced the reality of her situation. Just because he was right didn't mean she had to like it.

A smile curved her lips when his pen suddenly leaked black ink all over his fingers. The solid string of curses equaled a balm to her soul. Sometimes small revenges provided subtle relief.

When Sebastian first showed her the delicate knit costume and declared it a singer's garb, amazement at the soft material kept her from questioning his choice. Now, she hugged the dangling fabric to her body for the little protection it offered.

Alone and near naked with a man had never listed among her experiences except for one very conservative doctor. Her fingers shook in reaching for the bag sitting next to the man wiping his hands.

Jake warned of many strange changes and experiences to come but hadn't sketched details of what to expect.

For an instant, Nate froze.

Callie held her breath, lest the beast taste her fear in each desperate exhalation. Stealth didn't number among her talents, so she wrenched the garments from the bag and took a step back. At least the sports bra was familiar and comfortable as she pulled it on while contorting to maintain the dress as a visible barrier.

The shoulder rig Nate pulled from his desk made her gasp. Well-worn supple leather scented the air and signified frequent use. The holster fit snug under his left arm. His flight jacket yanked off the chair back would conceal its presence.

"You're not changing your clothes?" Whatever demon strangled her brain's filter needed a muzzle. "How come?"

Again, Nate paused. "No. Let me clarify. Whatever *you* had with you *before* your arrival tonight stays behind."

"Fine." Rough denim felt foreign to the touch yet fit the strategy Nate outlined. Clean start.

In two hours since her arrival, she realized the extent of her closeted and uninformed existence. Not only did she have everything to learn, she had to incorporate the new knowledge on the fly.

Hearing stories about covert ops was far different from experiencing them. Slipping off her low-heeled flats, she wondered aloud, "How will Jake find us?" Shoving into one leg of her jeans, she paused for his answer then hurried to pull on the other leg.

"We'll worry about that later. You finished dressing?"

"Um, Nate, these pants, they only come up to..."

"Zip 'em up, Callie. They're fine."

"But—"

A startled squeak escaped when he turned to face her, his expression implacable. Before she understood his intent, he gripped the waistband. Her breath sucked in fast as he zipped them up.

The impersonal grasp of her pants provoked an astonishment she couldn't define as she clutched the knit shirt to her chest. Without preamble, he snatched the pullover from her hands and shook it out. "Arms up, sweetheart, we've run out of time."

No one had helped her dress since childhood, yet she complied without question while garbed in denim jeans and a sports bra.

His expression bore no semblance to the man who'd cared for her in the restroom. No, this was a man caring for an incompetent relative.

The whisper-soft grazing of his touch down her flanks as he settled the hem tickled, with gooseflesh rising in its wake. A furtive glance at his face revealed a mask she couldn't read. From the muscle ticking in his jaw to the slight furrow in his brow, he remained a mystery she was determined to solve.

"Sit, let's get these on. You should have thick socks here." After sidling over to a nearby chair, she perched on the edge and took the bag handed to her.

Again, the brush of his fingers against her skin as he pulled thick woolen socks up didn't appear to register with him. Dumbfounded didn't come close to her reaction as he secured her tennis shoes. When he laced them up, she felt like a child.

"Here's a jacket. Now, let's go." Grabbing her bag, he gestured toward the hallway and walked out.

To leave with Nate would open a whole new world for which she hadn't prepared. Yet Jake had trusted their lives to him. She followed his lead.

With shadows invading from the hall came another voice, brisk and succinct. "Hey, Nate. Take this. It's all I have on me and from our offices."

"Thanks, Conner, I'll call when we're clear. The guy in the women's restroom, Daniel—"

"I'll take care of him and the ones from the parking lot."

The sounds of material shuffling and zipper teeth engaging accompanied the addition to Nate's bag.

"Well, that's what brothers are for." The older version of Nate smiled and winked as he handed her a drink. "Here you go. It'll help clear your head."

The can was cold in her fingers. "I've never drank one of these before."

Nate froze and turned to her. "You've never had a Coke?"

"Um, no. I don't do drugs, at least not knowingly."

Confusion, then amusement, flitted across his face. "Okay. Try it. If you like it, just drink half. Okay? Trust me, it'll help"

She startled when he opened the can for her. "Thanks. I think I can do the rest of the heavy lifting." Taking a tentative sip, her brows winged up. "Oh. I like this. It's good."

The right corner of his mouth tilted up in a grin. "Stick with me, kiddo. There's lots of great things to experience."

Sebastian waited at the head of the hallway, his fingers tapping against his thigh in a silent rhythm. A shudder traversed her shoulders at the fleeting frown cast toward Nate before something else darkened his gaze. Friction existed between the two men.

Because Nate's taking control?

In the next heartbeat, Sebastian smiled, the seething undercurrent camouflaged. Nate didn't miss much, but he hadn't seen the glimmer of animosity.

"Okay, Callie, let's get a move on." The heat of Nate's hand wrapping around her fingers added more confusion to her muddled mind.

Her thoughts traveled at warp speed, circulating theories with her focus clearing. Would life always be like this? Had she doomed others to forever looking over their shoulders?

Sebastian stepped before them to block their exit. "Let's take a breath here and discuss the plan."

Callie saw and shrank from the malevolence in Sebastian's countenance. As if expecting her response, he took a step back and maintained a distance of several feet.

"We're leaving. Plain and simple, that's the plan."

"I'll grab my bag from the car on the way. I've got some extra things packed for her. Who's driving?"

"No. She takes nothing but what she's wearing and the bag brought by the team. It's been checked." Nate's tone brooked no argument.

Spirit appeared by their sides, holding a black leather bag. "Everything's clean, Nate." The Native American held out the smaller bag.

"Wait. Will someone please explain to me what we're doing? This is the shoddiest briefing I've ever attended." Sebastian's voice gained volume.

In front of his office, Conner held up a restraining hand. "Nate, tell me where you're headed, and I'll catch up with you later. I assume you have a burner phone?"

"I do, and we're heading to our favorite place, bro. We'll take stock there and figure out something moving forward. Don't join us till I call."

"Hold on, here." Sebastian stood tall and sidestepped to block their exit. "I want an explanation."

"Short version. Virus followed Jake when he left. Jake ran into a problem. I don't know if either got out of the situation clean."

"Oh, shit. So, where are we headed?" Sebastian pivoted when Nate brushed by, but kept pace, keeping Nate between himself and Callie.

"Uh, sorry, Sebastian. Can't take you on this ride. Jake requested—"

"What? That's ridiculous. I've watched over her for years. I'm certainly not going to abandon her when she's in trouble." As Sebastian stepped around to face her, Callie shrank from his glare.

Before she could voice her objection, Spirit stepped between them. "Sorry, man, this is our fight from here on out. No need to put you in any more danger. If you could take care of her outfit so it's not seen again, that would help."

"No. She's my responsibility in Jake's absence. Callie, come here. Now." His shuffle sidestep to circumvent Spirit produced a mimicked step that again blocked his sightline to his target.

Spirit again proved her initial assessment correct. Their prior time spent in conversation built a tentative foundation of trust she prayed would grow to withstand any trial. Each team member now gathered and scowled at Sebastian.

"Hey, it's up to her to continue with the ones who freed her or adopt a completely unknown group. She doesn't know you people. She's safer with me. It's what Jake would want."

Nate pivoted to face her, invading her personal space. Their gazes locked. "Technically speaking, you are of age. You do know Jake asked me to—"

"Yes. Yes, I want to go with you, Nate."

Lost in a sea of confusion where rational explanations failed to come forth, an innate sense dictated Nate the safer option. Squeezing his fingers created a combination of warmth, security, and excitement.

"Then we do this my way." With a slanted grimace at Sebastian, he added, "Sorry, man. We need a clean slate, and we need to move. Got a long ride ahead."

Again, Nate lent much-needed assurance before gently tugging her away. The blistering string of curses filling the hall's confines noted Sebastian's opinion of the plan.

Maybe military experience stripped away pleasantries of simple interactions. She'd seen it in the mad dash across a courtyard that left Franklin dead and Jake injured. Now, she felt it in Sebastian's strange animosity.

One thing was certain. Each man carried responsibility to his last breath.

Chapter Nine

Spirit shoved the gear in park and cut the engine before slipping his backpack over his shoulder. Thinking ahead and the equipment needed to complete the job, he had a single paper clip and a piece of gum.

Assessment of the *easy* op ranked toilet high when Nate requested all his gear. It indicated an elevated threat. Beside him, Nerd fidgeted. The electronics guru was always nervous.

Instinct warned the current agitation was warranted.

"I'm concerned about Jake. He always ran a tight ship." Nerd pulled his balaclava down to cover his face and checked the .45 at his hip.

"Nate said the bastards from the Think Tank have the highest connections. We could be eyeball to eyeball against equals on this one. Let's stay sharp."

"Our opponents might have better and more current intel. Shame we can't tap into that."

"Who knows? We've got a hacker of our own. For now, let's hope we're in and out of here before company arrives." Spirit eased out of the truck into the brush hiding his vehicle and met Nerd at the hood.

"You ever been in Nate's house? Should we expect something that bites? His brother trains dogs for police departments."

"No to both. But we're good. He gave me the layout. Open span downstairs. Three bedrooms and two baths up. Said the oak tree on the southeast side takes us to the corner guest bedroom."

"Why not pick the front or back lock?"

Spirit sighed, also wanting to make quick work of the job but understood why Nate put him in charge. "There's a series of alarms. The only place to silence all at once without his thumbprint on the front door reader is to go through the window."

"Damn. The man likes his privacy."

"Can't blame him. Not with his field experience." Spirit snagged his vibrating phone and read the text. "Damn. We gotta move it. Something's happened to Virus. Blade and Whisper will cover Nate and Callie."

"Hells bells and fried monkey meat. These bastards are fast, accurate, and methodical. I'm thinking this girl is a hell of a lot more special than Jake let on. It's not like him to sandbag us."

"Problem solving later. Weapons and gear retrieval now."

"Let's get this done before bad weather slows us down."

Frozen ground with a thin layer of ice hindered their ability to move with little noise. Lacking foot traffic and daytime warming sunlight, the forest floor didn't radiate enough heat to thaw precipitation. If someone had entered the home before them, they'd left no telltale prints.

A full moon playing hide-and-seek with low cloud cover rendered periodic light on thin trails. Together, they padded through the woods, each wary of their surroundings. Nate's house offered a perfect secluded spot to unwind with plenty of cover for an enemy to hide.

Spirit paused twice, listening to the sounds of nature, then the lack thereof. A knack for searching out his enemies warned they weren't alone. Tiny hairs along his forearms and across his nape jumped to attention, his body tingling with the forerunners of an adrenaline rush. A quick hand signal conveyed his concern.

At the edge of the forest, Spirit halted, drawing Nerd up short. Everything around them was still. Too silent. A slight tilt of his head and shoulder shrug conveyed the warning.

His partner nodded.

Nothing stirred other than the breeze through bare limbs overhead, their creaking and scratching hinting of other threats nearby.

The two-story contemporary remained dark and quiet, with no shifting of surrounding shadows. If someone waited to ambush them, they were well-trained and patient. Perhaps they wanted something inside the house.

Together, they raced across open ground. Blade's unfortunate slip on ice and uneven ground sent him to his knees. A fast recovery saw them both flattened against the home's southern wall and beside a branching oak with an eight-inch diameter.

Quick study of the tree proved its leaning point, though slight, faced the home. Protected from the northeast storm front moving in, rough bark remained free of ice.

Keeping his feet and hands relatively close, Spirit laced his fingers together, wrapped his arms around the tree, and "walked" up the trunk. Close proximity of hands to feet brought more weight to bear on his forearms.

Only Nate would have the luck for the tree to fork near the second story window. A small penlight in his front pocket allowed Spirit to study the window. Nate's planning ahead for this type situation stemmed from his black-op days. The private investigator's foresight to drill a small hole behind the window's handle push, the pinpoint opening covered with paint, spared the expense and hassle of shattered glass.

Spirit straightened his paperclip and stuck the end through to push against the retaining lever, then slid the window open.

Once inside, he waited for Nerd to climb through amid grumbling about ice and cold weather.

"Don't worry, dude, we'll get you back with the bayou's snakes and crocs before you know it." Spirit retrieved his mini-flash and aimed it at the floor.

"Let's get his stuff and get out. This is giving me gator bumps."

"We'll have to go out the same way."

Nothing stirred Spirit's immediate concern in padding down the hallway and carpeted stairs, not until he stepped into the great room.

Air currents were still except the light stirring of window curtains over the floor's heat register. Ambient light through the bay window painted shadow outlines of furniture, two couches and three wing chairs.

A stone fireplace occupied a good portion of the opposite wall with a large screen TV above it. Thick patterned rugs softened their footsteps.

Nerd followed his path to the foyer where the closet held Nate's gear in a hidden rear compartment. Two heavy jackets and three lighter ones left most of the closet space bare. A plastic bin with Christmas wrapping paper hid the seams of the partitioned space.

Nerd shifted foot to foot while Spirit punched in the compartment's code, the release of the hinged door rupturing the silence.

"Here, you take the lighter one. Pretend you're dragging a baby croc by the tail." Spirit grabbed the second duffle and hefted it over his shoulder. Again, his sixth sense prodded him to pause and listen to the silence.

Well-tuned intuition rarely proved wrong. Nodding over his shoulder, he pressed his elbow against his flank, reassured with the outline of his shoulder rig.

Even Nerd's penchant for pranks didn't rise above the eeriness of the night's chore. In any other situation, the younger man would busy himself filling Nate's toothbrush with Orajel, putting powdered cheese in his orange juice container, or any one of a hundred stunts. His practical jokes edged manic when bored.

Back upstairs and at the window, Nerd tugged Spirit's jacket. "I'll go first. You drop 'em down to me."

Spirit moved aside to let Nerd out, his sixth sense screaming. The small wad of gum stuffed between his teeth and jaw had long since lost its flavor but not its purpose. "You're assuming I won't slip and land on top of you."

Soft, crunchy thuds announced Nerd's quiet landing in the damp bed of leaves. The smaller man caught each duffle and lined them against the foundation.

A small portion of Spirit's gum covered the pinpoint hole after exiting and closing the window. They had no other way to secure it.

At least it won't be visible.

Thoughts of Callie and what she'd endured during the past week bolstered his determination to see her safely tucked away in an environment where she set her own path. Maybe because she didn't yet know enough about the world she'd entered, but he hadn't detected signs of overwhelming animosity.

He landed with a soft thud next to his partner. Each slung a duffle over his shoulder.

Honed instincts necessitated a moment of silence to survey their surroundings. Nothing organic moved.

Spirit nudged his partner. "Don't see 'em, but we've got company. I feel them, so don't dawdle."

Halfway in their sprint to the tree line, Spirit's well-honed sixth sense compelled a quick sidestep just as a muffled *ffft* coincided with a sound of metal striking metal. The force shoved him cattycorner into his companion.

Nerd stumbled but regained his balance. "Shit. You're right."

Zigzagging their steps avoided another direct hit but increased their time in the open. Another round of shots failed to pierce Spirit's hide.

Once behind cover of a large tree trunk, Spirit retrieved his Glock. "You hit?" Even the low murmur carried.

"No. Fight or flight? We need information but—"

"Don't know their numbers. We've achieved our priority. Best to leave. Nate's probably facing an equal or greater threat and might need us. Better to consolidate."

"Who in hell are these bastards? How'd they get on him so fast?"

"Dunno. Doesn't sound like they're following. Can't see a target. Let's hoof it."

Speed over stealth. Frozen twigs and dead limbs crunched under foot in their bid to reach the truck first. Each carrying an extra few ounces of lead in their duffle encouraged speed. If not for Nate's hardware, they'd both be dead.

Circling wide, they approached the truck from a western angle. When within fifteen yards, Spirit halted and turned to Nerd, pulling off his balaclava. "It's a chance we need to take. They haven't pursued and probably don't want us."

"You're assuming they know Nate's approximate size and build."

"Safe bet. They knew to come here."

"They'll try to pick us up on the road. I'll check for trackers, you keep watch." Nerd whispered even as he handed over his duffel and retrieved a flashlight.

"We'll take as many back roads and four-wheeler paths as we can. I know the area well enough. I'll tell Nate we'll be delayed."

Jake hadn't known the extent of the Think Tank's resources. If the administrator pulled the current strings in this hunt, he was well-funded and hired the best.

Chapter Ten

"Where are we going?" Callie rubbed her eyes and sat up in the passenger seat.

Nate smiled at the determination in her voice. "To a place not registered in any of our names."

"You live on the coast *and* have a cabin in the mountains?"

"I like lots of space around me, along with nature." He needed it to breathe. The thought of living in a barrack-type situation made him cringe. He preferred either mountains or an ocean view.

"And we'll stay in the mountains? That sounds great. Can I go on hikes?"

The wistful tone of her voice reminded him of where she'd grown up. The change in tact symbolized her ability to compartmentalize.

Asking instead of making a declaration arose from a life of programmed living. He wondered how long it would take to change her way of thinking. She probably didn't yet recognize the difference.

Precipitation had ceased but created sparkling reflections from intermittent moonlight. Heat buildup during the day along with sparse traffic prevented ice coating the asphalt. That would soon change when they traveled the more remote route to his property.

"Of course. It's great exercise. We'll have to keep Faith on a harness though, until she learns to stay with you. She'd be easy prey to a lot of critters."

"Maryland gets snow, yes?"

Nate paused in his musing. "You've seen snow, right?"

"I have, but I was never allowed to explore it."

The odd turn of phrase matched his perception of her thought processes. "It's not supposed to snow tonight, but we'll get some soon enough. Maybe tomorrow."

"The rest of the team will meet us at the cabin?"

"Yes. Nerd and Spirit grabbed my gear from home first. Don't worry. Even if someone makes the connection from you to me, they won't know where to look for us."

"How much farther?"

Nate grinned at the universal sign of impatience. "Another couple hours."

The fact he'd run roughshod over her emotions in Ambrosia stuck in his craw. He knew of nothing she'd done to deserve the less-than-respectful treatment.

A few hours prior, he'd brooded under the onslaught of memories and curiosity of an old friend's cryptic request for help.

Now, he ran from an unknown, unseen enemy who followed an invisible trail. He may not know Sebastian's history and experience, but he did know Jake. The Jake he knew ran a tight operation, always well-planned and executed to the last detail.

"You worked with Jake in the military." Callie's tone was tentative, exploring.

"Yes. Then, after discharge, I joined my brothers in a private investigations venture."

"Are you married?"

"No." Adjustment to civilian life had led to what he thought would be a permanent relationship. His former girlfriend would've stayed if he'd asked, but the price tag included her fledgling career.

He'd set her free.

Knowledge of traveling the honorable path offered little comfort when the medical residency of her dreams took her across country. She'd received an equal amount of pain from the separation. The demand on her time plus the geographical relocation made continuing their relationship unfair to either.

Now, as he turned onto the expressway, intermittent headlights flashed across a whole new bundle of trouble in the making. Nothing disguised chaos better than angelic wrapping.

With Jake's first contact, he'd insinuated the young woman held talent beyond imagination and distinct from her extreme if selective intelligence. It all added up to secrets.

Secrets got people killed.

It's harder to protect what you can't define.

In retrospect, he'd yet to extend an olive branch. Instead, he'd barked orders and separated her from anything she'd thought familiar. It was up to him to figure out how to bridge the gap.

They wheeled through the night and into a future unknown. He'd have to earn her trust before seeking that which she held most dear. He should've confronted Jake at the club and demanded the whole story.

"Will you tell me what Jake's message said?"

Reaching back, Nate pulled a blanket from behind the seat after noting her shiver again. Each of his three brothers were intelligent, yet none compared to the young woman sitting next to him.

"It wasn't from Jake. It was from Virus."

Her inexperience in normal life screamed like a blow horn in his ear. The way she'd looked at him after their collision smacked of infatuation. The panic in her eyes when he'd dressed her like a child unveiled an innocence that clubbed him between the eyes. In between, he'd witnessed defiance with an edge of mistrust.

Eyebrows drawn low and pursed lips spoke volumes, yet she hadn't voiced her frustration.

"And..."

They didn't have time to do things the right way. Nate took a deep breath and considered his words. "Okay, here's what I know so far. After I tell you, I need to know what you're hiding. In order to keep you safe, I have to understand *specifically* why foreign asshats are hounding your trail. It'll help us narrow the suspect pool."

Translation—if you've created some type of bomb, I need to know where it's hidden.

Another glance revealed her frustration had morphed into the murky area of stonewall. He'd earned a stranger's trust before and could do it again, especially considering the stakes.

"Jake warned me—telling anyone would endanger their lives."

"Callie— we're already there, sweetheart." The vibration of his cell made him pause. "Just a sec." Snagging it from its clip, he took a deep breath after reading the message.

"Who's that?"

"Wow, you really don't trust easily, do you?"

"It's just that I've had one upheaval after another. I don't know when or where it'll stop. I'm not accustomed to so much change."

"Here, check it out." He'd already erased the earlier message from Virus, hence plopped the phone in her lap. "It's from Blade."

Startled, she fumbled for a second then read the message aloud.

"So, what supplies did Lightning and Nerd have to pick up and what does snag mean? Where will they meet us, and where's Virus? Is Jake with him?"

"Don't know where Virus is at the moment. Spirit and Nerd picked up gear we may need. Whisper and Blade will catch up with us."

"It's late."

"Not a problem." Every sentence she spoke clued him in to some aspect of her level of understanding concerning her new environment.

A lifetime of living by instinct forewarned their troubles had just begun. The likelihood of Jake's survival decreased with each mile they drove. He wouldn't talk probabilities when her mind would already be working them out.

Virus should've called with a sitrep by now, if only abbreviated.

They hadn't seen any traffic for miles and probably wouldn't on the back roads. Straight stretches became shorter as they wound their way through the foothills of Western Maryland.

Away from the hustle and bustle of traffic, there were no streetlights to grant intermittent glimpses of her mood. Soft blue glow from the dash furthered the mystery surrounding his enigma.

A straightforward and artless character revealed her current emotional status, as long as it didn't exist as a well-constructed façade. According to Jake, who excelled when it came to assessing personalities, Callie didn't do subterfuge.

Multiple upheavals in her life failed to shake what he sensed of her inner strength. Again, he marveled at the young woman beside him.

"Something's wrong."

Genuine fear laced her voice, the slight tremor reminding him of recent experiences. Her gaze lasered onto the side view mirror.

"What, Callie? Where?" He'd be foolish to discount the instincts of extreme intellect when not understanding what other surprises lay hidden beneath the surface.

"Behind us. Impact in less than forty-five seconds." Her gaze switched to the rearview mirror.

Did she just calculate the rate of speed from headlights in our rearview? At night? How?

Sure enough, twin headlights advanced and closed the distance in exponential fashion. A speculative glance at his passenger made him wonder at her sense of perception. *Damn.*

"Send a text on the cell to Blade, sweetheart. Just type bump."

To hit trouble so soon indicated either Jake employed lax security, presence of a mole, or a well-connected enemy. There wasn't enough information to differentiate.

Maintaining his speed, he reached inside his shoulder rig for his Glock then stayed his hand. "Scoot down in the seat, Callie, now. Leave your seatbelt on."

"Really?"

"Now, Callie. Do it and send the text."

"I am. I am." She dropped the phone twice after scooting down then sighed after hitting the send button. "Done. What does that mean exactly?"

"Bump in the road, a problem encountered. Blade and Whisper will join and escort us. We don't have much farther till we reach our pit stop."

"They got all that from one word?"

About fifty yards separated them from the approaching vehicle, a van judging by the size and set of the headlights. It closed in fast.

"Yeah, when you work with a team that closely, you can do that. They'll also give Spirit and Nerd a heads-up."

The strobe of light crossing his rearview mirror snapped his attention to the approaching threat. The van's course veered to one side of the road, then crossed to the other. Squealing tires and skid on the dirt shoulder preceded it leveling out.

They'd encountered no ice since leaving the parking lot of Ambrosia, and none since, except minor patches on bridges.

"Why is this happening?"

"Not sure yet, but we'll figure it out." The swaths of roadway cut by light beams canted an erratic path back and forth.

Drunk driver?

It made no sense. Beside him, Callie growled.

His mind worked to eliminate the unlikely: deer or other animal darting across the road, small patches of black ice, vehicle malfunction. Nothing fit. That left him with no plausible explanation.

After another dip to the uneven shoulder, the van careened back onto the road in a disjointed effort to avoid spinning out. Trouble in the form of inconsistent and volatile driving rendered Nate unable to form a viable defense.

The driver's speed didn't fluctuate, a giveaway for drunk drivers, *and* they regained control of its headed-for-the-ditch trajectory with skill and precision. Those maneuvers required training and experience to execute.

"What are we going to do?"

The fearful glance over her shoulder firmed his resolve. He would keep her safe.

"We'll be okay, Callie. We've got this."

Someone had either stuck a tracker on his undercarriage, missed by Whisper's inspection, or used satellite imagery. He hadn't picked up a tail from Ambrosia. However, Jake had mentioned foreign interests, which meant money. Anything could be possible.

Shit. Shit. Shit. What hell did you get me involved in, Jake old buddy?

"How close are the others?" She settled his phone in the cup holder.

With the quaver of her voice, Nate saw a little girl cowering within a woman's body.

"Just a few minutes away. We'll be okay."

Their pursuer closed the distance again in a direct approach, headlights beaming across Callie's headrest.

He needed a look at the driver, but a glance in his rearview revealed the headlights again jerked toward the ditch before cutting back to midline.

Callie sniffled. The last thing he wanted was a terrorized young woman to deal with while trying to keep them alive.

What is happening?

Whoever wanted her, would need her alive. They wouldn't risk a high velocity traffic accident.

A low groan escaped Callie as she peeked between the seats to see the vehicle change tactics and take position behind Nate. She held one hand to her temple and groaned.

The sudden jolt forward from the rear-end collision gifted them with a small whiplash. He'd soon return the favor, compliments of his fist.

Callie's rearward momentum stopped short with the seat, a thin cry escaping clenched jaws.

Faith's whining transformed into small yips as her crate jostled from impact.

"Faith," Callie screamed then reached to unbuckle her seatbelt, stopped with Nate's hand closing over her fingers.

"No. She's safer buckled in. Leave her. You okay?"

She whimpered.

"Callie?"

"Yes. Yes, I'm all right. Why are they doing this?"

"I'll remember to ask as soon as we finish this monkey dance."

The dark van slid into the oncoming lane and started to close the distance on his left. Both the driver and passenger wore masks. The van was black, nondescript, and lacked a front tag.

Just as Nate prepared to hit his brakes, a distinctive pop snapped his attention to the side.

The bastards had fired a round through his side window.

Callie screamed as the bullet's trajectory made a hole in the top six inches of the windshield.

Nate felt as much as heard its passage. Conchoidal fracture lines and hackle marks registered the bullet's position without a crimson stain.

"Incoming." The shooter hadn't compensated for height and skid discrepancy, hence failed to hit a soft target.

Had he been wrong about them needing her alive? Were they so careless as to risk hitting her by accident?

Callie's soft mewl echoed in the small confines.

Stomping the accelerator rocketed them forward in a risky bid to gain the lead. The vehicles were near equal in weight and size.

The van's position dropped back with Nate's acceleration then moved closer and to the side. Its front wheels aligning with Nate's rear tires indicated their intent.

"They're gonna try a PIT maneuver to spin us off the road." Before he could brake and counter their action, a low mewl from his passenger corresponded with the other vehicle jerking to the shoulder.

"Oh, God. That hurts." Callie pressed her palms against the sides of her head.

"Where are you hurt?"

"I'm not, I'm just scared."

Fishtailing sent the van's back wheels across the uneven rocky shoulder, increasing the chance of rolling. Expert maneuvering brought it back on solid roadway. The driver was experienced and talented behind the wheel, if not a bit crazy.

Fracture lines extending from the bullet hole reduced visual assessment in front. It wouldn't surprise him to face a new threat, head on. Nate flicked a button and braced himself for the inrushing wind swallowing the soft whir of his window's retraction. Cold air swept away the myriad questions assaulting his senses.

The driver handled the vehicle like a pro between intermittent, chaotic movements. There didn't appear to be a fight between the occupants, hence no logical reason for the sporadic fumbling at the wheel.

Instead of punching forward again, Nate hit the brakes hard enough for the rear vehicle to overlap his SUV by fifty percent. The maneuver was too fast for his pursuers to take advantage.

Once he'd taken away their leverage, he veered into their path, forcing them onto the shoulder.

Lateral force sent two of the van's wheels careening in the loose gravel. The driver hit his brakes to avoid toppling into the ditch. Again, the other driver had anticipated Nate's move.

"Someone's coming." Determination laced with uncertainty. Her voice quavered; her hands fisted in her lap.

Headlights flashed three times a short distance ahead. "There's Blade and Whisper." Unfortunately, the hunters would have seen the signal, too.

Headlights behind them faded as their assailant backed off.

I might not get another chance to end this hell.

Conner's earlier text declared those involved in Ambrosia's disturbance weren't talking. Public knowledge of the incident and assailant's detainment denied a personal *hands-on* interrogation.

"Oh, hell no. Not today, dirtballs." Screeching tires accompanied Nate stomping his brakes. Perfect timing derived from training lifted his foot off the pedal while spinning the wheel. It was a risky turn but needed under the circumstances. In order to shake their tail, he had to know who followed them, along with the *how* aspect.

Halfway through his spin, he shifted gears. Applying the brake again forced the wheels to a squealing stop.

Frustration culled his thoughts until anger expanded to fill the void as he looked ahead. The vehicle pursuing them had duplicated his maneuver and now headed away from him. He still faced a tinted window. Mud smeared the license plate.

Callie's voice filled the cab. "Wait. Please. I can't do this."

Whatever she thought she could or couldn't do didn't matter. He couldn't take her to a safe house until knowing they weren't followed.

"No, Callie. Sit tight. You'll be fine." The minute he took to dislodge her hand from his arm allowed his adversary to put distance between them.

Tires shrieked as the driver barreled ahead.

Nate did the same. Hunter became prey.

Flooring the gas pedal brought another surge of adrenaline. Only the silence of the woman beside him brought his gray cells' functioning to the fore.

Just when he thought his little enigma had reached her limit, Callie swore. The words were so foreign to his perception of her. The string of words equaled a common epithet from Jake long ago.

"We're okay, Callie."

"Are you nuts?" Panic in her voice coincided with a sniffling sound. She wiped her nose on her sleeve.

"Sometimes, yeah. Got to do something, or they'll just keep coming. You can't always hide."

"You think they won't give up... and we might not see them coming next time."

He could tell by her tentative tone she explored various scenarios and outcomes. According to Jake, she hadn't felt like a prisoner since she didn't know any other way of life. Now, the number existed to overwhelm her.

Instead of continuing the conversation, he concentrated on his driving. There'd be time for explanations later.

She scooted back up in her seat to watch. To make an angel cringe in terror earned him eternity in hell.

"I'm sorry. I can't let them go, Callie. We need information, and we need it now." This wasn't her world. She didn't know the rules of engagement. "They're too organized to stop short of success.

The problem is, they have to get it right *once. We have to get it right* every *time in order to keep her safe.*

"All right. All right. I get it."

Another inexplicable swerve sent the van to the dirt shoulder. Instead of compensating, it tacked harder until the front wheel dropped, and the van tilted. Unable to counterbalance, the vehicle bounced over rocks surrounding a small culvert and began a multi-revolution roll into the adjoining field.

The tortuous sound of twisting metal filled the air as glass shattered and each revolution modified its shape. Nate's headlights caught tiny reflections of reflective shards disseminating with each point of contact.

"They won't hurt anyone else. This ends, now!" Callie screamed.

The sudden fireball engulfing the vehicle took him by surprise. Rare was the incidence of an explosion from this type of accident, not that he could figure out the instigating factor.

Unless centrifugal force threw the passengers out the windows when the vehicle rolled, they'd be dead. Neither door had opened.

Callie's shoulders shook from the sobs she was unable to hold back. In less than a week, she'd seen more death than most saw in a lifetime.

After a final tumble of screeching metal and flying debris, the mangled vehicle came to rest on its side.

Silence reigned.

"No, no, no. I don't want to be like them. It wasn't supposed to be this way." Callie continued to cover her face with her hands, her mumbled words making no sense.

Confusion passed briefly through his mind, but he couldn't pass up the opportunity to unravel the source of the threat. As he picked up speed, he kept an eye on the van to make sure no one stumbled or crawled near the wreckage.

In closing the distance, the steady thrum of his tires created white noise reflecting his thoughts. From behind, his team advanced.

"Can we get out of here now?" Callie choked out between gasps.

"I have to check the vehicle and surrounding area." He didn't want to explain why he searched or what he expected to find. She'd seen enough death.

The crumpled vehicle lay on its side fifty yards into the field. Nate calculated the time needed to do a cursory search. The team could watch over his passenger.

"No. They have to have burned in the fire. I don't want to see it."

As if the situation wasn't bizarre enough, his vehicle began slowing—

even as he mashed the accelerator. They still had fifty yards to go before pulling perpendicular to the accident scene.

"What's happening?" A glance at his speedometer showed the steady dropping of the needle despite his efforts. The pedal wasn't stuck.

"What's wrong? Are we out of gas?"

"No... I don't know what's happening."

They rolled to a stop close to where the van left the blacktop. Before Nate could hit the brake and cut the engine, it went dead.

What the hell? This vehicle's maintenance is up to date.

Explanations would have to wait.

As soon as they stopped, Callie released her belt and retrieved her whimpering pup, cuddling Faith close and murmuring against the dog's thick fur.

Blade's truck pulled alongside with the engine idling, hence, no sort of EMP was involved.

"Everybody in one piece?" He leaned forward to scrutinize Callie before addressing Nate. "You do realize the fire is going to make identification difficult." He grimaced as he took in the scene. "We'll see what we can find. Why don't you go on ahead?"

"I've no idea why they crashed or why it caught fire, but I don't believe in freak accidents. One minute, they looked like an ad for drunk driving. In the next, the driver executed advanced maneuvers as well as any high-level operative." Nate thumped the steering wheel in frustration. Nothing added up.

"Looked like they had a chance of getting away clean. S'pose a deer ran out in front of them?"

"Along this highway? Quite possible." Nate snorted and glanced at Callie, still huddled in her seat. "But I sure didn't see it."

"This is getting into a whole lot of weirdness, boss." Blade tapped his steering wheel in time to his internal beat.

"It's not likely we'll find anything useful. I'll get Callie out of here and meet you at Parnell's. Need to check the undercarriage and get her some food."

"Just got a message from Spirit. Small hitch, but they're free and on their way." Whisper was already out of the truck and heading toward the van. From his back waist, he retrieved a gun.

"What about your brothers?" Blade paused in closing his door.

"I'll call Conner and give him a heads-up. For now, I want to keep them out of this. Watch your backs. Tell Spirit to call when they reach the Frederick County line, and I'll give them specific coordinates."

When Nate turned the key, his SUV purred to life. Slight pressure on the gas produced a smooth acceleration. The next one-eighty turn didn't involve screeching tires or a terrified passenger.

Callie and the pup remained cuddled, her soft voice crooning against her companion's neck. "We're alive, Faith. I'll protect you no matter what it takes. Jake said you're special, too."

In review, it wasn't pure fear Callie radiated. Frustration had morphed into anger bordering on rage, the type felt by someone backed into a corner. He remembered his brother describing canine fear-biting. Once dogs felt like they were backed into a corner, they fought with anything at their disposal, so panicked they weren't able to think in a reasonable manner.

Silence. Darkness. He didn't know whether to expect continued quiet or chatterbox Callie to pepper him with questions.

She kept her gaze facing the side window with a mass of curls covering her face, her version of shutting out the world.

"Callie?" The click of the overhead light sounded harsh in the cold stillness.

"Um, yeah. I'm all right. Just frazzled." A quiet sniffle as she wiped her nose on her sleeve was appropriate. The small line of blood left on the cloth—not so much.

"Callie. Look at me, sweetheart." He slowed, then pulled over and shoved the gear into park. Panic filled him with the thought of her having sustained an injury. A head injury. He'd thought she was crying.

Another misconception. He underestimated her at every turn.

She didn't move. Another sniffle.

With a slow, gentle touch, he turned her chin to face him. A good look at what his recklessness had wrought reminded him she wasn't a soldier, nor had she been exposed to talk about wars or even the violence of video games.

Bright light in the small cab highlighted the thin trail of blood coming from her nose.

"Shit. What happened? I'm—I'm sorry, hon. You don't deserve any of this."

"Guess I hit something when he rammed our bumper."

He couldn't hold back the disbelieving grunt. *Yeah, air molecules carry a heavy mass this time of year.*

She'd been huddled low in her seat, secured behind her seatbelt.

From the glove box, he extracted tissues and wiped her nose, satisfied when no more blood appeared, then held the rest out for her to take.

A gentle swipe of his fingers edged the heavy fall of hair away from her ears. No blood or drainage. For the second time tonight, he wondered about her extraordinary circumstances. "We'll talk about this later."

She offered no response, her gaze flat and empty.

Minutes passed as he contemplated recent events. The driver of the van had executed a perfect bootlegger turn, yet at times drove like a drunken sailor. No other signs of struggle existed. It appeared his concentration had come and gone on a whim. The vehicle ran off the road without apparent cause, then blew up. *Why?*

"How far is it to your cabin?"

"Not too far, but there're a couple of things we need to do first, like check this undercarriage again for a tracking device. Plus, I want to grab some chow. Hope you don't mind fast food."

"Um, fast food?" A puzzled look conveyed sincerity.

"Sorry, I keep forgetting. Slang is new to you." He clicked off the light and pondered things she needed to learn to survive in a world where spies and death lurked in dark corners.

He had taken her trust for granted, that she'd want his help. He hadn't considered her guilt over Franklin's death and perhaps she might have developed an agenda of her own. If she thought others safer without her presence and took off, she wouldn't survive long.

He'd promised protection, which meant he needed her secrets.

The very real possibility of betrayal glared like a beacon on the horizon and threatened them all. He didn't have a handle on the situation or his target. There was no way of knowing what information Callie held close to the vest, or if it would help him ferret out how someone tracked them.

One thing seemed certain. Someone had separated Jake from the herd for elimination. Another burden for Callie to bear.

The only thread he had to pull was the name Penny, sure to be a false identity.

Chapter Eleven

Callie's imagination outdistanced the headlights stretching into oblivion. She'd crossed a line that could never be erased, unofficially making her a member of the team. Whether they knew it or not didn't matter.

Faith snuggled against her chest, her warm breath and presence an unknown but welcome comfort. If she'd known weeks ago that the world was this dangerous, would she still have accepted Jake's offer of freedom? Her life had become anything but free still directed by strangers, but now with the burden of death lurking at every turn.

Nate had retreated into silence.

During their brief interactions, she'd discovered much about his character. He wouldn't suffer fools or subterfuge. He'd dig through her world until satisfied of knowing anything of significance.

The strange environment in which she now dwelled proved to be everything Jake promised, full of wonder and danger alike. Both men had spoken of cities with disdain but marveled at the majestic beauty of mountains. They also detailed friendships so strong to suggest worthiness of one's life.

She'd seen firsthand evidence of this with Franklin's death and the extent to which the others went to protect her.

Jake trusted Nate. That spoke volumes on a general level but didn't help in the moment-to-moment social transactions or protect her secrets. Giving him something to chew over might conceal her emerging ability.

In a moment of clarity or insanity, she blurted, "I can read binary code."

Silence.

"Did you hear me?"

"I can certainly see where anyone would covet such a rare gift. But just so I understand, you read it the same way others would read a book?"

"Yes."

He nodded. "How many know this?"

"Jake, Sebastian, Ray at the Think Tank, and anyone they've told."

"I suppose they tested you as far as speed and accuracy?"

"Yes. For a while—until it got old for them."

"Let me guess, they wouldn't let you anywhere near the internet. That must've frustrated the hell out of you."

"My life has been so censored. I didn't realize it until Jake let me use his laptop. Wow. There's so much out there to learn."

"You can probably hack anything you come across?"

"Haven't been stumped yet."

"Which would make you invaluable to so many."

"It makes me an oddity. People fear or hate what they don't understand."

"Not always." A half-smile quirked up one side of his mouth. "Sometimes, they're just plain out fascinated."

She waited for a stronger reaction, but it didn't come.

"The Think Tank's administrator would fear what codes you could crack with free access to the internet."

"I did do some snooping during the ride to Maryland. Jake was careful with where I went. Ray isn't as insulated as he thinks, but they must keep sensitive information on a standalone, because I couldn't find what I wanted."

"You couldn't find who was after you?"

"Not enough time. We didn't know anyone was tracking us across country, and thought we had time. Why didn't they try to grab me sooner?"

"Good question. I'll ask soon as we catch one of these bastards. It might be they wanted to root out all his contacts to avoid further problems. What've you learned about the Think Tank so far?"

"Not a lot. Ray's quite the paranoid bastard. Unless I'm mistaken, and I don't believe I am, he assigned key personnel false identities. Since I didn't have contact with many, there's no way I can connect duties to faces I haven't seen. He even segregated the employees according to assignments. I haven't had enough time to learn what else they did there. Neither has Jake."

"We'll figure it out, eventually. For now, we have other concerns."

"How are they tracking us?" If one of the team had turned traitor and Nate couldn't find the source, all their lives were forfeit.

"Don't know yet." The simplicity of his statement contradicted the intensity of his gaze, which promised retribution to anyone crossing his objective.

"There's so much I don't know, can't change, and can't predict." It'd been naïve to consider herself a decent judge of character, now realizing the lack of base for understanding. She'd jumped into a world where fear and death followed the joy of new discoveries with no break or warning between.

"Life will settle down. You'll be able to breathe easy and find balance. You've been torn in too many directions to know which way to turn. Decisions, even once made, sometimes have to be fluid to accommodate life."

Sensory overload didn't come close to describing what boiled inside her mind. No wonder her nose bled.

Nate was right about the difference between knowing and experiencing. Deciding who to trust necessitated careful consideration.

"Sebastian and Jake were careful. No one followed us from the safe house to Ambrosia. Sebastian seemed frustrated, but he, Franklin, and Jake were very close. He's as worried as I am about Jake."

"Callie." A momentary pause marked words he'd obviously chosen with care. "I don't know yet how they found us, but we'll figure it out."

"I can't hide forever."

"Won't have to. Once we eliminate this threat, I know someone we can approach for long-term support. For now, we'll pull off the road so I can check the vehicle."

"How will Jake find us? Does he know about your cabin?" Jake trusted Nate, but would Nate's loyalty survive tragedy befalling his teammate or would he deem the risk too high?

"No, but he knows how to reach me. Listen, Callie, there's a chance—"

"Don't say it! Jake has to be okay." She couldn't contemplate any variance, bending her head to take refuge with Faith.

"All right. You have enough on your plate for now. Listen, I'm going to park behind these big rigs at the truck stop. I want you to stay put while I check the SUV. I'll make it quick, but we need to make sure we're clear before proceeding."

"What about the others?"

"On their way. When they arrive, I'll go in and grab us a bite to eat. Cheeseburger and fries okay?"

"Right now, I'm intellectually and physically depleted. Anything is fine." How could life devolve into bedlam within a few short days?

Franklin dead, Jake missing, Sebastian feeling lost and adrift. A car chase, gunfire, squealing tires, fireballs of death. It all added up to a future she wasn't sure she wanted.

Sacrificing her friends wasn't a price she was prepared to pay. As far as the team, despite them being strangers and willing to help their teammate, they didn't know her or owe her anything. She didn't want to risk their lives.

In the space of five minutes, she'd become like them, willing to do whatever it took to survive.

During her cross-country road trip with Jake, talk about the future included a tranquil cottage by the sea or a lodge in the mountains, quiet days of study and most of all, freedom to do as she chose.

All she wanted now was to avoid a bullet in her skull and bleeding out from a cranial hemorrhage.

Ahead on the narrow highway, a large truck stop loomed, somber and forbearing. A dozen tractor-trailers parked in uniform consistency off to one side of a glass-fronted, low-slung brick building mimicked soldiers in formation. The sign out front, Jimmy's Chat and Chew, reminded her just how far out in wonderland she'd ventured.

"I thought you said we'd meet at a place called Parnell's."

"A guy named Parnell owns it. The hillbilly name is his idea of a joke we locals refuse to acknowledge."

Nate pulled behind the farthest truck and parked, leaving them in shadow. "Okay, Callie, I'll just be a couple minutes. Then, I'll grab us a bite to eat after Blade and Whisper arrive. You've already proven you have good instincts. So, one short honk if something feels off but stay locked inside. All right?"

"All right." She'd proven herself strong, self-sufficient, and able to take care of herself. Even if Nate didn't understand the what, why, or how of it, she'd become part of their group.

No ambient light divulged a stranger's outline lurking nearby when he opened the door, yet something in the shadows oozed menace with the cold inrush of wind. Its oily, crippling aura registered a presence with hostile intent.

Fear of the dark had never been an issue. If she were telepathic, she'd swear she'd latched onto someone's venomous objective.

"Nate, be careful."

"Always, little one. Always. Something you'd like to tell me?"

"Um, no. Guess I'm still shaken, but something feels *wrong.*"

Murky light cast half his face in shadow when he tilted his head. He knew she held secrets not ready for public consumption. Would he force the issue?

He opened his mouth twice, obviously thought better of it, then shook his head.

When a small thump issued from his door closing, she took a steadying breath and thumbed the lock.

He'd been part of a shadow company in the military, just like Jake. Even so, someone tracked them. Again, she questioned her decision to follow Jake and Franklin's lead.

The once-white building ahead showed its age in dingy stucco and peeling paint on its door.

Distance to the pseudo-safety of the sallow light mocked her fear. Between long strips of shadow created by trailers, blocks of light stretched from low-pressure sodium lamps on the building's block walls.

Cocooned in the dark swaths left by the big rigs should've engendered a sense of safety. A slight rocking motion brought her awareness back to Nate, now searching the vehicle's undercarriage.

Headlights again cut across the lot behind them. Blade's pickup pulled alongside and stopped. He and Whisper exited and visually scanned their perimeter.

This was her puzzle to solve, a characteristic in which she excelled. She couldn't solve it without obtaining more pieces.

She'd never managed access to the Think Tank's secure standalone, stored in the very bowels of the structure, if she were correct. Entrance to the mainframe hadn't revealed much more than the basics of their cover, including payroll, and a few benign projects.

With the right contacts and support, Jake suspected a raid of the facility's protected server would pinpoint other structures housing the genetic oddities like herself. He'd reported whispers and innuendos of others like herself being held prisoner.

Logic dictated Ray would see her dead rather than free. Perhaps the men in the van intended to kill them all since failing to capture her at Ambrosia.

Minutes later, Nate's stealthy shadow crouched beside the passenger door. With his fingers covering most of his flashlight's blue filtered lens, only a narrow backlash exposed his presence. Uneven steps marked his pace around the vehicle in checking for electronic malevolence. After a 360-degree tour, he returned to the driver's side.

As before, little sound betrayed his movements. The gust of cold air preceding his entry suggested an icy if not ominous forecast. Even in the low light, his grim expression held a semblance of frustration.

"Nothing?"

"Nope, no pucks, at least not that I can find. If they somehow managed to track you to Ambrosia, there's no way they could've known I'd be the one taking you away. In addition, there were dozens of vehicles on the lot. This one belongs to my brother. They couldn't have bugged them all. There just wasn't time. We should be free to continue to the cabin."

"They're too well-organized to not have a way of tracking us. I'm a danger to anyone near me."

"And yet they're batting zero."

"What does playing baseball have to do with spies and hi-tech equipment?" Not for the first time, she puzzled over basic human interactions.

"Ah, nothing. Just a metaphor." Taking pity on her frustration, he added while giving her fingers a light squeeze, "Don't worry. You'll get the hang of it. Just takes time."

Nate tilted his head to glance at the night sky. "Too overcast. No way could eyes in the sky see us, either. Not unless they've devised a quiet drone."

"None that I know of, but I could achieve that."

His unfathomable expression made her wince. Men at the institution frequently puzzled over her statements and assumptions, but she blew them off as curiosity. Nate's reaction made her want to hide.

Just as quick, his mysterious countenance transformed into an easy smile capable of eradicating all thoughts in her head. "I don't doubt that at all. You have quite an exceptional mind."

"I don't understand you." Frustration lowered her tone. Interpersonal relationships existed as a fathomless hole in her mind, but this one raised the hackles on her neck.

The longer he stared, the more bewildered she became. His look spoke of more than curiosity. His smile widened.

"And here I thought that would be my line." His jaw inched sideways, as if shifting thoughts around in his mouth, attempting to decipher inscrutable secrets. The rest of his body stilled when his mind went into overdrive.

"Huh, nobody ever understands me." The age-old stigma attached to her back battered her equanimity.

"Perhaps others have taken the wrong approach."

Again, his penetrating gaze sought to pierce her protective wall, crumbling pieces, littering her mind with excessive and ineffective junk.

An indelicate snort was her answer.

"Some challenges hold the most exquisite gifts."

Yeah, that doesn't sound good.

The man existed as one giant Rubik cube, different facets showing at a time, interchanging on a whim. This was a puzzle she couldn't solve.

Without flinching, he'd watched the van roll five revolutions before exploding, then swore to protect her. *Maybe it's a testosterone thing.*

Nate wouldn't ignore what he didn't understand, instead relating facts and events to the back burner. Those details would surface later in the form of direct interrogatives.

"Okay, we haven't been followed and we're not carrying a tracker. I'll go inside and grab some food. Blade and Whisper are right outside."

"I want to go with you."

"No, Callie. Until we come up with a fitting disguise or eliminate the pricks after you, we need to keep you under wraps. I won't be long. I promise."

As if the most natural gesture in the world, he reached over and cupped her chin. "You'll be fine."

Warmth billowed and spread throughout her body. She was thankful the hot sting of her blush wouldn't be visible.

"No more bleeding. Good. I don't expect your trust yet as I haven't earned it. However, I will. Count on it."

"Umm." A mere touch sidelined her thoughts. She had nothing to offer.

A new chill settled in her bones when he withdrew and cleared his throat.

The quiet snick of his door opening brought more than a cold wind. Trepidation cleaved her hard-won composure, settling a knot of foreboding in her chest.

Unlike the danger she sensed earlier on the road, the current angst lacked substance, existing as smoke and shadows in a world where men like Jake, Franklin, and Nate dwelled. She found no valid reason to call him back.

Sight of his retreating form instigated an onerous rhythm in her chest, the nature of it organizing a tangle of crystalized dread shooting up her throat. She'd rather go without food than endure his absence.

Settling Faith back in her crate, she prayed her instincts were wrong.

Chapter Twelve

A minor victory rose from the ashes of fear. She'd trusted enough to offer Nate a tidbit of insight into her mind. It didn't matter Jake had disclosed that particular skill.

Regardless, he sensed it's position at the top of a very deep well.

Flashbacks of the van's occupants and gunfire narrowly missing his head instigated various scenarios where Ray ordered Callie's capture or death. To deal with a threat of this magnitude, he'd need more than his team. He'd need resources obtained through his ex-commander.

Steam from the hot chocolate in his cardboard tray drifted upward to warm his cheeks, bringing back childhood memories of sitting around a table with his siblings. Not that they were carefree days, but he wasn't responsible for others. Despite a rough start, he and his brothers had managed to stick together, which created a new sense of awe concerning Callie's upbringing.

Without brothers or sisters, she'd never simple rivalry or comradery. No wonder she viewed the world as a mechanized puzzle. Still, she displayed a remarkable range of emotions. Frustration over her differences, wonder at small things like simple conversation and her pup, and the blush of first infatuation provided multi-pronged distractions.

Extreme and unique intelligence created an entire host of issues he couldn't assess until she'd settled into her *new normal* and provided a baseline from which to compare new experiences.

Regardless, he admired the way she interacted. Not only did she connect with others utilizing a well-rounded affect, she also demonstrated character traits he admired.

How much of that traced back to Jake, Sebastian, and Franklin's influence?

Years of private investigations after the military sharpened his instincts, which suddenly alerted with extreme intensity. He hesitated in approaching the division of the parking lot where gravel met blacktop.

The urge to draw his weapon had never proven a mistake.

Ten yards ahead, the line of big rigs blocked his view to the SUV. Neither Blade nor Whisper stood in the shadows.

Without announcing his presence via turn of stone, he set the drink tray and bag of food on the gravel. Sweaty palms arose from anxiety over his team's safety, which now included a blue-eyed enigma. He wiped them on his jeans.

No one had followed them, and the night's heavy overcast prevented satellite imagery. A restless energy coiled in his chest. Loose pebbles slowed his progress, but he wouldn't give away his advantage with hurried, careless steps. Circling behind the trailer next to his vehicle, he approached from the rear.

Two forms lay on the ground, deep in shadow. Motionless.

No!

From twenty yards away, the outline of the open passenger's side door stood in bold relief against the distant lights of the restaurant.

How did they get the drop on both Blade and Whisper?

All pretense of stealth gone, he bolted toward his men. Strong pulses and lack of obvious injury on the two inert forms offered little relief.

He rolled Blade onto his back and lifted an eyelid.

"Ah..."

"Damn. What happened, Blade?"

"Stun guns. They attacked from atop the friggin' trailers." Blade groaned then looked for his friend. "How'd they get up there without us sensing them?"

Nate helped Whisper to sit. "You okay?"

"Yeah. But the bastards took her."

A quick search of the SUV revealed Callie's bag, the contents emptied on the seat, along with the clothes she'd been wearing. Faith yipped from her crate.

Shifting position rolled a small cylindrical object under his foot, a hypodermic needle on the gravel. It hadn't been there when he'd checked for trackers.

Earlier, he'd suspected her intent to run to avoid collateral damage. Since they'd been together every moment after receiving Virus' message, she hadn't contacted anyone. At this point, she wouldn't know who to trust.

Nerd, the closest backup, answered on the first ring. With hindsight came the prediction for a less-than-satisfactory outcome considering the speed and organization with which the kidnappers worked.

Either a mole constituted part of his team, or he had stumbled upon some extra clever bastards with vast numbers and resources. A third possibility rose. What if Jake hadn't scrambled her chip's data as well as he'd said. In retrospect, the timing didn't fit. They wouldn't have waited three days to reacquire her.

Time was critical in obtaining a lead.

Each man entered the cheesy motel room bearing frowns and tight postures. No sign of hesitation, avoidance of gaze, unusual restlessness, or other indications of deception pointed to a conspirator.

Virus, Blade, and Spirit stood around the table as Nerd booted up the computer still in its case. Anxiety manifested differently in each, from beads of sweat dotting Virus' face to Blade and Whisper's aimless, restless movements. Spirit remained unflappable, consistent with his usual demeanor, which irritated them all.

"Spirit, Nerd, what happened at my house?"

"They weren't there before us, but tried to nail us as we left." Spirit stuck his finger in the duffle he'd carried. "Good thing you packed hardware boss. Better it than us."

"They didn't give chase?" Nate murmured in contemplation. "Odd."

"Must've noted the differences in our build. Nerd's shorter, and I'm wider. Probably wanted to find you. Suggests they have another inroad to you."

"Yeah." Virus lugged a case full of electronics onto the makeshift desk. "Years ago, the bastards at the institution inserted a pea-sized GPS tracker through her navel. I have the new code."

"Jake told me he scrambled the data, not changed it for his own benefit." Nate slammed his fist on the table. "Still, if the Think Tank bastards caught on to what he'd done, they wouldn't have waited three days to snatch her."

"Jake was planning on telling her and taking it out as soon as we got settled. Sorry, boss." Nerd's fingers flew over the keyboard. "We don't know much else. Jake was really tight-lipped on this one."

"He had the skill to competently alter the records?" Nate tapped Nerd on the shoulder. "You knew him best."

"Yeah. He gave me enough detail to make me believe no one else could get it."

"I guess we can thank the foundation of asshats when we find her. How long before you have her location? It's been twenty-three minutes."

"Workin' on it, boss," Nerd mumbled, his face lit by the screen's eerie glow.

"Where's Jake?" Whisper's concern echoed in the small confines. All eyes turned toward Virus.

A low groan escaped Virus as he scrubbed both hands down his face. "FUBAR from the beginning. Fucked up beyond all recognition. I couldn't stop them all. Jake walked into an ambush. Damn if they don't have significant numbers. They nailed him as soon as he met his contact. You think they somehow got the number to his burner phone and knew where he was headed?"

Waves of helpless anger blossomed in Nate, shaking the foundation of his soul. The smothering effect forced a deep breath and heavy sigh before he could continue.

"Jake said he was gonna meet someone named Penny. Supposedly a long-time friend of Callie's. Only problem is, Callie has no known friends outside the institution." Through the large picture window, bare-branched trees loomed over the dark parking lot just as the night foreshadowed Callie's demise.

For the umpteenth time, Nate searched his memory. No one followed him from Ambrosia, yet the bastards found her soon after. "Nerd, did Sebastian know about her chip?"

"Sebastian? Not sure. I doubt it. I don't think he had the clearance unless Jake told him," Nerd replied.

"Possible, but unlikely, Whisper declared. "What happened out there?"

"I'd followed the bastard on Jake's tail."

"Jake didn't recognize a tail? Since when?" Whisper asked.

"The guy hung far enough back not to be picked up. Wouldn't have seen it myself if I'd left a minute sooner."

"Then?" Nate made a hurry up gesture.

"Parked and under the pavilion alongside Schwartz's park outside Bowton. The guy following him was fast and organized. When he set a bead on Jake, I took him out, but wasn't as quiet as I would've liked. He was one of three.

"I never saw the third shooter, but he took Jake out with one shot. I heard a lot of rustling in the woods. Must've been this Penny he was supposed to meet. Don't know if they wanted her dead or just scared, best guess is the former. They might not have known she was there if she hadn't screamed."

"She get away clean?" Whisper asked.

Virus briefly closed his eyes before continuing, "Don't know. Couldn't help her 'cuz of the angles and obstacles. Figured this involved Callie, hence my priority to return."

"Maybe she shares common ground with Callie," Nate suggested.

"Dunno. Where'd they pick up Jake's trail?" Blade wobbled the knife balancing on the back of his knuckles. He concentrated best when his hands were busy.

"About a mile from Ambrosia. At the rendezvous, I couldn't get close enough to distinguish specific features, but the dipshit fiddled with the undercarriage of Jake's car prior to slipping through the tree line. Might have removed a tracker."

"Sounds like they didn't want to risk more interference at the club. Which means they could have background information on us. I'll call Conner and see what he found out from Callie's assailant."

"Sounds logical." Whisper's rhythmic finger tapping blended with the patter of freezing rain just beginning. Showers would wash away any chance of a dog's ability to track through the woods.

"Wonder if this Penny looks like Callie?" Nate needed to make sense of the meager information, fast, but there were too many questions, too many angles to consider.

"Don't know. I got the impression of dark hair, slim build… and now that I think about it—her reflexes were incredible. It was as if she knew the shots were coming. But only a split-second ahead of time."

"And you don't think she set Jake up?" Nerd asked, his flurry of keyboard tapping increasing.

"Doubt it. Not the way they went after her," Virus replied.

"Okay, let's find Callie. Spirit, you get the gear from my house?"

"Yeah. All of it."

"Good. Nerd, got a lead on her yet?" Nate had never failed in a protection assignment. Kicking off a mission with the death of a team member added significant weight to everyone's emotional toll.

Tight expressions revealed them on the same page. Spirit began pacing, his form of extreme anxiety.

"Got it! She's stationary, twenty miles west. Coordinates show a cabin in the middle of nowhere. Nothin' but deer trails and dirt paths."

"She's probably unconscious. I found an empty hypodermic by the car."

"I can put a drone in the sky, but it'll sound like a flying weedeater. Flip side, the noise will keep them under cover. They wouldn't risk us catching them in the open." Virus arched a brow, waiting.

"If they move out instead of take a stand, they'll only have one path, farther west on a dirt road. Problem is, it leads to open highway, which doesn't clue us into their plan." Nerd traced the possible escape route on his computer's map. "Looks like someone followed a black snake to make this trail."

"Damn, they've prepared for everything else ahead of time. They wouldn't box themselves in now." Hair on Nate's neck prickled once again. They would face a dicey situation without knowledge of their opposition's strength or numbers.

"Got a bad feeling about this, boss." Nerd shut down his computer. "I'm thinking air transport."

"Sounds about right. Let's get going before they move out. Spirit, Blade, you two come from the west. Nerd, take south. Whisper, you come from the east, and I'll move in from the north. Virus, you're in the van, monitor movements until we call for pickup. Let's go."

* * * *

Abdominal pain reacquainted Callie with her living nightmare. Tendrils of anguish spread from belly outward like fire over an oil spill, fanning out and consuming everything within its path.

Concentrating on a faint and distant voice weakened her tenuous grasp on lucidity, the words and tone berating all within earshot. Interpretation surpassed her ability to concentrate, the inflections and excitement resonating a familiarity.

Who is that?

Unable to clear the web of confusion from her mind, she couldn't name the speaker but assumed she'd heard him before. If only he'd talk above a whisper.

Her eyelids refused to function in the most superficial capacity. Hazy recollection formed a scenario of a black-clad figure opening the SUV's door before something sharp had pierced her neck. A dart.

Someone had ripped at her clothes, filling her with a panic her mouth couldn't voice. A cloth over her nose had issued a sweet smell and decreased her ineffectual clawing. She'd ceased to care when darkness loomed tight.

Another pinch and warmth flooding her forearm brought her back to the moment, yet unable to hold onto it. A black void yawned in front of her.

One she couldn't refuse.

Chapter Thirteen

"What are you doing? This isn't part of our agreement." Kyu-chul leaned over the unconscious young woman to watch the proceedings, his right hand drifting to the pistol at his waist.

"Take it easy. I'm not maiming the twit. Treat her right, and she'll come to appreciate this someday. A nice piece of jewelry is every girl's dream, isn't it?" Spy Man, the acquired moniker give by these idiots, suited him. Maybe he'd have it engraved on a ring.

Filth of the one-room cabin took him back to his roots, a bastard born in the sticks. It'd smelled of mold, rot, and rodent droppings, too.

This time when I go, I leave it all behind, never to see its likes again.

The little bitch was no more than a hefty paycheck. He'd forget her the minute fresh air brushed his face, but she'd remember this night for the rest of her life.

Naïve little nerd.

With the money earned, he could buy an island, some place warm, outside U.S. boundaries with no possibility of extradition.

"She's not destined for the slave trade. We pay good money."

A thick foreign accent obscured some of his contact's words. The merchandise was bought and delivered, the new *owner* had a right to ensure nothing prevented his objective, to breed the little genius to another and guide the offspring.

The military would brand his actions traitorous, not to mention the dozens of federal laws broken. In light of both, he might as well make this final venture worth his while.

"Ah, but this has a purpose. I guaranteed you a genius free of microchips, hence the removal of that nasty piece." He nodded toward the tray holding a small glass cylinder the size of a grain of rice.

In response, Kyu-Chul retrieved the tracker and dropped it to the floor before stomping it.

"With the addition I'm providing, if she ever gets away from *you,* she'll not trust another for a long time to come." He knew all about instilling doubt and mistrust. He'd been taught by the best.

It was time to show the terrorist bastards a new trick. "Watch, Kyu-Chul, and learn from a pro. Come and gather round, men. I know some of you like your women to wear jewelry. This isn't a new fad and not difficult to do." As he worked on his unconscious patient, he couldn't fault the new owner for worrying, not with such an exorbitant price tag.

Advance preparation ensured everything lay at his fingertips. He grabbed the disinfectant and wet another gauze. The service now performed was new to him, despite the lie he spoke.

"She's going to enjoy that?" Kyu-Chul's dubious look said otherwise.

"Yep, something to ease the sting of being kidnapped. All finished, just a quick wipe. Tell her when she wakes up, I gave her the parting present. She'll think of me every day until she dies." A knowing grin accompanied the next question. "How many times are you planning to breed her?"

"We will take good care of her. She won't lack for necessities. Why this? Do you hate her that much?" Kyu-Chul's puzzled frown darkened as he pulled Callie's sheet up to cover her naked form. "This will not get infected? Interfere with pregnancy?"

"Keep it clean with a saline rinse and she'll be fine. Oh, and yes, I hate her that much."

"We've already selected a breeding mate. As soon as we're out of here and on the plane, we'll see it done. Think of the advances we can make, grooming the offspring to our specific needs." Rims of the foreign agent's glasses reflected the meager light as he continued. "And you Americans think us barbaric? We paid for her—intact." He snorted in disgust.

"Relax. She's still a virgin, without a GPS chip, and with the added bonus of a belly ring. Everything done in clean fashion. No infection. Consider it a gift that keeps on giving from her American family. And really, on the plane? Not wasting any time, are you?"

"You did say she should be ovulating now. Why wait?" Kyu-Chul's brushing of hair from her face indicated a fatherly gesture.

Odd.

"Yes. Yes, of course. I can't blame you for wanting to begin as soon as possible." The last injection ensured Callie wouldn't interrupt his ministrations, yet the twilight anesthesia wouldn't hold for long. She'd wake up in pain from the probing needed to remove the chip despite using the reader. It was time to get moving.

With an expectant look at his benefactor, he asked, "Has the transfer to my offshore account completed? I believe I hear your interim transportation approaching."

Outside, the muffled *thump-thump* produced by the twin rotor blades of a helicopter reverberated in his chest.

"Yes, ironic that we appropriated one of your own. And funds transfer to your account is complete."

The Oriental's smile acquired a distinct smug appearance.

"Good. Then I'll say adieu and leave you to dress and remove the little bitch from American soil. Nice doing business with you."

They called him Spy Man.

Ha. With a soul-deep cockiness, he left as quietly as he'd come, headed for a new life.

Not the original plan, but it'll suffice.

****

Strong downwash from the descending chopper's rotor blades buffeted Nate as he tapped his mic. "One exiting the front now. Let him go. Not a priority." With the team nearing position, anxiety compelled a fidgeting he couldn't control.

A brief stab of light resulting from the front door opening revealed little of the interior through his field glasses. With no time to prepare, he had little in the way of surveillance equipment.

Letting one asshole escape to rescue an asset equaled a small price to pay, even if it sucked.

The tall silhouette offered no telltale means of identification, merely someone above average in height. A long trench coat topped with a wide-brimmed hat pulled low over the face prevented a glimpse of the shadows or shape within. The unknown tango ambled toward the first of two vehicles, a dark-colored SUV.

Something about his posture and walk struck a chord of recognition. Gait correlation analysis remained impossible due to visual obstructions. It didn't allow time to get a recording.

Scrub brush hid the vehicle's plate from his angle. If one of the others could get it, they would. Otherwise, they'd find the bastard another way.

History dictated fate seldom favored the unprepared. There were so many ways tonight's strategy formed on the fly could detonate and kill them all. It wasn't just the life of a young woman, but the fate of nations involved. If forced to do the unimaginable, Callie could rewrite history.

Light drizzle mixed with sleet drove mini spikes against Nate's face with the turbulence of the blades and thickening storm. Ice would slicken the roads and make escape more difficult if pursued. He sure as hell wouldn't take the risks to the earlier thugs.

Hive mind thinking asserted no assailant be left alive, an advantage to long-term working relationships his teammates understood. Considering the kidnappers' connections and meager windows in the cabin, they could only guess at the number of occupants.

The pit stop in the woods didn't make sense if it were Ray's men. Neither did killing her here. They'd carried out their assignment with precision and forethought, despite the few but distinct irregularities. Flashbacks of the van's wreck contradicted the kidnapper's execution of timing. In counterpoint, the two events might not be connected.

Since this group wasn't likely from the Think Tank, they must be the foreign bastards from Jake's forewarning.

There still existed a missing piece to the puzzle. The traitor. Nate's brother had kept an eye on Sebastian, who'd stayed to listen to the music—and sulk.

The pilot no longer hovered, turning the chopper's nose into the wind with the next strong gust before beginning its descent.

"Naterz, good to go. Fifty yards until skids touch down." Nerd's voice over the mic barely surfaced above the chaos of swirling leaves and force of freezing rain.

"How much company are we expecting?" From his angle, Nate couldn't define the cockpit's occupants.

"Three," Nerd replied.

"Blade, help Nerd roll out the red carpet for the newest arrivals." Nate kept a mental template of his men and their positions while assessing visible and blurry movements via the cabin's filthy window.

Nerd and Blade have the south side covered.

Blue glow inside the cockpit cast an eerie effect on the occupants while the landing light detailed the rooftop and surrounding trees. Port and starboard sides couldn't have much clearance, which left the back. Even considering experience pilots, not many would attempt this maneuver.

Seconds passed as the pilot navigated to the cabin's rear.

"Sitrep. Twenty yards of open ground out front. One window." Verbal shorthand saved time and effort. If destiny favored them, there'd be less space around the back. Nate wanted each conspirator with a passion, but timing and circumstance negated rash action.

"Twenty *on the east side, one window,"* Whisper murmured.

*"Twenty-five on the west, two windows, one blocke*d," Spirit advised.

"Just enough to light out back." Nerd's bad news arrived on cue.

"Nerd, help Blade introduce our visitors to a warm welcome as soon as the skids touch. Angle your position to avoid crossfire. Spirit, Whisper, ready?"

"*Ready*," they answered in unison. Each tapped their response on their mic.

Significant crosswind shifted the chopper's position, forcing the pilot to compensate with a deft hand on the cyclic control. A few feet would make the difference between landing and crashing.

"On the count of twenty, go. Blade, don't let their reinforcements exit the bird. Virus, we'll signal when we need wheels." Double tapping his mic received like responses.

Nate pulled in a deep breath. Adrenaline pumped through his system and narrowed his focus. Every mission entailed hazards and unexpected twists. He could count the number of times an assignment followed the plan on one hand.

His flat-out run and sure-footed landing on the front porch raised no audible alarm, the soft thuds lost in slashing rain and the helicopter's blustering arrival. If the chopper's occupants caught sight of his team's movements, the cabin now blocked their shot.

With his internal clock on five, Nate gently palmed his Glock and tested the doorknob. Locked.

Paranoid bastards.

Age and rust furthered his goal when he kicked. His muddy boot left its outline on the weathered wood planks close to the knob. The ill-kept portal splintered and crashed inward with the force of his first kick.

Breaking glass from either side of the house signaled Whisper and Spirit's simultaneous entry.

Low light didn't hinder piecing together the scenario. Five men had locked their gazes on the unconscious figure lying motionless in bed.

For a single heartbeat, his mind stuttered. The darkest reaches of a twisted imagination couldn't prepare him for the sight in the one-room structure.

Without extensive training, intended actions would've faltered, his body paralyzed with shock. It took a split-second to register the foreigners surrounding the small bed taking up most of the space.

Golden curls tangled around Callie's face and fanned out on the mattress. Beside it was a tray bearing a variety of surgical instruments and bloody gauze.

Callie lay silent and still with her eyes closed, her jaw slack.

Two men stood on either side in the process of dressing her unconscious form. Each froze with the intrusion.

Their fractional pause provided split-second timing needed to squeeze off one round. As the second guard cleared his weapon, the first one dropped, still holding a jacket sleeve in one hand.

The *thwack* of a bullet slamming into the doorjamb by Nate's head sent splinters flying into his shoulder as his gun bucked again. The thud of the second guard falling registered as an afterthought.

Three more shots rang out as Whisper and Spirit took out the remaining three men inside. Headshots resulted in five dead bodies dressed in black, sprawled on the scarred floor.

Automatic rifle fire outside signaled resistance for Nerd and Blade. Whisper strode to the shattered window, and Spirit cracked open the back door after flipping off the light.

Soft glow from the cockpit's dash outlined the occupants' positions. The pilot lay slumped over the cyclic pitch control.

Fish in a barrel came to mind.

Two passengers behind the pilot opened their glass doors, one on each side. Nate saw feet descending as the first hopped out.

From Nate's perspective, Whisper's bead on the cabin-side gunman proved dead center. A double tap jerked the body like an unruly marionette against the aircraft before it slumped to the ground.

"All clear wood side," Nerd's rumble over the ear bud gained intensity as the rotor blades came to a halt.

"All clear." Whisper's voice resonated with the energy of post-mission adrenaline.

Nate's focus returned to Callie when Spirit flipped on the light. Four strides into the room offered time to collect details. Pain etched her features as a mewling whine spilled from pale lips. The bruise blooming on her right cheek contrasted the creamy, soft translucence of smooth skin.

Skeins of silky tresses tangled in the t-shirt hiked to her breasts. He tugged down the hem after examining her torso for injuries.

Dread knotted his gut at the thought of what the bastards might already have done. The lowlifes had pulled sweatpants up to her thighs before his team's intrusion.

Rage choked his thoughts, leaving the need for revenge to consume him. Before his actions registered, four more shots fired from his weapon. Two dead recipients gained their weight.

"Nate. Not now. We gotta collect her and go before reinforcements arrive." Spirit's voice sounded distant, calm.

Shouldering his weapon, Nate turned to Callie. A harsh glare warned his teammates not to advance. "I have to look to see if she's... hemorrhaging."

Nothing could've stopped the tremor in his fingers as he tugged at her cotton panties. No blood stained the cloth or smeared her thighs.

His gorge rose. He swallowed hard.

"Nate, you know I have medical training. Let me..." Spirit's murmured words drifted off when their gazes locked.

"No. This is my fault. She's my responsibility." With gentleness born of compassion, he inspected her groin to discern injuries.

Seconds later, one possible scenario spun him around and emptied his stomach. The purge couldn't clear his mind. When he turned back, Spirit had pulled up the stretchy pants.

After brushing a lock of hair from her face, Nate's fingers still trembled while his mind fumbled for the right words. He wanted to kill—something. Anything. He barely registered another of his team entering.

"Whisper, grab that blanket." The flannel throw over the only chair present depicted a peaceful woodland scene, contrasting the reality of their situation. "I'll wrap her up before we split. Tell Virus we're ready to roll. Whisper, you drive, and I'll sit in the back with her."

"She's been drugged, but the hospital—" Whisper tucked the soft blanket around Callie before heading out the door.

"No. We'll go to my cabin and assess her there." Grinding under

Nate's boot brought his attention to the small smattering of shattered glass on the floor, then to the tray with bloody gauze. "They took the chip out."

With infinite care, Nate cradled her against his chest. "What they did this night, you will not reference in any way. Not unless she asks, then direct her to me. I'll take care of her and anything she needs. Got it?"

"Sure, Nate. We see how it is," Whisper murmured as he helped check the downed men's pockets. "No one's got ID."

"Tell Nerd to get their prints when Virus arrives." With the silence screaming recriminations, Nate could do naught but hold her, whispering words of her bravery and strength.

She would need all that and more to come to terms with her ordeal.

"Let's go. My place is titled through an offshore corporation, so we won't be traced." Nate turned on his heel, cringing when Callie cried out with the slight jostling. Sudden physical contortion confirmed her pain.

She would suffer until the muscles healed, then have a physical reminder for the rest of her life. The crude incision from removing her chip would leave a scar. Nerve damage would be permanent, her skin tingling with every brush of cloth against it.

He'd failed her.

He'd help her recover.

Chapter Fourteen

Waking up in a soft bed would've felt wonderful if not for the sharp pain blasting from skull to belly and back. A moment of panic followed when Callie tried to get up, yet a soft voice and gentle hand covering hers halted the effort.

"*Shh*. You're safe. It's still the wee hours of the night. Close your eyes. I'll watch over you while you sleep."

Nate's voice, soft, soothing, reassuring, and an offer she couldn't refuse. Her mind conjured a chair beside the bed with Nate sprawled in it.

"No more drugs." Her mind registered lying on her side. Nausea burned through her stomach.

Her left hand rested on her hip with the slight buffer of soft cotton that encompassed her torso. She shifted then whimpered.

"Why do I hurt so much, everywhere?"

"You've been through an ordeal. Right now, you need to rest. We'll talk in the morning. You're safe now. I won't leave this chair while you sleep."

"Promise you won't let go? Are we in your cabin?"

"Yes, hon, we are. I swear I won't let go until you wake up."

"I hurt."

"I know, but I can't give you anything yet. We're not sure what drugs are still in your system, and we can't risk taking you to the hospital for anything less than an emergency."

With the speed of a diving peregrine falcon, memory of recent events flooded her mind. Tendrils of fog released its grasp with each breath.

"Faith?"

"Downstairs with the guys. I'll bring her up in the morning. I'd really like you to get some undisturbed rest till then."

"Oh, God, those men..." A choked sob erupted as the flashback replayed in slow motion. She'd been too slow to react and had paid the price.

Nate's gentle touch grazed her fingers and back of her hand as she collected her thoughts.

"Did you recognize any of them?" His hesitancy sliced through the quiet.

"No. One of them talked in a whisper. He seemed familiar. I think he was from the institution. I think I'd have recognized the voice if he'd spoken in a normal tone, yet he never did, at least not while I was conscious."

"I'm sure you didn't know, but someone inserted a microchip in your abdomen many years ago."

"What? I was chipped—like a dog?"

"It was removed and smashed in the cabin."

"Jeez, I am subhuman. Did Jake know?"

"Yes. He'd managed to alter your records at the facility so they couldn't track you."

"He would've taken it out once we got settled. I know he would."

"Yes. He didn't want you overwhelmed from the start. So much has happened."

One after another, sobs wracked her body. "I was sitting... someone knocked on the driver's side window. He held a gun. Another man opened the door with a lock jock. They were so quick."

A broken mewl disrupted her speech. "I thought it was a regular gun. I was shocked and couldn't react fast enough. They stuck me with a needle and put a cloth over my nose and mouth. I passed out. Oh God, where are they?"

The men in the van are dead and others still captured me. When does it end?

"Where they can't hurt you ever again. They're all dead but one. We'll find him, too. He'd smeared his license plate with mud. Still working on that one."

"The rest of the team is here? What about Jake?"

* * * *

"Callie, Jake went to meet someone. Do you know a young woman named Penny?"

There was so much terrible news to divulge. He wished it could wait until the drugs cleared her system, but grief washed her face in tears, glistening in the glow of the nightlight.

"No, why? Did she set him up?"

"We don't think so, but we don't know why she requested the meeting."

"What happened?"

Ripping off the bandage seemed the kinder approach. "Callie, I'm sorry. There's no easy way to say this. Jake was gunned down at the rendezvous."

The silence greeting him expanded until the atmosphere felt thick. Tension in her thin frame built with the force of hurricane winds.

"No." Her whispered cry carried the weight of overwhelming anger.

The broken sobs that followed shredded his heart. How could he fight this? Hell, he'd rather slit his own wrists than witness such physical and emotional defeat.

Between the seconds of seeing his open passenger door and stepping on the syringe, it'd crossed his mind she might have taken off, escaping from the new world where Jake promised she could thrive.

When he'd stepped on that small barrel then later witnessed her defilement in the cabin, exposed and disfigured, shame engulfed him.

Months prior, when his girlfriend embarked on her new career, she'd accused him of lacking the capability of a full range of emotions. Now, the cataclysmic rupture of his invisible shield left him raw and vulnerable with guilt probing his internal organs.

Outside, the storm punctuated his frustration with a deluge of sleet rattling the windowpane.

The vibration of his Glock on the dresser brought his attention to everything shaking around him. The mattress shuddered under his forearm while the capped bottle of water rolled off the nightstand to the floor.

What the hell is going on?

Instinct tightened his hand on Callie's fingers. To his knowledge, there'd never been a significant earthquake in Maryland. There were no major fault lines nearby to cause concern.

Two pictures on the opposite wall hit the floor in consecutive crashes with glass shards skittering across hardwood.

"Callie, it's just a little quake. We're okay." Even nature conspired to frighten his ward. "I'm gonna cover you." There was no sturdy table or desk to shield them, so he leaned over her body, using his larger frame for whatever protection he could provide.

"What? Oh, uh... s-sorry. Death is following me wherever I go."

Within seconds, the shaking stopped, and Callie's hand squeezed his fingers. Nate leaned back and flicked the lamp switch to survey the damage.

What the hell? You're sorry? Why?

Heavy footfalls down the hallway stopped short of his bedroom. *"You guys all right in there?"* Blade's light knock on the door preceded, *"You need anything?"*

"We're fine. A couple broken picture frames, but I'll take care of them in the morning. Everything else okay?"

"Yeah, no problem," Spirit replied amid murmured comments from Whisper and Blade. In any other situation, they'd refer to earthquakes and noisy sexual activities.

An angry swipe of Callie's hand against her face left a thin trail of blood.

It seemed her physical responses wrapped tightly to her emotional state. Nate grabbed a tissue and held it to her nose. She grabbed the tissue and held it for a minute. When she pulled back, the bleeding had stopped.

Soft sobs quieted in time with gentle strokes along her back and arms with tears drying up until only sniffles remained.

His life had never been normal but didn't compare to the transition Callie endured.

As a child, he'd enjoyed books of dragons and knights where heroes rescued women and children from certain death. Strong characters used magical spells and potions to protect those under their care. They'd been his escape from a drunken father and domestic violence.

His thoughts flitted to the peculiar occurrences continuing to surround Callie. In his mind's eye, he again replayed the moment she crashed into him at the club. Both should've tumbled to the floor.

They'd remained upright.

In addition, there was the matter of the pursuing van's erratic driving followed by its roll and explosion. Contrary to what popular movies portrayed, car crashes seldom resulted in fireballs.

Not a believer in paranormal abilities or ESP, he surmised some other plausible explanation other than Callie prevented them from landing in a pile of tangled limbs in Ambrosia.

"Do you think it was Ray who sent men after me?"

"Don't know yet, but I doubt it. Did you have much interaction with him at the Think Tank?"

"Once a week. He always treated me like a prized specimen, something he grew in a lab experiment. For all I know—he did. I don't remember anything other than life there. I'm sure he'll never stop looking for me."

"He's on our to-do list to ferret out. With the right ties, we can end his penchant for acquiring people like lab rats." His thoughtless choice of words echoed in the quiet confines.

"I believe there are others held captive. I'm not sure where, but if I could access Ray's standalone, I bet I could find them."

"We'll find them together. In the process, we'll expose all those involved. Can you tell me more about the institution?" It was obvious she wouldn't sleep. Perhaps talking about what felt familiar would ease her plight. At least the institution had kept her safe and free from mutilation, which was more than he'd done.

An hour passed as she detailed the routines of her life before the cadence of her breathing evened out in sleep. With his hand clutched between her two smaller ones, she'd bent her elbows and curled into a ball.

He could count the number of botched missions on one hand. Each one left invisible scars etched on his chest. This time, his asset survived, but with a terrible burden.

Another failure.

The ineffable strings binding them would never break regardless of the path either chose. With each light puffy breath on his forearm, he realized a part of his soul remained tangled in her web and trapped for eternity.

He could do naught but watch over her. She didn't trust him. Not completely. *Therein lies the rub.*

How could he ask for something not earned? How could he protect her without knowing what secrets she held? There was more to her than extraordinary intelligence. So much more. He'd bet his life on it.

Dawn's faint rays filtered between the curtains' gaps to spear his eyes and remind him of all that had passed. His charge's soft snores shifted a lock of curls across her cheek as he stretched his legs and crossed one ankle over the other. While the chair wasn't designed for sleeping, it proved better than other places he'd rested.

Unless he could help her battered psyche heal and find a positive path around her experience, she'd never trust another soul. No woman could rationalize her experience and remain unaffected.

Injured nerves would regenerate to a point, but there'd always be reminders, the small scars. She'd forever suffer a tingling sensation from severed nerves every time something touched the skin around her navel.

Two stabbings during the course of his missions taught him the consequences of damaged nerves. Flesh healed yet often led to paresthesia, or prickling sensations surrounding the scar.

She hadn't indicated knowledge of the belly ring. He hadn't brought it up, not knowing the extent of her tolerance.

Her future included horrific nightmares awaiting her at the end of every day. Her imagination would conjure all manner of possibilities to prolong the suffering, and there was nothing he could do other than provide support through his presence.

Her attachment to the pup would provide a positive light through the darkness. While she slept, he tapped out a text to Whisper for another item to give her tangible reminders of hope.

Unless he could encourage at least a neutral outlook on intimacy, she'd shun an important aspect of life, a crime against nature for any young woman. The next few weeks were crucial in healing both body and spirit.

A longer-range plan had formed during the wee hours when monsters of the night held sway against sanity and civility. At the kidnapper's shack, he'd found no evidence of rape, but that would enter her thoughts sooner or later.

Why the bastard performed crude surgery, then inserted the belly ring on someone considered a prize, remained a mystery he'd solve at knifepoint.

Chapter Fifteen

Nate checked to make certain Callie slept before snagging his phone when it vibrated. She'd drifted into an exhausted sleep after their talk.

He didn't recognize the incoming number.

Is Callie okay?

Who's this?

Penny. Is she safe?

Yes. And you?

I'm... okay.

What happened at the meeting?

Assassins. I'm sorry about Franklin and Jake.

Who's pulling the strings?

Don't know. I'll look into it.

No. Too dangerous.

My fault Jake and Franklin are dead.

You set them up?

No!!!! But I failed to protect them.

Not your responsibility.

Nate tapped the side of the screen. He couldn't risk giving away his location, but if Penny was like Callie, she needed help.

I'll have Marc call you. He'll provide protection.

No. Too many have died. I'm tossing this phone.

Give me a way to contact you.

No. No one else dies because of me.

More women held prisoner. Need your help.

Working on it. Take care of Callie. She's special.

Like you?

Nate waited for the icon bubble to start bouncing.

A minute passed with nothing. Dialing the phone yielded no answer.

Damn it.

One texted conversation told him part of what he needed to know. Penny was like Callie, in some fashion. She also carried the guilt of death on her conscience.

Another minute passed.

Nothing.

Late-morning sun shed light on horrors previously endured as each explanation tumbling through his mind rejected the smallest slice of sanity. A night spent in contemplation left him drained and exhausted. Soon, he'd have to find the words to untangle Callie's confusion.

She'd remained in fetal position and clutched his hand as he sat in the chair by her bed. Now, after a groan, she pushed the cover aside and reached for her belly.

Gently, he wrapped her hand in his and held it over her hip.

And so it begins.

"*Shh,* Callie. You're safe. We're at my cabin, remember?"

"I hurt. There's something on my stomach."

"It's a bandage."

Her assault wasn't the ultimate corruption of innocence. Nate earned that distinction when he failed to protect her.

When she'd bumped into him at Ambrosia, he equated her character to an unsullied waif. In one night, the wonders of mutual attraction and discovery were ripped away and replaced with fear, pain, and uncertainty.

Her two words brought back the image of the guard pulling up her sweatpants at the cabin.

"I know, sweetheart. Let me grab some Aspirin off the bedside table.

I have a bottle of water for you here."

Snagging the bottle off the floor reminded him of the tremors that toppled it last night. Another mystery to solve, along with the pile of glass shards against the baseboard.

"Here, drink a bit so you can swallow these. They'll help. Then, we'll talk."

Tears marked time as she fisted them off her cheeks.

After swallowing the pills, she covered her mouth as if to prevent damning words from escaping. "Last night, someone said they were going to breed me. Did they—"

"I found no evidence of rape." He prayed she understood his reasoning for saving her the humiliation of the intimate if cursory exam. Small consolation she wouldn't become pregnant or suffer venereal disease. "I—"

"You examined me?"

"I realize I had no right, but I didn't know what they'd done and wanted to spare you." Jake explained how she could compartmentalize her emotions. It was again time to test that theory with logic.

"Thank you." Confidence and determination left with a sigh in her settling back against the headboard.

Now was the time for disclosure. Finding the right words to divulge specific information and avoid further damage to her spirit challenged his mind. "I'd like to hold your hand while we talk."

She took his offer like a lifeline and clutched it tight.

Careful to not jostle the bed, he perched on the mattress. The silken mass of her hair lay tangled around her shoulders, her eyes puffy.

"If they didn't rape me, why does my belly hurt? What aren't you telling me, and why don't you want me to see it?"

"Their assault wasn't sexual. They performed a minor surgical procedure." Drugs muddled her memory of their previous conversation. Expensive dogs were microchipped. Horses were microchipped. *Things* were microchipped. Human beings should never be subjected to such barbaric behavior.

"What kind of procedure?"

Jesus.

Neglect to reveal the extent of her ordeal straight away could lead to a complicated web of deceptions and half-truths eventually choking the life from their tentative relationship.

"They removed the chip and gave you a piercing. Looks like they did it aseptically, so you shouldn't develop an infection." He sounded clinical, detached.

"The microchip is how you found me. Maybe I should be marked."

"No, I believe it was inserted when you were much younger. They're animals, Callie, plain and simple. Above all else, you need to remember that. You're going to heal. We'll help you through this."

"Damn bastards!" Her entire body shook with the rage bubbling up from deep within.

This was something he could work with. If she'd given up before starting, that would've led to a different ending.

"Listen. We need to check and make sure you don't develop an infection. If you'd rather see a doctor, or have me remove the piercing now, we can do either. If you'd rather wait and avoid the manipulation for now, that's up to you. If we leave it, it must be cleaned and dressed every day."

Evident was the fact—regardless of being raised in captivity, she'd been afforded a certain level of independence concerning her body. That much he'd gleaned when compelling her to change clothes in the same room the prior evening. He'd taken away so much, and wanted to offer as many choices and as much control as possible.

"I don't want to even think about it now, much less deal with it."

Higher than expected emotional quotient worked against her with the lack of a logical explanation for the piercing. Rationalization wouldn't help her process what a psychopath had done. She'd need to see the changes to avoid her imagination making it worse.

"Nate?"

Prepared for the storm of emotions, he snatched tissues from the bedside table to dry her tears. "Yes?"

When she lay motionless, he waited to see which direction the pendulum swung.

"I want to find the men who shot Jake..."

Again, she choked on her words.

"Okay. We're stronger together, as a team." Stroking his thumb across the back of her knuckles did nothing to calm his nerves, yet it seemed to help her. He'd known many women in his time. No one had ever affected him as she did now.

"They shot me with some type of dart. Why would they do that *and* drug me with a cloth?"

"They may not have wanted to take any chances. Dart-delivered drugs can take longer to work. Different absorption rates. Are you remembering something else?"

Maybe they knew something I only suspect.

"At one point when I started to wake up, I thought I heard something about... twilight? The only people who knew our destination was Jake, Sebastian, and the team. Sebastian wouldn't have taken me. He helped me escape. He's always been good to me. I-I trust the rest of the team. I know I haven't known them for long, but I do. There was this thumping noise I felt in my chest at one point."

"The guys are looking into Sebastian and others connected with the Think Tank, especially Ray, the administrator. The thumping sensation was from an appropriated helicopter."

A low feminine growl filled the air. "The microchip. How do I know there's not another one? I never thought about that."

"We checked before coming here. You're clear. I didn't know about it until after they took you. I'm sorry. Jake scrambled the records at the Think Tank, but they probably had had backups he didn't know about."

Standing and replacing the water bottle on the table redirected his focus. "Ready to get up and start a new day? A new beginning?"

"Might as well."

"Good. We'll get you cleaned up, dressed, then go down, and grab something to eat. How's your head feel?"

Uncertainty radiated from her gold-flecked violet gaze. Lack of intimate experience with men relegated this to new emotional territory as well.

"We can do this, Callie. Let's go in the bathroom so I have better light to check your incision."

She needn't say more when her lucid gaze told him everything. Her stance wobbled in gaining her feet. With remnants of drugs still active, she wasn't steady enough to leave to her own devices.

Waiting to scrub the memories away wasn't an option. Every op had a middle ground. It was small comfort that she leaned on him without hesitation.

Spacious and elegant, the master bath proved a blessing with plenty of room and decent lighting. She sat on the counter while he gathered supplies, curiosity drawing her brows together.

With no further mention of the belly ring, he wondered what she thought about it.

When she made the decision to take it out or leave it, he'd comply. It would take manipulation to remove. She didn't look like she had the stamina yet.

Her fists tightened at her side, yet she remained mute.

"You okay letting me take a look?" Reminding himself of her innocence kept his demeanor professional.

"I can take care of myself after you check for infection."

"Okay, but you're shaking from head to toe. I don't want you falling and cracking your noggin'. I'll wait until you're seated in the shower. You can drop your clothes on the floor and use the handheld sprayer. Deal?"

"Fine, we'll compromise as long as I wash myself."

For a fleeting thought, he considered asking her to skip the shower but realized she'd need it to *feel* clean.

"You're very brave, Callie. I'm proud of you."

Tears splashed on her sweatpants as she studied the jewelry and steri-stips from the minor surgery. She leaned back against the mirror and studied the ring. "Damn. Women really like this crap?" A sigh escaped before she added, "I'm not brave. I'm a coveted... thing."

"No, hon. You're brilliant. You can't put any of this on your shoulders. The pricks who did this are—"

"Soon to be dead," she finished.

"Yeah. Count on it." He didn't know how to make the situation better. Hell, nobody could.

"By my hand, though," she pressed.

He overlooked her growing need for vengeance. It was a short-term crutch but long term disaster left for a later conversation. " know it's difficult. We'll get through this and make a plan moving forward."

Angry swipes whisked the tears from her cheeks before her shoulders drooped. "I'm so tired of all this. And we haven't even begun yet."

"You're one of the strongest women I know. Keep in mind, you have friends." He didn't budge when she leaned forward and wrapped her arms around his waist. The silent request for strength lasted mere moments, but again bonded them in a way he couldn't define. Not sexual. More akin to a team member.

Neither spoke. Words proved unnecessary during a sharing of warmth and support. When she gazed at him again, he perceived a gradual return of earlier strength.

"Your color's a little better."

"I'm too tired to deal with all this now." A wave indicated the jewelry.

"We'll talk about it later."

"What are we doing today?" Callie stood and turned to stare at her reflection, her face a study of determination.

"I thought we'd take it easy, play with your pup, put up some Christmas decorations if you feel like it. If you'd like to read, there's a library downstairs. Not sure what you'd prefer. If you want to veg out in front of the TV, we can do that. There's a variety of movies. I also have something for you."

A half-smile slid into place. "I've not watched much TV." The uncertainty in her voice increased. "Do you have Wi-Fi here?"

"Sure do. It's spotty at times, but we manage."

"Spy Man. I remember hearing that name. He's a spy?" Nate thought about a military buddy who'd once worked both side of the fence. Nobody trusted him.

"The men who took you were foreign, so yeah, it'd make sense."

"To hell with them. To hell with them all. I'm keeping the belly ring." Her stance steadied as she studied herself in the mirror.

"That's my girl." Nate winked as their gazes collided. "You're stronger than anyone could guess."

Her gaze snapped away in an instant, her hair falling forward as she took a deep breath.

"Jake once talked about piercings. Despite the *way* I got it, it kinda makes me feel like I'm blending in. The people at the club, I saw some there."

"I've got some plastic wrap to keep most of the water from your dressings. When you get out of the shower, I'll change the bandage."

Diluted crimson fluid had stained the prior dressing. The new one applied would collect less as the wound healed.

"I can't believe they chipped me like a dog."

Anger and determination rose to the fore.

"Like everywhere else, people come in all different sizes, shapes, and mentalities. It doesn't make them all freaks, just different."

"I understand."

Despite her intelligence, she'd still surf the varying stages of grief, some days forward and other days reverting to helplessness over her friends' deaths.

The falter in her tone let him know she felt more than mere pain. Her anger was growing.

"Teach me to fight. When I do come face-to-face with this *Spy Man*, I want to be the one to take him down."

Now was the time to set the record straight and steer her toward a new outlook, before she traveled too far down a dark path. "Callie, you can see the situation from two angles."

"Wh-what? How do you mean?"

"Just this. You've been victimized, yes. However, it's over. What you do now, how you deal with this—is up to you. Your decision. You can cave to the need for revenge, or you now have the power to take back your life."

"I want to kill all those bastards." His shirtsleeve twisted in her grasp.

"Anger is expected. You're smart enough to see past that. I'll help in any way I can, but your attitude will determine your path and progress. This anger won't last forever, but what they did won't be forgotten. You did what you had to do. You survived."

"Not by design, action, or without help."

"Doesn't matter."

Something ill-defined overtaking her expression in tilting her head reminded him of their first meeting when she'd worked out the cubed puzzle.

"What are you not saying?"

"That we make a pact and a plan. Nothing is set in stone. You'll have good times and bad, but you're not alone. You can come out of this stronger than you imagine."

Her intelligence made her a target. It could also be her ticket to greater inner strength.

In mulling the situation over, he considered alternative possibilities in moving forward. Her lack of choice in how she'd spent her time at the institution offered no direction in providing specific distractions. On the other hand, the possibilities were endless.

Three loud knocks on the bedroom door brought their discussion to a temporary halt.

"Yeah, what's up?" Nate answered as he let her shirt hem fall in place.

His sixth sense kicked up a notch with the creak of the opening door. No one would interrupt them without good cause.

"Hey, Nate. Need you downstairs a sec." Whisper's calm tone belied a major situation taking place. From her vantage point, Callie couldn't see the hand signal flashed in their direction.

"Sure. Be right down."

Stiffness in her shoulders seeped away with the click of the closing bedroom door.

"Callie, I'm going to help you back to bed. Don't try to get up by yourself, okay? I promise I won't be long. When I come back, I'll stand outside the bathroom while you wash up. Okay?"

"Please, don't make promises. Jake promised he'd come back and..."

The desolation in her eyes nearly crushed him, yet he needed to address each concern as it arose. How could Jake have been so reckless in not taking appropriate backup?

"I rarely make promises. However, I will promise you this. As long as I'm alive, I will help you in whatever way I think best. Fair enough?"

Her rapid blinking prevented moisture from falling but pulled him deeper into her web. He'd already broken one promise. She stood there in pain because of his incompetence and lack of foresight.

Never again.

Silken skin, so soft under his touch, held a quality he couldn't fathom, drawing from an unknown source deep inside to expose feelings he'd never experienced.

"Little one, let the pain pill have time to work. I'll be back after I speak with Whisper, and we'll get you straight for the day, okay? Let's get you back to bed."

Whisper had better have a damn good reason for interrupting.

Chapter Sixteen

"Bad news, boss. Some dipshit decimated your home, blew it off the map, deep fried in the cosmos." Spirit's stiff posture and clenched jaw spoke volumes as he typed on his keyboard. "I'll pull up an aerial view."

"Sonofabitch! Who are these people? How did they find me so freakin' fast? I'm damn sure no one escaped that van last night."

Because of a previous semi-nomadic lifestyle, home equaled sacred ground. Nate's sitting occurred as much from legs giving way from exhaustion as from intent. The chair screeched in protest as he pulled it closer to the massive kitchen table.

Multiple keyboards produced constant clicking as each man pursued a different angle of investigation. A box of donuts sat open with several remaining. He couldn't stomach food at the moment.

Spirit sighed. "Dunno. Might be a bug somewhere, or a mole. Maybe they had access to Callie's chip information? It'll take time to sort this out."

Every close-knit unit put their lives in each other's hands, the bond between them near unbreakable. To suspect a traitor in their midst put them all on edge.

"Jesus. Maybe they have the numbers to cover lots of bases. We won't know until we find out more." An undercurrent of anxiety filled the room as he looked between Whisper, Spirit, and Nerd. He'd known and trusted each man with his life—and still did. "Where's Blade and Virus?"

"Blade's checking our vehicles again. It's driving him nuts to think he might've missed something. Virus is monitoring the usual bands, hacking through God only knows what." Spirit rotated his laptop to show the crumbled remains of Nate's home.

"Oh, shit. My house...please tell me it was empty. My brothers have a habit of dropping by without notice, especially if they think trouble's brewing." The thought of a family member buried under the rubble drained the heat from his face.

"Nobody home. Conner called to make sure we're all okay. Said he didn't call you 'cuz he didn't want Callie to hear. Guess he knew you'd stick by her side." Whisper rubbed the back of his neck as he shook his head.

"Who else could tag me as part of this? You all know Sebastian better. Think he turned renegade? Hell, he helped break her out of the institution. The way Jake explained it, Sebastian could just as easily have been killed that night."

"Doubt it. Last Conner saw of him, he was trying to get lucky with one of the wait staff," Blade offered, never taking his gave off task.

If Nate had taken Callie to the house, they'd be dead. "It doesn't make sense to abduct her after helping her escape. Sebastian spent three days with just Callie and Jake. Logistically, *that* would've been the time to make his move."

"He came on the unit as we were getting out. None of us knew him well. Seemed all right... took an instant liking to Jake." Nerd's distracted words met with confirming nods from Whisper and Spirit. "Yeah, a *real* good liking."

"What time did the explosion happen?" Nate's thoughts slipped a cog as he calculated distances and the time needed for set up.

"Not long after we got here. We didn't come get you, nothing we could do. Marc called. I gave him the short version of the past twelve and told him you'd tag him bright and early. I guess Conner got antsy. He called again, still a den mother, I see." Nerd scrubbed the stubble on his chin then continued with his research.

"Yeah, Conner's always been that way." Nate explained his texted conversation with Penny. "I'm thinking she's like Callie, but somehow gained her freedom."

"Another loose thread. Let me see if I can track the number. Maybe they tagged Jake through her. Conner said they'd work this from their end and let us know when they found something. I sketched the highlights about Callie. I figured you'd go into detail... or not." Nerd made a low humming noise as he worked.

"Not. Good luck tracing the number. Said she's gonna ditch the phone."

"Friend or foe playing games?" Nerd asked.

"For now—a friend we need to find. She got the number to my burner phone. How? Think she was among the guests in Ambrosia?"

"Damn this is gettin' spooky kind of weird." Whisper kept his gaze on his keyboard.

"Also, the colonel is looking for you. According to your mother hen, your brothers are banding together in a front line." Nerd's gaze slid to Spirit, looking for affirmation. "You think the colonel's gonna be a problem?"

Shafts of light streaked Spirit's dark hair and cast half his face in shadow. "Whatever the colonel knows, he wouldn't betray us. Though, he obviously suspects our team is helping out on this end if he called Conner. It all smacks of military precision."

"Colonel Kenson is solid. Unless something has drastically changed, he won't let anything slip even if Ray has contacted him. He'll want to know every detail about Callie, then form his own decision on best course of action." Nate stood and stretched. "All right, I'll check in with my brothers. Meanwhile, let's look at Sebastian and the Colonel for shits and giggles. If either's mixed up in this and the one we saw leaving the cabin, he didn't have time to set up the explosives. Neither involvement makes no sense—but check them out anyway."

"What about the foreigners?" Spirit frowned and punched at his keyboard a little harder. "And what about Ray, the administrator of the Think Tank? Obliterating your home might be his idea of a friendly warning."

"The foreigners are dead, minus one. Those in the van who tailed me are dead. I'll get a message to Kenson for cleanup. He'll jump at the chance to scour the wreckage for evidence."

"With bodies burned to a crisp, Kenson's gonna do a wide sweep, both for the asshats and to locate us," Whisper added.

"Don't fret. We have enough distance. Spirit, Whisper, you two look into the foreigners. See what pops. Virus can help you hack records. Nerd, you look into Ray. It's a shame we couldn't bring Jake's computer. Apparently, he had info stored, but I don't want to ask Callie about that just yet. I do, however, want to know everything that administrator has seen, done, and who he's talked with in the last six months." It occurred that Callie could probably make short work of hacking, but not until she found her equilibrium.

"I ran the prints of the asswipes at the cabin." Nerd spun the laptop back around. "Here's the dirt on them."

Nate whistled when he saw the dossier on her abductors. "Hell, it could've been directed from anyone at the brain trust in league with these guys. I'll talk to Callie again and see what she remembers about the employees."

Too much information was missing to navigate the maze to a logical hypothesis. With the drugs clearing her system, maybe Callie would remember something else.

"Nerd, can you pry into the Think Tank's files and scramble anything they have left on her? Some will be on a standalone, but I'm betting they have other records, maybe coded."

"Virus already snuck past their firewalls and deleted what files he could find on her after copying them. We'll go in the back door he left and poke around. Hopefully, we'll learn more about Ray." Nerd stuffed part of a donut into his mouth and resumed working.

"I'll call my brother before heading upstairs. When I bring Callie down and settle on the sofa, let's keep everything low key. She needs normal and routine till she finds her equilibrium."

"What's with the glass shattering earlier? Everything okay?" Nerd's gaze never left the keyboard, yet the weight of his measured words expressed volumes.

"Nothing broken down here from the small quake?" Nate looked to each man for confirmation.

"Quake? There was no quake. I checked the National Earthquake Information Center site. They registered no activity in the area, but we all felt something." Whisper opened a new screen and pivoted the laptop for everyone to see.

Nate felt their gazes bearing down on him as he answered, "Damn, this situation gets stranger by the minute. That's the least of our problems for now. Start digging and build a file. Callie needs to hear the basics to know we're not keeping information from her. It'll help her start processing."

"Okay then, let us know when and how we can help," Spirit added while grabbing a donut. "I made more saline solution for her incision's aftercare. It's on the counter."

"Thanks." Though Nate considered all three men hardened warriors, they each drew the line when it came to innocents and women.

Years of working together in the military and private investigations furnished the Crofton brothers with a wealth of resources. On the other hand, sometimes comradery proved a liability. It was a stroke of luck his house was empty prior to exploding.

Telling them to stay out of the current mess would triple their curiosity and make them more apt to stick their collective noses where they didn't belong. At least if he shared knowledge, they'd be cautious.

They were supposed to meet and spar at his brother's house today. After the fiasco last night, they'd be waiting for a call.

Marc's ring back tone made him smile.

Yep, I'd like to do bad things to someone right about now.

"Hey, Nate. How much is bail? What kind of trouble did you find this time?" Marc's early morning snark proved habitual.

"Ah, I haven't done anything wrong."

"Of course, not. Someone blew up your house for munitions practice."

"Maybe I forgot to tip the cleaning service."

"And maybe one of the cleaning staff has an irate husband. Tell me this is not about a woman."

"Um—not like you think."

"Thought so. Conner's spinning some wild yarn about girl geniuses and Think Tank institutions. And for the love of God, please tell me this guy Sebastian is not your new BFF. I've had enough of his poor-me ranting. Sure you don't want to take him off our hands? He's trying to attach himself to any of our hips."

"Listen, Conner can explain in more detail, but the stuff about Callie is true yet only skims the tip of the iceberg. For now, I need you to keep an eye on Sebastian. I'd be surprised if he's involved, but we haven't ruled him out."

"Yeah, I get it. Sometimes you gotta feed people bullshit just to see where they go to tattle."

As the oldest of the Crofton brothers, Conner had the most experience with spies and counter-intelligence work, but Marc's ability to connect with others made him a valuable asset.

"Ahh, friends close."

"And enemies closer," Nate finished.

"You and Callie, huh?"

"Focus, Marc. Also, get word to the colonel about the cabin with foreign agents, assuming they haven't been cleared already. Oh, and there's a mangled and burned van along the highway from when we left Ambrosia."

"Hell. You've been busy."

"Damn straight, and I'm tired of it. I'll check back with you tonight but call me if you find anything significant, especially concerning the outlanders."

"Stay safe, little bro. I don't wanna collect your life insurance."

"Yeah, you'd love more beachside property..."

"Not when it's in small, chunk-sized pieces."

A few minutes of shorthand conversation put them on the same page before Nate ended the call. Top-notch investigators with advanced skills, each of the brothers had military and civilian contacts they could tap.

Now, to deal with Callie.

Nate grabbed a broom and dustpan from the closet along with the saline rinse before heading upstairs.

A primal scream not heard since watching a teammate die at the hands of his enemy energized steps muffled by carpeted stairs.

Heavy scraping across the floor followed cessation of music from his clock radio. Glass shattered with something heavy thudding against the wall in his bedroom.

He wasn't sure what to expect upon entering the space but didn't anticipate seeing his king-size bed shoved *into* the wall. Enough power such that the headboard post went through the wallboard. A ceramic lamp lay shattered, its pieces strewn in linear fashion parallel to the long edge of the room. Bedding draped in tangles over the dresser, whose contents also lay scattered around the floor.

Knowing Callie had surpassed her breaking point didn't explain how a slip of a woman could ram the heavy frame with such force. "Feeling better?"

With hands fisted at her sides and crimson spreading across her face, she closed her eyes and hung her head.

"Sorry. I'll find a way to pay for the damage."

"Nonsense. A little mud, a piece of wallboard, and a few minutes time, it'll be good as new. Can't say it's the first time there's been a meltdown in this house. I'm sure it won't be the last either."

Nate shrugged like it was a common occurrence. There was nothing common about the strength and time needed to demolish the room. Her position relative to the damage done didn't add up any more than the timing to accomplish so much carnage. It was a mystery for another time.

"I didn't peg you for a fan of western swing music." The corners of his mouth tipped up.

"I can quote any number of studies showing the health benefits of music, from decreasing perceived pain, stress, and anxiety, to improved cognitive performance, decreasing insomnia..."

"Maybe we should leave it on?"

Deeper crimson colored her cheeks and contrasted the bright violet of her eyes, guilt and fear filling their depths.

"Your nose is bleeding." Slowly, as if approaching a cornered animal, he advanced, snatching a tissue from the box on the floor.

When she dabbed under her nose, her gaze landed everywhere but on him. "Um... sorry?"

"No problem. We've all had a few." Nate assessed the mess and considered the timing of the various noises heard. It appeared multi-tasking ranked high in her abilities.

The *how* of it along with the timing added up to more than one person's carnage.

"I just want to be normal."

"Callie. We are what we are. We each have to learn to live with that. It's *how* we do it that makes our journey interesting."

The sense of wistful longing gracing her gaze as she turned to the window filled him with guilt. Jake's death lay at his feet, not hers. As head of their unit, he should've sent more backup.

"Guess I have a lot to learn."

It appeared in his absence she'd gathered the remnants of emotional strength and swept the floor of glass in a pile.

Using what?

"Feel like talking?" Nate gestured toward the room, eyeing the wallboard.

"Please no. Not now."

"Okay. But eventually, we will."

"All right."

With someone perceived as average, he would know better how to proceed. The fact she'd pulled herself together as soon as he stepped into the room dictated she hid much, which necessitated taking a different tack.

How deep did she bury her pain— physical and emotional? *Better to deal with it now than let it fester.*

"Callie, about Jake." While deciding on the best approach, he took the bottle of saline solution to the bathroom. Spirit's thinking ahead saved time, a precious commodity.

"Jake's dead. We're not. It's time to figure out who's going to pay."

In one sentence, she summed up her priorities and intent. Strength of character matched beauty. Detailed discussions on revenge versus justice could come later.

At the moment, they needed information and a plan in order to survive.

"We'll talk downstairs. For now, let's get you clean, dry, and dressed, unless you want to eat first."

"No, thanks, I couldn't stand to look at food right now. I'll wait until lunch."

Her widened eyes and sudden nibbling on her lower lip told him her energy focused on anything but her own circumstances. A pale face and tight expression betrayed exhaustion and frustration.

She needed a distraction.

"I have a question for you." Even though she watched him approach, she jumped when he touched her arm. "Did anyone at the institution ever talk about your parents?"

"No. I asked Jake once. Apparently, Ray works with some very distinct and shady individuals. We were going to find out if I have any relatives."

Hmm, table that conversation for later.

"We'll look into that when the dust settles. Tell me what types of physical activities you enjoy." Mindful of the discomfort she'd feel with each step, he led her to the bathroom while observing her body language. "This won't be as bad as you think, Callie. How's your head feeling?"

"*Um,* a little better. At the facility, I went to the exercise room every day, weight machines, treadmills, and such. I used to bug Jake about his daily activities in the outside world. It kind of became an obsession with the way he described things."

No doubt about it, Jake's final decision proved ill-advised and poorly thought out. It also presaged extensive and substantial consequences to the woman under his care and guidance.

"What did you and Jake talk about doing? What things do you want to experience first?"

"I want to play with Faith. I'd like to have a garden in the spring, maybe a greenhouse. It'd be nice to see what it's like to have a day with no structure, to study the stars at night and breathe crisp clean air. Not sure if all that would be comfortable, but something to experience. I want to hike several times a day and see if bird song differs at various hours."

"One of my brothers has a telescope. I'll get it sent up in the next day or so."

"I saw the starry sky while we drove east. Jake told me that no, they're just holes poked in the top of a jar so we could breathe. It was his way of reminding me one day we'd sleep under them, when the weather's warmer."

"You'd never seen stars?"

"Not before my first night of freedom, I spent hours just studying them. They're fascinating."

"Okay, then we'll take it one hour at a time." Gently, he leaned her against the counter, then turned on the shower taps and grabbed a washcloth from under the sink. From the medicine cabinet over the vanity, he retrieved a stack of gauze pads for after she'd cleaned up. "I'm sorry I don't have any special shampoo for your hair..."

"Soap is fine."

"If you were mine, you'd be pampered with sweet-smelling oils and lotions." Not only would he try to bolster her self-esteem, he wanted her to absorb the difference between experiences at the Think Tank, with the kidnappers, and a complete new lifestyle. Otherwise, she might grow to think of *all* men as evil.

"Mine? As in—"

He held up his hands before she could finish the derogatory thought. With a sad smile, he addressed her underlying concern. People should never think of themselves as subhuman or owned.

"Mine as in girlfriend. Where I'm from, women are pampered and protected."

"Oh." She tilted her head to the side in thought.

"Your color is a little better, but you're still not steady on your feet. I'm going to cover your bandages with plastic wrap for now." A deep breath steeled him for the argument to come. "I'll straighten the bedroom while you clean up. There's a towel within easy reach for when you're done." He nodded to the rack beside the shower door.

She stared at him as if he'd grown a third head, then shrugged.

"I don't want you falling and hitting your head. You've already had several nosebleeds."

He understood her need to wash away the filth of the kidnapper's touch.

"This bathroom's huge. You could host a party in here."

"You've been to parties?"

"No, but Jake described them."

"Hmm, actually my brothers and I designed this. We each like our space. They have similar cabins nearby."

He didn't want to explain about his home's obliteration yet but knew she'd eventually inquire.

The party idea had merit, a Christmas gathering of family.

"I love looking out the windows and seeing so much green."

"Sounds relaxing. And Callie? This'll get better—a little each day. You okay for now?"

In response, she wrapped her arms around his waist. "Thank you for all you've done and are doing. I wish I could pay you back."

"You're fine." He topped her height by half a foot, but she stood equal in every way. "Can you scooch out of your pants after sitting on the shower's bench?"

"Sure."

She didn't protest as he held her hand when stepping over the rim and waited until she sat. Her expression displayed more resignation than defeat. The movement instigated pain, judging by her quick inhale. She had a long road ahead.

Chapter Seventeen

Never in Nate's imagination could he have foreseen the present scenario during initial discussions of bathroom design. Two rainfall showerheads, check. Spacious with lots of storage, check. A beautiful woman in need of help, not so much.

In counterpoint, Callie's inner strength was amazing.

By the time she called his name, she'd already dressed and had wrapped a towel around her hair. "I redressed the incision."

"All right. Let's go downstairs. You can comb out your hair and by the fire."

She moved a little better as he escorted her downstairs and to the sofa facing the fireplace. "Better?"

"Yes, the Aspirin and getting cleaned up helped. Nate, I know you each risked your lives to rescue me from those pricks. I also know you're not going to hurt me. I do trust you."

Her choice of topic surprised him as she combed the tangles from her hair. "Is that the only basis for your belief?"

"Kinda. Hurting women is not in your nature. I usually have good instincts about people."

"Figuring this out will give you closure. Meanwhile, we'll look at new activities for you to explore." Nate watched her changing expressions then retrieved her pup after she'd finished braiding her locks. Faith curled in her lap and groaned. Mere days and they'd formed a strong bond.

"In future, I pray I'm always there when you need me, hon." Though he hadn't known her long, he'd discerned in her tone when fear and trepidation began to dissolve into a tentative trust.

"I don't want anybody else hurt because of me."

"None of this is *because* of you. It's because of the greedy, power-hungry bastards after you. No one has the right to mark or track another as if they were some kind of *thing*." He threw out her own words to mark his indignation.

"I see that, but I want to understand the world."

Her curiosity about new experiences drew an uncertain path moving ahead. He looked forward to the journey.

"Let's set that aside until we know more. We can talk, and I'll answer whatever questions I can."

She'd just thrown down a gauntlet. He could teach her so much and take care of her, all under the guise of protection. Though he had no intention of sexual intimacy, he might be able to change her viewpoint on a future relationship instead of letting cynicism rule her perspective.

"Jake thought I could thrive. Just because I can figure out puzzles better than most doesn't give me the social skill set to understand and flourish in your world."

"It's just as much your world as mine."

With her steady gaze piercing any obstruction to his heart, he couldn't say no to anything she'd ask. Inexperience ensured she had no idea what life entailed, but she'd learn. Persistence and inquisitiveness wouldn't go away. At least he hoped not.

"What projects were you working on before you left the institution?"

"Um, they wanted me to build a bomb that's undetectable using current methods."

That brought him back to reality. "Did you ever see any men in uniform? Military men?"

"No. And the only administrator I saw was Ray."

"Ever?"

"Actually, no. I did see Ray with another man on occasion, but I didn't know his name or affiliation. He wore jeans. There weren't a lot of people who interacted with me, but Ray was the one in charge."

"Ever hear the other guy's name?"

"No."

"And your work with explosives?"

"Jake was the only one who knew the extent of my research since I didn't keep much in the way of physical records. I think I've got it figured out. Though nothing's been tested."

"Do you think Jake would have told Sebastian?"

"I don't know. They were close."

"All right. Anything else, maybe other projects someone might want you to finish?" Nothing explained the reason behind the belly ring.

"Yes, a bioengineering application. I was in the early stages of developing a plant-based toxin, a paralytic agent."

"Weapons and chemistry?"

"I won't finish that either, but I do want to study botany—not for that purpose. I'd like to delve into holistic medicine."

The revelation shouldn't have come as a surprise. In counterpoint, if any government agency learned the extent of her talent, she'd never see the light of day again.

His little enigma had just added another reason to keep her under wraps.

Callie blew out a breath that brushed wispy bangs from her eyes. "Will you teach me self-defense?" Running her fingers through Faith's fur, she tucked her feet under her and held his gaze.

"I think it's wise for every young woman to know the basics. Let's give you a few days to heal before we start. My gut tells me you'll be a unique student."

"Can we sit on the porch this afternoon?"

"Whenever you like. I have some heavier clothes you can borrow till we get you more in your size. They'll be a little big but will keep you warm enough." Swiveling to face Whisper at the kitchen table, he asked, "When's the last time Faith went out?"

"'Bout an hour. Probably ought to try her again. She's been really good and catching on faster than any pup I've known," Whisper continued his research, not looking up.

"Can we take a short hike through the woods?" Her fascination with various ideas reminded him of a toddler holding a bag of candy, uncertain which piece to eat first.

"Sure. My brother left his winter coat in the closet on his last visit." Nate collected the jacket along with his shoulder rig. He wouldn't venture anywhere without protection.

Once bundled up and outside, Callie took a deep breath, closed her eyes, and tilted her face toward the sun. "Freedom. I wish Jake were here to see this." Faith pulled at her leash toward the woods and barked.

"I think someone's impatient and wants to explore." Nate marveled at her perceptions. She and the pup had so much in common, both experiencing new things.

Callie selected and picked her way along a well-used deer trail leading to a breathtaking overlook. Many paths crisscrossed the gentle incline where prints detailed the various creatures using them. At the top, the view was one where he'd contemplated the vagaries of fate on occasion. Now, he could almost envision it for the first time. *Breathtaking.*

Gauging her endurance and stamina over the next fifteen minutes, he didn't ask if she needed a break, instead pondering her strength. Still, in no universe could he see her strong enough to shove his heavy bedframe *into* the wall. She hadn't even been out of breath, nor close to the bed when he'd opened the door.

How'd she do it?

If she withheld some kind of super strength, it would blow his teammates' minds.

A soft but high-pitched moan drew the pup's attention off-trail and to their right. Faith stood on her hind legs trying to gain forward momentum, her harness tightening around her chest.

"Faith, no. That's not something you need to tangle with, I'm sure." Callie picked up her pup and visually probed the deeper shadows of the woods. "What is that sound?"

Nate slipped his arm around Callie's waist and tugged her back. "C'mon. Sounds like a—"

"Oh, hell." Callie stumbled back at the blowing sound to her left. "Are we between momma and her cubs?"

As Callie spoke, a large black bear emerged from the brush, standing on hind feet and chuffing out in sharp breaths.

A dozen feet away, the bear pounced forward, blowing explosively while slamming both front feet on the ground.

"Back up, Callie." Nate nudged her back and behind him. "Keep backing up. Don't run."

"She's growling at us."

"No, she's moaning, a lot of people misinterpret that as a growl. Keep going, hon."

Behind him, Faith sent up a racket in ferocious yipping barks. In front, the bear slammed her paw against a tree.

"Ah, Faith. No!"

Callie cried out and tried to scoot around Nate as her pup hit the ground and bolted toward the bear.

Nate grabbed her arm and palmed the Glock in his shoulder rig, noting Callie's move to stand beside him.

Several things happened at once.

Faith charged forward, stopping three feet from the bear, who once again stood on her hind feet and roared, classic Hollywood style.

"Shit." Nate moved one step forward and took aim.

"Don't shoot, Nate."

His thoughts stuttered when the bear toppled over onto its back. The animal's paws flailed in the air in trying to roll over. Its natural agility should've righted it in short order, yet it continued to struggle atop mashed winter vines.

Dumbfounded, he froze, never having seen or imagined this scenario.

Callie latched onto Faith and together they stepped back.

Nate kept his gaze on the animal, who continued its chorus of loud sharp snorting, woofing, and huffing, jaws clacking and popping.

"Let's go, Callie." Seconds later, they'd moved out of sight. Nate turned around and hustled his charge to the base of the trail and the wood's edge.

"Wow. Never seen a real bear before. She sounded furious."

"That's an understatement. Though, I still can't figure out what happened."

"We're safe. Faith is safe. That's all that matters. I'd like to go inside now."

Nate grinned at her insistence. "As you wish."

As soon as they opened the back door, Spirit glanced up from his screen. "What happened? Callie's all flushed."

"Got caught between a momma bear and her cub. Then, Faith decided it'd be a good idea to protect us." Nate shook his head as Callie further explained what happened.

"Damn. Never a dull moment around here. How could a bear fall over backward? They're very agile. What happened?" Whisper removed a casserole from the oven and set it on the table.

"That's the damnedest thing. Looked like it got punched in the gut—lifted her right off her back legs." Nate cast a speculative glance in Callie's direction.

"It was all Faith's doing. Old momma bear didn't stand a chance against this ferocious little protector." Callie picked Faith up and snuggled.

Flashbacks of the bear's flailing legs in trying to right her position surfed his thoughts. She hadn't lost her balance. Something shoved the bear, plain and simple.

"Food's up. Let's eat." Spirit nodded to the rest as he sat.

"Smells great." On cue, Callie's stomach growled as she set Faith down. "Can you teach me to cook?"

That halted the conversation between Blade and Spirit sitting at the table.

"You face off with a pissed off momma bear and want to talk about cooking? Well, okay then. Better ask Whisper or Spirit. Otherwise, we might starve or suffer recurrent food poisoning." Nerd didn't look up from his laptop screen. "Unless it comes to the wild stuff. I'm hell on wheels with gator or possum."

"Ew." Callie studied Nerd as if *he* were the odd duck.

Nate held the chair for her, determined to demonstrate the difference between being a prisoner and a guest.

A frown revealed her confusion. "Oh, that's your seat? Sorry, I didn't realize." She pointed to the end. "I'll sit over there."

Commotion stopped with all eyes on the interaction.

"Callie." Nate halted her progress with a light touch on her forearm. "You don't understand. A gentleman holds the chair for a lady and waits to seat her. It's part of social etiquette."

"I don't want to be a lady. I want to be part of the team."

"Can't switch sides of the stream, darlin." Nerd arched a brow then reconsidered, "Well, you can, but it's a difficult swim."

"First of all, I don't know how to swim. Second, I don't see how that would make a difference. Is that part of the training?"

The round of chuckles ceased under her glare.

"What he means is this. You're a woman—" Nate began.

"Good to know and glad everyone noticed. Now... do you seat your teammates?" Her challenge earned a round of snickers.

"No. Can't say that I ever have." Nate admired the defiance in her gaze and chuckled when she pulled out an adjacent chair and sat.

"Quite an attitude, Callie. I like it," Blade snickered.

"I don't have an attitude. I have a personality he doesn't know how to deal with. I want to be considered equal."

"We'll see." Nate smiled at her burgeoning pride.

"I want to be part of the team."

"You don't have the training," Nate returned with his own challenge. "What makes you equal?"

Callie huffed.

"Look, I understand you want justice. However, when you don't have all the pieces of the puzzle, it's dangerous to show your hand." Nate waited, hoping she'd divulge some tidbit to lend a better understanding of their situation.

"You want information."

He didn't expect to stay ahead of her. Keeping up would do just fine. "If we make a move now, lives will be endangered unnecessarily."

"There are other people being held prisoner. I know that much."

"But you never had contact with them?" Ignoring her change of subject, Nate went with the flow.

"No. I don't know what level of which facility to search."

"There are other institutions holding captives?" Blade asked, accepting and dishing up a heavy scoop of sausage and egg casserole.

"Yes, from what I understand. Well, at least one."

"Okay, we'll deal with that when the time comes." Nate accepted the platter of bacon after Callie helped herself. "Let's back up and talk about the unconscious man in the restroom."

Intelligence, whether intuitive or through study, didn't pre-empt emotions. He didn't need to search her gaze when she squirmed. Whatever she was hiding, it was big, and she didn't trust anyone with that secret.

"I don't know who he was or what he wanted, well, not specifically."

"He had a gun, still in his holster, and lay unconscious behind a locked stall door—locked from the inside. I'm a bit confused as to how that happened." Nate quirked his head to the side.

"He wanted me to go with him. Said if I didn't, he'd kill Sebastian and anybody else who interfered."

"He wasn't dressed like the others at the cabin. Ray might have sent him. If they picked up the discrepancies of your GPS chip at the facility, they might've been prepared, thinking to catch whatever foreign agents are on your trail." Blade offered the insight without looking up from his plate.

"If that were the case, they would've attacked the men who'd kidnapped me."

"Depends on how long it took to muster reinforcements. Ray knows by now you have allies in his command," Nate countered.

"*Had* allies. Damn. We don't know any more now than when I escaped. You said Sebastian's all right?"

"Yes. He's with my brothers and is concerned about you."

She lifted her chin, brushed her braid over her shoulder, and met his gaze head on. "I'm fine, and while I'm here, I want to help with cooking, cleaning, and other chores."

Determination was an admirable trait.

"Why not? Have you ever done domestic duties? We all take turns and share the load. That's how teams work," Blade agreed with the others nodding approval.

"I don't have much experience. Jake showed me how to make scrambled eggs. Judging by his expression, they didn't quite turn out as expected."

"Okay, then. All learning starts with 'I don't know,' and this'll be no different. None of us are gourmet cooks, but we each have our strengths and get by. Unless he's lost his touch, Whisper is pretty handy in the kitchen."

We'll find out at dinnertime. As far as me? Mustard greens and possum innards so good you'll want 'em the second day is my only specialty." Nerd's cheerful tone said he welcomed her into their group.

Callie's look of horror instigated a round of chuckles, but Whisper took pity on her. "He's kidding, I think. Nerd's from the bayou and used to living off the land—or swamp."

Conversation passed with each man detailing their strengths and weaknesses and how they worked as a unit.

The next few days would prove entertaining as well as enlightening. Nate figured memories of Jake was the reason she hadn't asked to use a computer. With her skill, she could shorten their workload. It wasn't worth risking emotional strain, as they were set for the time being.

When finished, Virus and Blade stood to scrape their plates.

Callie's voice held none of her earlier insecurity. "I can prove I deserve to be an equal member of this team."

Both Whisper and Nerd looked up, frowns wrinkling their brow.

Nate grinned. His little enigma surprised him at every turn.

"Since when does an asset fight on the front lines?" Nerd's jaw moved side to side as if tasting a theory.

"Well, can't say I'm too surprised..." Spirit's half-grin indicated partial acceptance.

"Let's give Callie a week to heal and get to know us. Teamwork is a partnership, which means complete trust, open communication, and absolute honesty," Nate confirmed.

"You're seriously considering this?" Whisper rubbed his jaw, a speculative assessment underway. "What've you been smokin'?"

"What the hell, Nate? She's a girl! Have you lost your freaking mind?" Virus's viewpoint hadn't changed over the years. In his book, women performed best in the kitchen or bed. "Do you know what they'd—"

"Not to mention the fact, we're supposed to *protect* our asset." Blade's attitude hadn't changed either.

"True, yet we've learned the safest place for her is with us. Hence, it would help us all if she could pull her own weight, even though she'll have to stay to the rear."

Nate's mollifying words met with grumbles until he added, "Unless I miss my guess, I believe this'll be the most extraordinary unit ever formed. Our official mission days are over, guy. But it doesn't mean we slack off. Training will keep us disciplined, alert, and in shape." He expected opposition to his plan, but it would soon melt under the revelation of the suspected secrets Callie held close.

"Then we should have backup. I, for one, am not willing to risk her safety." Virus's words brought mumbles of agreement.

"Okay, let's give it some time. We can revisit this conversation next week." Nate's thoughts spun with a thousand what-if's, a headache forming from trying to pick one and follow it to its natural conclusion.

In his mind's eye, he conjured the erratic path of the van trailing them, bursting into flames, then Callie's nosebleed. Subsequently, the bedroom furniture shook, the bottled water on the floor, and pictures falling from secure perches on the wall. Again, a nose bleed followed. Finally, the bear. Its instinct was to charge, yet some force punched it in the midsection and knocked it over.

One revelation, though minor, would stun his men into silence. Both Virus and Nerd were experts in the electronics arena. Once told about her digital prowess, they'd pester her until the end of time.

Her closed-off attitude confirmed something extraordinary engulfed his enigma, something defying his experience and testing his imagination. Still, there was more. He would distract and cajole, teasing the finest details into light.

"We've rarely had women join our missions." Virus's curious stare at Callie met with calm assurance. "What special skill set do you bring to the table, hon?"

"You're forgetting something, guys. I have a working knowledge of the institution. I *can* help." Self-assuredness resurrected her earlier tenacity. "Also, I can read binary code. I'll break down any firewall you put in front of me."

Four sets of chair legs hit the floor. Four mouths sat agape.

And so it begins.

"Like, as in how we read a book?" Virus's soft question filled the room, echoing Nate's earlier reaction.

"Yes."

"That doesn't make you bulletproof. We can tap into surveillance footage from anywhere. Don't need to be part of the squad for that," Nerd countered with a sense of wonder. He wanted more. "Can you show us after we get cleaned up? It'll open any and all digital files."

Frowns from Virus and Blade suggested their interest and curiosity outweighed any reservations at the moment. They each knew Nate wouldn't accept her as a team member without reasonable backup.

The half-smile tugging the corner of Nerd's mouth confirmed his begrudging if reluctant challenge as he stood. "Welcome to our little group, sis."

"Want some more coffee?" Blade and Virus each gathered dishes and took them to the sink.

It would be a long morning where they each tested her abilities, not knowing she held more in check, if Nate's supposition proved correct.

Chapter Eighteen

The rest of the team had either delved into research or were checking perimeter guard after two hours of show-and-tell. Exclamations and wonder declared Callie a member on probation.

When she plopped down on the couch, exhausted, he tried to hold his own questions in check. Wanting to brighten her outlook, he held out a box. "This is for you. Didn't have time to wrap it."

"Why would you disguise a gift?"

He shook his head with a smile. "Consider it an early Christmas present."

Callie's eyes lit up. "Jake talked about Christmas, but I don't understand it."

With a deep breath, Nate launched into his perspective of the holidays, the distraction encompassing family traditions, food favorites, and decorations.

When she opened the box and lifted the device out with reverence, he smiled.

"A camera? How thoughtful. Thank you." A wide smile graced her face. "I can take pictures of you all and Faith. Memories fade with time. This way, I'll always have a reminder."

She'd understood his intent, inserting the memory disc and snapping pictures of Faith first.

"I'm sorry you weren't able to connect more with the outside world while under Ray's thumb." Nate moved to put another log on the fire, turning to watch her rapt expression while his team made silly faces for the camera.

"You can't form a server and internet connection from thin air. Ray was neurotic about no one having electronic devices that could connect. He saw that ability as a shortcoming."

"A shame you never got into their standalone."

"Not even close. Jake said we couldn't risk it, wasn't a priority."

Even a grudging acceptance as part of the team seemed to settle something in Callie's mind and clarify her resolve.

"How did you find out about the other women?" Nate asked.

"Jake said he'd heard rumors of another Think Tank. Once I get into the standalone, I'll know more. Nate—"

"Hon, you don't know what's involved in day-to-day living, yet. First step includes healing and research." Boisterous vocal agreement declared the team on board and wanting to help. "If the guys start drilling you too much or asking too many questions, you have to be comfortable saying anything without concern of reprisal. For instance, if there's something you're not ready to discuss, you can say so and know we'll back off."

Her gaze slid to the window when he referenced the secrets she withheld. "Okay."

"This is a two-way street. There are personal things I'm not comfortable talking about either. So, instead of a white lie, I'll be honest and say, I'm not ready for that conversation yet."

With the last sentence, her expression closed off as she nibbled her bottom lip. "Understood. I get it."

Ah, hit the nail on the head.

"Give it time, Callie. Trust is earned, not given with title or circumstance."

With confirmation of her understanding, he continued, "I keep my promises, good or bad. You'll see that in time. You've already gotten a glimpse of how teams work, but adding another to a unit requires adjustment from all on board. Remember, communication is key. We'll start with the basics and move forward."

Further conversation wended through her studies at the institution. Callie reflected on her work with equations and scientific jargon far above his basic knowledge.

Science lacked the moral base of right and wrong while ambition outdistanced qualities such as ethics. Callie voiced her dislike of many projects. For all her mysterious knowledge, every visible part of her body became a canvas displaying emotions roiling inside.

Under no circumstance did he want her to complete a bomb, detectable or otherwise. Aside from the obvious, it wasn't in her emotional makeup. Together, they'd find other, more appropriate avenues of study.

"Ya know, I get a sense that besides your obvious beauty and extraordinary mind, there's something else I should know. Anything you'd like to discuss?"

Her body stiffened. With arms wrapped around the pup who'd

jumped into her lap, she held herself in check, scarcely breathing.

"Well, um, that's a conversation I'd like to hold off on. Is that all right?" Lip nibbling gave her that adorable let-me-hug-you look.

"That's a perfect answer. I'm proud of you." Nate smiled.

"But I need to earn your trust to be part of the team. It's a catch twenty-two."

"It may seem like that at the moment. Give it time." It was difficult not to smile when she scrunched her nose up.

"Can we talk about military strategies? I want to learn as much about the team as you're willing to share."

As the midday sun projected its brightest streaks across the hardwood floor, Callie loosened up, smiling when relating particular conversations with Jake and several others at the institution.

To keep her hands busy as well, they drug out boxes of Christmas decorations and the artificial tree. Her exclamations over each ornament drew detailed explanations from Nate including family anecdotes of the four brothers. It likened to sharing of spirits when she gravitated away from shiny balls and toward handmade decorations featuring animals to complete the woodland theme.

Frequent trips to the backyard with the pup demonstrated development of her innate nurturing side. Gentle and caring, she'd make a good mother someday. When she stood in the yard and studied the mountainous landscape, Nate held his breath at the sheer wonder in her manner.

Never had he spent so much time in casual conversation with anyone other than his siblings. "The breadth and depth of your understanding of normal life surprises me, even if you lack experience."

"At the institution, I spoke with various people about different things—yet my knowledge base is spotty. There was so much Jake and Sebastian wanted to show me." Again, her mind directed their conversation on a tangent, grief followed by frivolous yearnings, the latter he intended to explore.

Back in the kitchen, Nerd stooped to pet Faith. "Time to eat."

"I'll help. Tell me what to do. Jake used to sneak me some of his goodies and promised to teach me how to cook. Can we bake some cookies?"

"Why not? You can pull a recipe off the net, and we'll give it a try. All you lack is experience." Nerd pointed to his laptop on the table. "Help yourself."

She'd avoided in-depth discussions concerning Jake. Thinking back, he knew his friend hadn't gotten the opportunity to discuss his thoughts of marriage. Callie's descriptions of Jake entailed a type of admiration and fondness, not love. The combination of her responses made it obvious she'd never participated in a physical relationship.

Late afternoon shadows capered along the opposite wall when she appeared to need a break. He'd moved them to the den to allow the others room to spread out in the great room.

She'd slept off remnants of the drugs on the couch, curled into a ball with Faith burrowed against her side.

"Knock, knock." Light thumps on the doorjamb preceded Nerd stepping inside as he continued in a whisper, "She asleep?"

"Yeah, totally worn out."

"Marc's on the line. You want me to stay with her for a sec?"

With a negative shake, Nate accepted the phone. He'd promised to watch over her. Keeping his promise would help earn her trust.

Callie grumbled in her sleep.

He smiled. "Marc. What's up?"

"The colonel's getting antsy, looking for you. Said he'd settle for me under the circumstances. I didn't tell him squat since I'm not sure who's on which side."

"Thanks. Did he give any specifics to work with, like, who rattled his cage?"

"Bare bones. I told him I'd look for you only if I knew why." Marc's snort declared he'd scored little information. *"Apparently, the asshat administrator, Ray, is searching for Jake and his old team. And before you ask, no—they can't trace this call. I don't know how the institution knew to contact Kenson. Looks like Ray has solid military connections."*

Figures it would come to this, Nate figured. "Did he give any indication Ray knows my identity?"

"Word has it, no one has nailed you, or that you're associated with the package. If Sebastian is our culprit, he's keeping information tight. The colonel certainly isn't gonna kiss and tell. Ray's men are beating all the bushes, though. They want her real freakin' bad."

"Maybe someone should talk to Ray about illegal confinement and how it's frowned upon." Nate adjusted his position to lean up.

"Be glad to relay that message."

"No. I don't want to give Kenson any more reason concerning national security to pressure you. He may not be certain I've got her if he's not aware of the decimation of my house."

"Nate, does he know about your cabin?"

"Nope. Just you guys. Let's keep it that way."

"Will do. Need anything else up there?"

"Information. Anything about Sebastian raise red flags? He's the connection between my identity and Jake, formed at the club. Think he's playing both sides of the coin?" Beside him, Nerd shifted his weight one foot to the other. None of the team liked life on the wrong side of details.

"Dunno. On paper, he looks square on. I'll keep digging."

"Jake said at least one other who helped her escape went missing. Maybe that's where we find the link. Her exit involved four employees. Press Sebastian and find the fourth." Nate winced when Callie repositioned herself and mumbled in her sleep.

"I'll get Julien and Conner on it."

"Good, but leave the colonel in the dark. Plausible deniability."

"You got a long-range plan, dude?"

Marc usually wasn't the worrywart. Something else was on his mind.

"Yeah, deal with the remaining asswipes responsible for grabbing her last night, then attach to one of the colonel's groups."

"Any ideas about last night?"

"No. No definite leads."

"What about short term?"

"Got a plan for that, too. Listen, how about a daily check-in? Let me know what you find. And don't let Conner push his military contacts too hard."

"You got it. Later, bro." The line disconnected.

"Hmm, Nate?"

"Hey, sleepyhead. Good nap?" Before the first stirrings of recent memories clouded Callie's eyes, trust and serenity held sway. He prayed for their swift return.

With a slight shift of her body, her brow furrowed and lips pursed.

"Yes. I can't believe I fell asleep. I never nap during the day."

"You didn't sleep well last night. How are you feeling?"

"It doesn't hurt as much. How long was I out?"

"Just a short while. Hungry?"

"Not much. What's the plan?"

The passage of time would be her friend in the healing process, but her unique mind would need stimulation. He'd never met anyone as intelligent. In counterpoint, her spotty emotional quotient provided an opportunity to explore the depths of her personality and still keep her mind occupied. Thirst for knowledge ran deep and included the need to experience life.

"I thought this afternoon we'd talk about the next few weeks' schedule. I know you want justice."

"I want vengeance for myself, Franklin, and Jake. I realize we can't go to Jake's funeral."

"No, we can't, but at least there will be one. It'll be videotaped. I'm sorry, but it's the best we can do to give you closure."

"Closure will come with vengeance."

"Did you love him? Jake?"

"Love? I don't understand what that is, but I would've given my life for him."

"I'm sorry for all you've been through. I know you want to be proactive but for now, heal and adjust. You need balance. Tell me, do you know Morse code?"

"Yes, Jake taught me."

"Good, we're gonna practice that and hand signals."

"Okay. Nate? Mind if I ask you a question?"

"You can ask me anything."

"All right. Tell me about your family. I've never had one. I want to know everything, the good and the bad."

"Sure. Well, of my three brothers, Marc, Conner, and Julien, Julien's the youngest and the biggest practical joker you'll find. Careful when you meet him."

"Good to know. I used to have a bit of a streak there myself. It's one of the first *worldly things* I learned from Jake."

"We were each in similar military units. As we were discharged, we started a private investigations firm and opened Ambrosia. Between the two businesses, we've done well enough to each have a cabin in the mountains."

"Where'd you learn about construction?"

"Conner got a job as soon as he was old enough to wield a hammer. He pulled each of us into it, partly to keep an eye on us, in part to earn money and stay out of trouble."

"What about Marc and Conner?"

"Hmm, Conner is the oldest and most serious. Marc has good self-discipline but also has a touch of Julien in him. He trains dogs on the side, considered one of the best in the area."

"Will he help me with Faith?"

"Absolutely. Until she's ready for advanced work, I can help you with the basics."

Chapter Nineteen

Growing up at the institution, Callie hadn't realized how far life outdistanced her until meeting Jake. The mere concept of family and friends proved a powerful motivator to become a homogenous unit with the team.

"When will your brothers visit?"

"We'll get together as soon as this threat is neutralized."

"Have our guys or your brothers found anything useful?"

"Not yet. They're working on it. No one's gonna find you here, Callie. We deeded our properties to offshore corporations and alternate identities. My brothers and I each set up a safe house when we left the military and started the PI firm."

"I could help with research."

"And you will, but not until you've got your feet beneath you. You've been through a lot. We'll set you up with a laptop soon."

Callie looked at her feet, then the couch where she sat, then at Nate.

"Sorry, metaphor. As far as research, we'll get there."

"I can't stay here forever."

"No one's gonna force your hand. Once we're squared away, we have several options. One is for us to leave the country."

His inflection on the word *us* offered as much comfort as sitting next to him. Close proximity lent strength.

"I'd like to stay in the States. There's so much opportunity on so many levels..."

"Fine. I have a friend, an ex-boss I'm sure would help. You can pursue whatever field interests you, and we can become a shadow arm of his unit. Only a few trusted people will know of your existence. That would be our safest option."

"Would they direct my studies?" She hoped he hadn't noticed her stiffen. Aligning with any part of the military held no appeal and offered no confidence in security.

"No. You'd have complete autonomy, unless you want to design bombs, or any form of WMD."

"Never. No weapons of any kind, mass destruction or otherwise. How can we attach to the military without falling into the same trap?"

"I have a history with Colonel Kenson. I know how he thinks and operates."

"Jake explained how teams were family, of sorts. That was the first discussion that made me question my circumstances. He talked about family units."

"You'll be a good mom someday."

The words spilling out of his mouth so casually, punched her in the gut. That scenario had never occurred to her, nor did she have a fitting reply. She tabled that direction of thinking for a later time.

For the unit to realize their full potential, she'd have to divulge facts never brought to light. They already knew she was different. In Ambrosia, Nate setting aside the freak status offered a new avenue to explore. Virus was a nerd, and well liked.

Her preternatural talent, emerging weeks prior, remained unwieldy and unpredictable. She needed time, but did she have it?

One thing she'd lacked, and Jake couldn't provide at the institution, was an internet connection. If the team accepted her abilities and her place among them, she could help protect them, and they could help her fine-tune her other talent. *Or curse.*

"Nate, I don't feel things the same way normal people do. Jake explained that much to me. I don't even come to decisions the same way, apparently. So, I guess my responses don't seem normal either."

"Everyone deals with grief and new situations in their own way. There is no right or wrong path."

In her mind's eye, she pictured them working as a unit, integrating her abilities.

"Hey, guys, dinner's on in fifteen." Spirit strolled in, the small grin tugging one corner of his mouth negating the gruffness in his monotone voice.

"Yeah, I've been listening to Callie's stomach since the smell of roast beef started drifting in."

Conversations on various aspects of the men's training, along with practicing hand signals, filled the following week. Each day, she nearly burst with the desire to show them what shes could do, how she could help. The possibility of their shock overcoming the ability to cope kept her mouth shut.

Nate's demands were simple. Heal and relax. It was a new world where she dictated her own activities, worked with Faith, searched the internet for proof of other prodigies, and followed any leads, however vague.

Evenings provided time to gather in the den and watch TV, play cards, or engage in simple conversation, each with fond memories of family and past escapades.

For reasons she didn't want to examine, she lay on the edge of a great chasm, a threshold of endless possibilities. The time had come to trust or "cut bait" as Jake would've declared.

Even the snowy vista outside couldn't relieve her stress.

"The air's water vapor is freezing. It's like a living snow globe. How deep is it supposed to get?"

"Don't like playing in the snow?" Virus studied her from across the room. "You won't melt."

"Play? How do you play in frozen water crystals?"

"Oh, darlin'. You haven't watched *Frosty the Snowman?"* Nerd tossed a pillow at Virus. "Don't mind him. He's all hat, no cattle."

"What? What does snow have to do with cows?"

"Means he's all talk, no filter, and no brains." Nerd held a warning finger up to shush the team. "All right, tonight we're watching a cartoon. Tomorrow, we play in the snow. I'm sure we have extra gear that'll adjust to fit you, Callie."

"You want to go out in that? And... *play*?" Last week's abdominal discomfort had downgraded to a strange tingling sensation when her shirt rubbed her abdomen. Physically speaking, she was ready.

"Yep. We're gonna have a snowball fight." Whisper's smile belied his words.

"We're going to fight? Start training?"

"We're going to *play*. We'll start training when you trust us." Nate's pointed look spoke volumes.

Am I ready?

From her perch on the sofa, the scene outside should've taken a more ominous aspect. Exposed tree branches bared their souls in preparation for spring, seeking the meager light and warmth which the sky's gray veil denied.

A certain yearning for change revealed in the reaching branches spoke to her on an elemental level. Perhaps now *was* the time to disclose her deepest secrets. It was a risk, in that once done, she could never turn back.

If she wanted total equality with the team, she'd have to bare her soul and pray for acceptance.

Moment by moment, she sat oddly transfixed as the heavens opened their gates to release the landscape-altering fluff. Rock, limb, and earth would become one homogenous unit under the blanket of white, declaring it a new world. An appropriate time for her own new beginning.

While small critters huddled in dens, burrows, lofts, or lairs, she remained cosseted among the group she'd come to know, safe and sound. She prayed to feel the same after her confession.

If not for Nate and Jake, she'd still be in the institution or with last week's abductors. Nate offered a new life. The strings he attached, revelation of her genetic oddity, seemed reasonable.

That realization brought a sense of peace permeating every limb and ligament. It felt—right, to explain the more peculiar aspects of her nonconformity.

"Nate, can we talk, later on? Just you and me."

His smile held warmth, curiosity, but most of all, acceptance.

"Sure."

"This thing, reading binary code—" Nerd screwed up his face as if not knowing how to continue.

"Which I, for one, will never get tired of watching." Virus smiled, eager as a schoolboy preparing to open a present.

"The government finding out about it wouldn't be a good thing," Nerd admonished.

"Exactly. We'll make sure they don't. I think the best place to hide is in plain sight. Show them what Ray had you working on, and they won't look elsewhere," Whisper supplied with a shrug, but underneath, he appeared as eager as the rest of the team.

"That is *so* cool!" Virus's prior reserved tone had changed with one revelation. "I wanna see it again."

Before anyone could object, he'd retrieved his laptop and booted it up, nudging Blade aside to make room on the couch.

"Holy hell." Virus's heel bounced on the hardwood as he swiveled his screen to face her. “Go to my bank and log in.” He repeated the bank’s name.

“I’ve not dealt much with the internet so far. It might take me a little bit.” Callie lifted the computer to her lap and started typing.

Minutes later, she swiveled the screen back to reveal the digital ledger. “You’re very methodical, Virus.”

“Damn. This is fantastic.” Virus accepted the laptop back with a wide grin. “C’mon, guys. Let’s sit at the table where we can all see.”

“We’ll be out in a minute.” Nate shook his head as the rest of the team stood.

Each man grinned their acceptance as they filed out.

Once alone, Callie met Nate’s gaze. “That’s not all I can do. It’s not even the best thing.”

“You’re telekinetic.”

“What? How’d you know?”

“All the circumstances since our meeting. Once I eliminated all the possible scenarios, it was the one remaining explanation, however improbable it sounded. You use a larger portion of your brain. Stands to reason that it might be feasible.”

“Well, I d-don’t control it very w-well.” How was she supposed to concentrate when he stayed one step ahead?

“You’ve been wondering if things would’ve turned out different had you’d told Jake. You did pretty well at the club when you sideswiped me. In the car, that was you again, wasn’t it? The van pursuing us?”

“Yes. That was me. The club was more of an *instinctual* thing, except for the ink pen leaking.” A violent shudder rippled across her shoulders in thinking about the van.

“Which is probably why you had better control in my office. In the SUV, you were scared, more emotional. And now you feel guilty.”

“Yes.” It was difficult to concentrate when she didn’t know what he was thinking. His stoic expression gave away nothing.

“Do you have any doubt the end result would be different if you hadn’t intervened?”

“I hadn’t considered that.”

“Don’t think for a second I’d send your kidnappers into the justice system. This group’s too organized to take chances. *If* they survive, they’ll go into Black Site seclusion.”

"I know in the military, you've had to..."

"Yes. Understand this is still a war, of sorts. We need to be prepared. We'll talk to the rest of the team in the morning over breakfast. You should take the night to consider it, make certain it's what you want. As a *team,* we can work out how to help you fine-tune your talent with practice drills."

"You think they'll accept me?

"Oh, Callie. You are so wrong to doubt them. They've already accepted you. When you show them the rest, they'll go ballistic wanting demonstrations. The late hour is why I think you should wait till morning."

"Ah, let me guess—they'll test me with snowballs?"

He just grinned. "*Hmm,* you must be telepathic, too."

"No, just beginning to understand team dynamics."

"Tell me, have you ever practiced Pilates?"

"No, though I've always had a good exercise regime." As he spoke, his gaze assessed her frame.

"Yes, I could tell that in Ambrosia. You're well-toned. We'll build up your core strength, balance, and flexibility. It will help with martial arts training."

That sobered her in an instant. She'd never practiced self-defense except for the few moves Jake had demonstrated. She'd never seen herself in that light while at the institution. "Martial arts? I thought we'd be working with my telekinesis."

As if sensing her bafflement, he lightly touched her arm to enforce the point.

"More of that initially, so we can learn your capabilities and limits, but if you rely too much on any one aspect of training, it'll be your downfall. You'll practice not just with telekinesis, but train your body and mind in other ways, too."

"The rest of them will think I'm a freak."

"No, they're gonna love it. However, it will challenge them to come up with unique drills. Divulging your talent is a monumental step. Make sure it's what you want."

"'Kay." She'd made her decision based on logic, but also on instinct. No way in hell would she back down now.

Chapter Twenty

"Morning." Nate's amusement held an undercurrent of anxiety as he knocked on her door, smiling at Faith's yipping. "Looks like having no schedule suits you."

"Coffee smells wonderful. In a little over a week, you guys have me addicted to the stuff." Her yawn paralleled a silent scream for a caffeine infusion despite having showered and dressed. Sitting on the bed, she'd played with Faith for the last half-hour until the pup settled on the blanket beside her.

Leaning against the doorjamb, he gave the impression of relaxed contemplation, strength, and confidence, but his gaze held a coiled tension.

He's wondering if I've changed my mind about revealing my secret.

"Today's a big step for me." Tossing the blanket aside, she scooped Faith up and placed her in Nate's waiting arms.

"You mean by coming out of the closet?"

"Why would I stay in a closet? I'm not going to hide."

Par for the course when their conversation went over her head, he smiled before explaining, "Exposing your talent, I mean. Nervous?"

Uncertainty made her hesitate. "Nate, what if the team believes I'm too bizarre after thinking it over?"

"Seriously? It's taken dire threats to keep them from waking you and pestering you every minute of the day for more computer demonstrations.

"Since they know there's more in store for them today, they're literally vibrating with excitement." Nate adjusted his hold when the pup squirmed. "They're gonna want continued demonstrations with your abilities, and I don't want you strained by it. Remember, it's your choice to fill them in and become a full part of the unit or stay on the fringes. No hard feelings, no judgment either way."

"I understand. I'm just excited—and nervous."

"You should ask them for help in protecting the other prodigies once we locate them. I've known these guys for a long time. They'll jump at the chance."

"You don't think it's too much, too soon?"

"Not hardly. Gives them something else to think about besides bugging you."

"I'm ready to help with the research. Wasn't sure I'd ever look forward to touching a computer again. Jake was the first person to give me unlimited access."

"You're fine, no pressure. I hope you understand why we've been holding you back, well, until last night. You've endured an awful lot of adjustment."

"It's not too much. I'm good with assimilation."

Nate tilted his head in understanding. "So we've learned. We'll be waiting for you in the kitchen." Offering an encouraging smile, he rubbed Faith's head in turning, the soft footfalls of his exit a remnant of his training.

Using a relay system to maintain their cover, Nate had acquired additional clothing and necessities for her through his brothers. It hadn't come as a surprise when the BDUs fit and were more comfortable than anything previously worn.

The lure of food and coffee urged her through her morning routine and down the steps. At the edge of the kitchen, she paused as each man at the table scrutinized her like a new microbe.

He's told them already?

"Have a seat." As he spoke, Nate held a chair for her.

She accepted without a quip.

"Here, eat. I think we'll all need our strength today." His smile, warm and knowing, lent encouragement.

The bacon smelled great but not as good as the coffee Spirit set before her. Each man around the table smiled, their bodies tense, their expressions expectant.

No one spoke.

"Anything new with the background checks?" Anxiety filled her chest. She didn't know how to begin.

Nate failed to cover the chuckle as he rubbed his chin. His hooded gaze made her heart beat a trip-hammer pulse. Every nerve ending hummed with excitement.

"Only thing of interest concerns Ray, the institution's administrator. The bastard has a pile of debt he'll never pay off. Guess he's counting on winning the mega lottery." Nerd shook off his frustration as he took a sip of coffee. "Of course, there are a couple sites I couldn't hack..."

"I'll check them after we eat. Do you think Ray was planning to sell *me* or the results of my work?"

"Don't wanna jump to conclusions." Nerd chuckled as he sat back in his chair. The air of nonchalance in his posture didn't match his intense, narrow-eyed gaze. "What's the news, sis? Must be important to have Nate looking so constipated and down here before you. He's already warned us not to pester you."

All gazes fixed on her presence, waiting, barely breathing.

Virus and Whisper each leaned forward, the front legs of their chairs thudding on the tile floor. Blade balanced a knife on his forefinger, the easy sway of his hand kept the weapon in constant motion, yet its equilibrium never wavered. Spirit's half-smile seemed to hide some mysterious knowledge native to his heritage.

"I figured it's time for you all to know a bit more about me."

"Knowledge is power, except in Nerd's case. Flushing a toilet is—"

Nate's brusque throat clearing brought them all to silence. "Guys, this is going to tax all of your minds... in many ways. She's now a part of our team and in need of *specialized* training."

"Her mind is unique." Spirit's wide grin and throaty laughter preceded his napkin's slam-dunk in the corner trashcan. "And now she's emerging from her cocoon."

"What? She's not a lesbian. You're nuts. Don't know what goes in that pipe you smoke, Spirit, but maybe it's time for a downgrade." Nerd's comment earned him a rear head slap from Whisper.

"Darlin', I can handle anything but aliens. You just tell Uncle Virus what's going on in that pretty little head of yours. We'll figure out how to deal with it."

"If Virus is your uncle, then one of your parents shared an unnatural relationship with a donkey."

The knife balancing on Blade's finger suddenly flew up and imbedded into the drywall ceiling. The wobble of its handle attested to the force of impact. His hand hadn't moved.

The shock registering around the table—priceless.

Each open-mouthed quick inhalation accompanied their heads jerking back to look at the ceiling, then to Blade, who stared at his hand, then at Callie.

"Holy shit! How'd you do that?" Blade shoved his chair back to stand then leapt on the seat to recover his knife.

"With her dick, you dumbass." Whisper clapped Virus on the back before adding. "She did it with that incredible mind."

Spirit slammed his hand on the table. "Ah-ha. I wondered if this is what you withheld." Spirit unfolded his long and lean body to close the distance between them.

"You knew? How could you've guessed? I've never told anyone before last night."

"At the club when you crashed into Nate, both of you should've landed in a heap, yet neither did. Then when we had the *quake,* it was localized... to your room." Now standing before her, Spirit held out his hand, the warmth of his shake chasing away any doubt of his acceptance.

"I wanted to ask you all for your help, well, more help."

"Sure. What do you need?" Blade set his knife on the table to offer his full attention.

"I believe there are other women, like me, kinda."

"What do you mean, kinda, youngin'?" Whisper drummed his fingers on the table in rhythmic tapping.

"Others who are unique and have various talents. I'm not sure where they're being held. I do think either Ray has the information, or it's in the Think Tank's mainframe. There could be another girl there now. I'm not sure." The thought of returning to the institution to retrieve the data brought back images of Franklin's body sliding down the chain-link fence.

"Damn those bastards. I'm in," Spirit affirmed.

"Our team may grow even bigger if other prodigies decide to join us," Whisper suggested to each man's delight.

Each gaze bounced between the knife now resting on the table to the ceiling where the small slit of a hole remained.

"Do it again, Callie." Virus smiled while the rest of them nodded their excitement.

Despite the circumstances, she didn't feel like a monster. Each man present held their own special talent, despite being limited to one of the five senses. They were unique in their own right.

Again the knife flew up, but didn't strike blade first. It bounced off the ceiling and clattered back to the table, each man shifting back in their seats then roaring with laughter.

"Damn. Can you like, move people and other heavy objects? Or just little things, like turn the hot water faucet to the shower off?" The excitement in Virus' voice was a little unsettling.

"Do you have to see what it is you're affecting?" The wheels in Blade's head were spinning like a top, evidenced by the glazed look in his eyes.

More questions followed so fast Callie couldn't keep them straight, until Nate's wolf-whistle silenced them.

"I'm just learning to get a handle on it, so you can see I'm not very accurate. I don't have to be close, but I do have to see it, if only once."

"Told you it wouldn't be so bad." Nate's throaty whisper near her ear sent a shudder from shoulder to shoulder. The unsettling sensations evoked with his close proximity grew stronger each day.

"Well... I had a difficult time believing it could happen like this. No one's ever really accepted me for what I am—besides Jake. Even he didn't know about this."

Slowly, deliberately, Nate reached over to brush the tear from her cheek. "I know he meant a lot to you, sweetheart. Rest assured, not only would he have accepted you, but he suspected you held much more talent than you'd shown."

"Before you guys, he was the only person I'd ever considered a friend."

"Now you're rich. You have six." The creak of the chair as Spirit took his seat punctuated his statement. "Some people go a lifetime and not share what we have. It's more than trust. It's the essence of family, distilled from years of relying on each other as a unit. Even though Nate hasn't been around for a while, he's still as much a part of us as ever."

"I don't know about you guys, but I'm ready to go plot and play in the snow. How about a snowball fight?" The ready smiles elicited by Whisper's suggestion resulted in them all stirring. "When Nate told us we'd have to devise ways of integrating an untrained woman, I thought he was nuts. This is a whole new ball game."

"I want Callie on my team. I figured out her secret before she spilled." Spirit's smile hinted of devious and perhaps painful tricks. "I can think of several ways to exercise and fine-tune her talents, though it might prove a little awkward for you guys."

"All right. Callie, Spirit, and me against Whisper, Nerd, Virus, and Blade. You all get an extra man to even things out."

"Yeah, right. That makes things even, for sure." Blade gazed at the ceiling, then back at Callie.

The prior late-night discussion concerning her talent and future training brought to light Nate's substantial knowledge of tactics and strategies. To learn each of these men shared or experienced such varied situations offered a wealth of information to absorb.

Something in the undercurrent of their tones and expressions told her they played rough, each accepting it as not just their due, but also a type of release from the stress of their work.

The significance and implications of their experience opened her eyes as Blade frowned at the knife balancing on his knuckles once again. His grin hinted at scenarios she probably wouldn't like.

"All right, but we get a fifteen-minute head start." Nerd pushed to his feet. "Since Callie's new to our games, we need to set ground rules until she understands how we play."

"Wh-what are you planning?" It sounded like trouble approached fast from men accustomed to dirty tactics.

"With just us, it would be anything goes." A wisdom beyond his years emanated from Spirit's calm façade. "With you, well, we'll just see how it plays out. I'm thinking you'll give as well as you get."

"No head shots and no water, guys, or I'll encourage her to develop her own games while you sleep." Nate's ultimatum delivered as a casual remark received mixed reviews.

Sharp, icy wind failed to penetrate layers of tightly woven nylon, loose-fitting fleece, and insulated long johns, but Callie's wind-kissed cheeks would be red before the morning was over. The Mad Bomber hat Nerd pulled on her head completed the appearance of a mountain dweller.

After giving Blade, Whisper, Virus, and Nerd a head start, Spirit and Nate ushered her through an open window on the side of the house.

"Shouldn't we talk about this first, Nate? Like, have a strategy or something?"

"Can't make a plan until we know what we're working with. This is just play time, so have fun."

"Fun? They're going to throw frozen balls of ice at me."

"Yeah, but look." Spirit scooped a handful of fluff and threw it up in the air. "It's powder."

Nate's grunt cut off her thoughts as a snowball exploded into a white cloud of diamond crystals shrouding her in cold, wet fluff.

"Aren't they going to give us a minute?"

"All's fair in love and war, Callie." Virus's triumphant chuckle echoed in the quiet air, spoken as he took refuge behind the corner of the house.

"But—but this isn't fair."

Nate used his body to protect her from the next flurry of powdery missiles. "Head for the woods. It'll give us temporary cover."

As Nate spoke, Spirit pelted Virus with a volley using enough force to make her doubt their sanity. Gentle didn't seem to be in any of their vocabularies when dealing with each other, yet she might as well have been a precious vase with the way they had treated her so far. Would they bombard her as hard in days to come?

The forest setting was idyllic for relaxing with thick pine branches covered in white. The scene created equaled the perfect composite for a postcard—or hiding an opposing team member waiting to rain snow and ice down on their heads.

Shielded on either side by Nate and Spirit's bulk, her body and mind recoiled in the calf-high snow, waiting for confirmation of her suspicions. From the other corner of the house, Whisper stepped clear, holding two giant snowballs.

The first nailed Spirit. His last-minute spin to protect her created another shower of white sprinkles dusting her hat and face.

Nate wrapped one arm around her shoulders. "Come on, Callie. The woods."

"Wait. I have an idea." In her mind's eye, a wall of snow formed and moved briskly toward Whisper.

Beginning at her feet, the white wave of wind grew into a small swell of snow. As the wave grew in height, the frozen upsurge swelled into a giant breaker six feet tall and spanning twice the width.

"Holy shit. That's definitely not playing fair." Whisper's voice faltered with the indecision in his expression.

Just before the snow wall obscured Callie's view, Whisper eyed the safety of the corner of the house, lacking time to duck and cover.

Maybe she'd get the hang of her talent sooner rather than later. The last thing she heard before impact was Whisper's growl. The white barrier of powder collapsed over him, sending a hail of flakes outward like an ocean wave smashing into a jagged outcropping of rocks.

As the roar of blood rushed through her ears, Whisper's laughter twined with dire threats of retaliation.

Her gaze flitted over to Virus, who held one snowball in his hand poised as if frozen by Medusa's wintertime cousin. His shocked-shitless expression begged for a camera. As his gaze met hers, he reared back to let the snowball fly.

This time she pictured snow parting underneath Virus' feet. Her mind put thought to action.

Howling as he landed on his ass, Virus' arms flew wide, the snowball crashing against the dryer vent on the cabin.

The choked yipe as he tried to regain his stance brought chuckles from her protectors. With a glance at first Virus then Whisper, Nate warned, "Okay, guys, you two are done. Any further interaction and she'll put you in the treetops."

Can I do that?

To feel Nate's arm tighten around her shoulder in a hug renewed her courage.

"Way to go, hon. How do you feel?"

As if nothing said would be taken seriously, he brushed the hair from her face and cupped her chin. "No blood. Good. Any headache?"

"Nope. I'm having a ball."

"All right. Let's head for the woods. We still have to find Nerd and Blade. They won't be as easy. Nerd's gonna have some kind of trap set for us."

Callie hesitated, thinking about Nate's previous outlined strategies. "They'll have the advantage of cover, but I have an idea how to draw them out or trick them into giving up their position." Having watched a cartoon about an animated snowman, she chuckled at the idea taking shape. "They have the advantage of ambush if we go straight for the woods without cover."

Spirit's smile and narrowed gaze preceded his chuckle. "What're you thinking?"

"Watch this." Within the next minute, three balls of snow formed in front of them. The largest one rolled to a stop before her. The next largest flew up to land with a solid thud on the first. A slight dusting of snow showered the ground surrounding the base.

Nate's laughter echoed in the silent morning as the third, smaller ball of snow landed on top of the previous two. "*Ahh*, I see you enjoy classic television."

"Yep. With a little modification. How'd I do?"

"Needs arms and a mouth." Spirit's chuckle joined her own as he reached over to give her a light hug.

Nate growled.

"Okay, now for the rest." Two trunk-shaped arms formed from the middle ball of snow. On the ends, short chunky appendages flailed in the morning light. On the head, a horizontal, elliptical shape opened and closed. Its haunting theatrics sent a chill slithering across her shoulders.

"Perfect, sweetheart. Can you reshape the bottom sphere into legs?" Without asking this time, Nate turned her face into the morning sun, checking her ears and nose. "Unlike your stint in the car, no blood. Good. Any pain?"

"No." The concentration needed to accomplish the modification was slight.

Several sidesteps gave her creation space to maneuver in disjointed fashion. The snowman's animation required more focus, its uncoordinated efforts resembling a clumsy baby elephant on two white tree trunks.

A little practice moved it forward with a precarious balance then shuffled on stilted legs like a white golem.

"What the hell, Callie?" Nerd's muffled voice ahead held a new strain—panic. "Please don't tell me that thing can climb."

"Judging by sound and prior experience, he's probably high in a tree in that direction." Nate pointed toward their right. "Let's track him down and see what we can do."

"I didn't think training would be so much fun."

Evening time at the dinner table yielded more drills and exercises along with a sense of pride, accomplishment, and encouragement. Gone was the cold and methodical moment-to-moment mechanical existence of the institution, exchanged for life filled with warmth, animation, and optimism to experience the world on her own terms.

"I'd like a little salt on my beef please, Callie." Virus's smile couldn't hide the childlike wonder in his expression each time her talent came into play.

"Keep harassing her and you'll end up with the spooky package while asleep tonight," Nate warned.

"Spooky package? Really? Make sure you turn off his superhero nightlight first." Nerd's forkful of potatoes paused in midair as he considered his next words. "On second thought, better not, he'd be lost in the dark."

"How did you find your way out of the birth canal?" Virus's retort resulted in verbal endorsements around the table. "You'd make a better candidate for midnight pranks."

The dozen peas Nerd flung in Virus' direction froze in midair. One by one, each quivered in place, not gaining or losing altitude.

"Callie, don't do it." The warning in Nerd's voice sounded hollow. Shaking shoulders negated the steely threat.

"But you know I don't have good control with fine motor skills."

All but one of the buttery batch of rounded missiles landed in Nerd's iced tea with laughter erupting around the table. The last pea floated down gracefully, the top of a baked potato the intended perch.

A moment's distraction evoked a savage shudder, both between her shoulder blades and in the trajectory of the falling vegetable. Nate chuckled in rubbing her back.

The last pea landed with a splat in the beef gravy.

"Ha! Now I know what to do when confronted with her talent." The slight smudge of gravy on Nerd's shirt didn't seem to bother him.

"Do and die, buddy." Nate's smooth baritone generated more chuckles. They all sobered with his arched brow.

Nate's protectiveness filled her being with the comfort of belonging.

The following day and for days thereafter, additional layers of snow thickened the white mantle covering their previous tracks. Callie had never dreamed of having so much fun.

They each taught her their version of Christmas carols, often ending with pillows thrown at Blade for singing off-key.

Though the team shifted other members each day, Nate always remained by her side. By the end of the following week, teams consisted of Nate and herself against the others. She rose to each challenge as she learned tactics and strategies with explanations of what to do under various circumstances.

"Okay, Callie, I think that's enough for today." Again, Nate took her chin between thumb and forefinger, turning her head side to side as he examined her face and ears. Only once had there been a spot of blood from her nose after trying to lift Spirit up into a tree.

"I've never thought of snow as a working medium, nor tree limbs, or pine cones. Can we do it again tomorrow?"

"Sure, but you know these guys are going to step up their game now that they have a handle on your ability. Remember, use whatever's handy."

"So, we're going to start training?"

"Hon, we've been training for the last two weeks. We've designed each exercise to help fine-tune your control, and your progression in self-defense is admirable. Your kicks are strong with quick recovery, your strikes accurate with good strength and follow through."

"What about guns and knives."

"You'll learn to shoot eventually, as a basic skill, but you'll never be on a front line."

"*Hmm*, always protect your asset?"

The tightness around his eyes contradicted the smile slipping into place. She'd inadvertently hit a nerve and raised the question of his viewpoint. He had explained how and why he wanted her to be able to defend herself, but never intended it to become reality.

"Exactly. Let's go inside and warm up."

Despite learning strategies inside and layers of clothes outside, Callie's learning always ended in a cloud of snowflakes or a light tap with a padded glove. Melted remains of snowballs seeped through her gloves to leave her cold and wet. Achieving the upper hand took strategy and determination learned through experience.

Chapter Twenty-One

"All right. Who turned my computer keyboard into a damn furry seed starter? And where's my encrypted Bluetooth?" Menace radiating from Virus' voice filled the kitchen in the early morning.

Nate rubbed his eyes to chase the clinging remnants of sleep as he discerned the problem. If not for Callie's revelation and unique training sessions, the computer tech would've gone stir-crazy.

A few quiet snaps saw the keyboard lying in two pieces. Narrow strips of paper towels covered in green fuzz lined the rows between the keys. Bits and pieces of broken seedlings littered the kitchen table.

"Looks like Nerd was bored last night. Good thing you have a spare. Who made the coffee?" No need to volunteer as a guinea pig when Nerd's prank streak ran manic in the wee hours.

Another glance at Virus' keyboard revealed the darker depths of stir craziness. Seeds took days to sprout, making it a planned assault.

"Spirit was here earlier, probably him, but I don't know for sure."

"Probably? *Hmm*, think I'll wait. You know, memory impairment is the free prize after days of little sleep." A bottle of water would do just fine.

"Tell that to Nerd, his overactive thyroid is gonna drive us all insane."

"Where's Callie?" Blade looked up from sharpening his knife. Narrowed eyes held more than a little concern. "No headaches? She's turning into a workaholic. Any way to moderate her pace?"

"Still asleep, we talked late into the night. She's still having a hard time turning it all *off*."

"Like any newbie to a team such as ours. It'll take a while to adjust." Virus sent the furry keyboard soaring into the trashcan in the corner.

"She's getting there, but still having nightmares. At least she'll talk about them now. Understanding we control our conscious mind doesn't grant us access to the subconscious where we deal with tragedy and stress."

"She opens up to you more than us."

Nate paused in taking a swig of water. "Jealous?"

"No, I prefer women with mammary glands large enough to feed a family. Besides... wouldn't wanna be with a woman after you've put new memories in her memory foam mattress. Not to mention the fact it'd be like doing it with my sister."

"Idiot. I sleep in the spare bedroom between her and Spirit."

Nate had always been a man ruled by instinct. The combination of Callie's innocence and vulnerability called to that primal part of him designed to protect. Not that he didn't appreciate her from a holistic sense, but she hadn't yet found her place in the world, hence was in no position to figure out who she'd want by her side.

When she'd asked if his sleeping in the next room was because of her telekinesis and fear of causing damage during nightmares, he'd denied it.

Her talent had yet to destroy anything of significance, yet he wouldn't take the chance on her adopting a negative outlook on such an extraordinary ability. Keeping everything in a positive light helped them all.

"Nate, message here posted on social media, shitload of numbers. I assume it's from one of your zany brothers since I can't decipher it without the initial random word." Virus' frustration plus his own cabin fever sharpened the edge of his voice.

"Here, print it out. I'll translate. The fact we've gone to code means someone's watching my brothers. This'll take a while. Careful making calls out." Nate eyed the coffee pot with longing before snagging a second bottle of water.

The list of numbers indicated a rather long message, each line a short sentence. The last word in each line provided the code for the next sentence. A serious message overall, it likely ended with the final line: *Cow tipping tomorrow at noon. Be there.*

"Blade, can you start some breakfast for Callie while I decrypt this? I'll check on her before heading to the office."

* * * *

By the time Callie woke, Nate was dressed and sitting in the bedside chair. The team's early morning banter from downstairs confirmed all was normal.

"Sleep okay?"

She'd gotten used to his checking her ears for bloody drainage each morning then asking about nightmares, which had become fewer and less violent.

"Yep. All night without a nightmare."

"Okay. I'll meet you downstairs. Breakfast will be ready soon."

"Thanks, I'm starved."

She made it down the stairs in record time.

"*Mmm*, smells wonderful, Blade. Where's Nate?" He was usually at the table, either conferencing over the phone with his brothers or talking with the team.

"In the office. He'll join us shortly." Whisper toed a chair out for her to sit.

"Coffee first. Can I help?" It'd become an addiction for her.

"*Um*, about the coffee..."

Callie poured a cup of the strong brew then gazed at the snowy wonderland framed by mullioned windows. Bright sunshine bared a few tree branches of their icy covering, the overall effect a glistening paradise. The view offered a different perspective than what she would have considered a month ago.

"Before you sip, something you should know. I'm not sure who made that coffee." Blade held both hands up, palms out.

"If anyone's messed with this, I'll dump a load of snow on them while they're sleeping." Coffee was sacred.

"All ready, Callie. Heads up." Without further warning, Blade tossed the food-laden plastic plate over his shoulder just as she glanced back.

Scrambled eggs, bacon, and jellied toast arced over the kitchen table creating a multicolored stream before its motion froze midair. Bits of egg and small globs of jelly separated from the bulk of the food, extending the cloud of protein, carbohydrates, and fat suspended over the table.

"Ha. I'm getting better with the small stuff." Steam rising from the coffee welcomed her to start the day. Her gaze slid back to the savage beauty of the woods. "See? I don't need to observe something to hold it once I've locked on."

Now, the coffee beckons.

At the institution, she'd drank milk with meals and bottled water in between, without questioning or even knowing she had options.

The loud crash from behind reversed her direction of focus. "Hey, since when do you toss cups of liquid?"

In the last few days, they'd all delighted in finding new ways to challenge and distract her.

"Never turn your back on an enemy, Callie." The quiet reproof in Blade's voice reminded her of his earlier warnings.

"Since when are you my enemy?" Drops of milk beaded on pieces of shattered mug while the rest pooled in the grout lines. Motivation for finding their traitor renewed her enthusiasm for fine-tuning her talent.

"In training, we are all enemies. Remember that. Now, let's see how good you are at cleaning while multi-tasking." A narrowed gaze betrayed the challenge in Blade's voice.

With a heavy sigh, she set her drink aside. Since the airborne food remained in her conscious thought, she placed the previously unbroken mug of milk to her mental template and set them both on the table.

"Close your eyes. You've already seen it." The arrogance in Virus' voice made her yearn for a ball of snow—or more chia seeds and Nerd's twisted sense of humor. She'd caught him setting it up and made a few suggestions.

"Can't we ever just have a simple meal?" At least Nate wasn't present to witness her lapse in patience.

"Sure. Life is as simple as we make it. I love eggs and bacon in the morning." The kitchen chair squeaked under Blade's bulk as he sat. His food hadn't undergone a fluff cycle.

Minutes later, the echo of footfalls brought a smile to her face. Nate's easy stride halted her cup of coffee halfway to her mouth.

"Okay, boys and girls. We have a meeting to attend."

"With who?" She knew at some point she'd have to face Ray again. The thought created a fine tremor throughout her body.

"Hey, no sweat. We'll all go together. Right Nate?" Blade paused in eating.

Nate frowned, studying her like a suspect in a criminal investigation. Maybe she should stop watching crime shows.

"Blade's right. And if things get twisted, you could tie all their shoelaces together while we make a run for it," Virus added. "He's been harping on how you need practice with the small stuff."

She gulped. Confrontation and defense were the costs of freedom. How high would the tally go?

Blade snickered, and a moment later wore the rest of his scrambled eggs.

"Hey, what the hell, Callie?"

"Sorry, reflex. As you've said, all's fair..."

"Okay, I'm hungry. No hands, Callie," Nate advised.

Not accepting the risk of stabbing his mouth with fork tines, Callie envisioned the spoon scooping up eggs and delivered them accordingly.

"So, who sent the crazy message, boss?" Virus asked.

"Conner. Looks like we have a date with the brass and a degenerate who's pulling heavy-duty strings."

"Huh, who else is attending?" Spirit's sudden soft voice behind her resulted in Nate's lap full of eggs.

"Thanks, Spirit, for sneaking up behind me." A deep breath settled her enough to regroup the food, replacing it on the plate.

"Looks like the colonel is under a lot of pressure from Ray and whoever's backing him. They're making a lot of noise about a kidnapping. If we don't produce her, shit's gonna hit the fan."

"Does Ray *know* we have her, or is this an attempt to flush her out?" Spirit padded to the counter and eyed the coffee before looking around.

"Coffee's safe," Callie confirmed.

"Not sure about Ray. Seems he and Sebastian are combining forces to a point."

"What? Why?" Callie shivered with flashbacks of witnessing Franklin's demise, then running through the woods holding Jake's bloody hand. Death was never far away, and now she'd have to face the icon who'd held her prisoner.

Spirit paused in drinking his coffee. "Maybe he fancies himself a double agent? Maybe Ray has put some kind of screws to him. Dunno."

"What if he demands to take me?"

"Not gonna happen. We'll have a private meeting with Kenson first." Nate reached over to curve his palm around the back of her neck and turn her head, his narrowed gaze revealing a fraction of his intensity.

"We'll make it known to all that you're off-limits and well- protected. When this is over, we'll set up some place quiet, where you can work in peace."

"Sounds wonderful. Here in the mountains?"

"If you like." Nate arched a brow at each man in turn.

"The guys and I've talked about building cabins up here. Close enough to call for backup if needed." Quiet grunts from Virus and Blade supported Spirit's assertion.

"Nice place to setup. Colonel could pull some strings, put us on active duty, after a sort." Nerd's voice held too much cheer for someone who'd been awake most of the night.

"'Bout time you got your tail in here. We have a meeting later this morning, needs some prep. Have a seat. Not near Virus." The amusement in Nate's voice garnered a scowl from Virus.

"Hey, I've been trying to get him to throw that keyboard away for a month. He's lucky I didn't make a giant gelatin jiggler out of it."

"Is Sebastian going to be at the meeting, too? I probably wouldn't be here if it weren't for his help. I owe him a debt of gratitude. Is he deflecting Ray's focus elsewhere?"

"Hope so, sweetheart. My brothers are gonna stick a puck on his car, though."

"Puck?"

"Tracker. We need to learn a little more about Sebastian's goals and intentions, where he goes, who he contacts," Nate nodded to each of the team, their unity solidified.

Chapter Twenty-Two

"Don't be nervous, Callie. We've got this covered." Nate slipped his arm around her waist to pull her closer as his gaze flitted from the utilitarian block building to the other vehicles on the lot.

Those bastards won't get a hold of you again.

"I'm all right. It helped meeting the colonel earlier. I have a better idea of what to expect and appreciate knowing how he feels about Ray."

Patches of snow dotted the quarter-acre blacktop surface, the mound created from initial plowing rising two-thirds up the security light pole.

A gray, slushy mix of ice and loose gravel slid down the icy hill as the sun's rays reduced its mass hour by hour. Small rivulets of dirty water drained toward the open fallow fields surrounding the almost clear asphalt.

"We needed the private face-to-face to let him evaluate the situation before others start spouting accusations. And like I said, the man keeps his cards close to the vest."

"You think he was able to forge papers for me?"

"He's a man of many talents and even more contacts. I'm sure the documents will stand up to the most discerning scrutiny. I'm glad we'll have them handy before dealing with the administrator."

"At least I kept my first name, not that I'm sure if it's really mine."

"It's yours if you want it. If down the road, you'd like to change it, we'll work on that. I'm hoping we can locate your birth parents when this is over."

The slight hesitation in her step gave him pause. With a hand on her shoulder, he gently turned her to face him. "What is it? Something's dropped your stomach into your boots."

He shook his head when she glanced from her stomach to her feet.

"No. It's a figure of speech."

"*Um*, well, I'm just worried about meeting Ray. He's the type who's always prepared.

"Anything in particular?"

"No. It's just the extremes of current events, I guess."

Brushing a stray lock of hair from her face and checking her ears, he added, "Callie, I trust your instincts as well as your intellect. If it becomes more, let me know. The rest of the team is on the perimeter. We have plenty of backup."

"Okay." A tremulous smile spoke of courage overcoming fear.

"Let's go on in. I'm sure the colonel's other team is anxious to meet you."

Anyone comes too close gets decked.

The growing protective streak within concerned him as much as Ray's persistence in reacquiring Callie.

"I'm surprised we're not meeting somewhere on base."

"This is an off-site operations post, easier to secure with less traffic, both human and otherwise. Less likely to get surprised by unwanted company."

"The colonel sounded confident when he accepted me as a special consultant. Are you going to tell him about my TK?"

"No. The research you've done has secured your placement. Keep in mind that it won't preclude Kenson from asking questions. As I said earlier, be prepared for that. He's a crafty SOB."

"How does he know the extent of what I've done at the institution? And what's a SOB?"

"Callie, he can be a son of a bitch, but he has contacts everywhere, and by now he knows at least the high notes.

"Ray has kicked up such a ruckus to get you back, that alone dictates significant worth and an investigation into your work."

"Then Kenson might know what happened to the other man who helped me escape?"

"We'll find out eventually. Now that foreigners are after you, Kenson won't take chances. That's why there's another team inside. I've assured him we had the outside covered."

As he guided her around a puddle and up the walkway, tension tightened her shoulders. Pulling her to a stop and pivoting to stand before her, he felt as much as saw the fear she couldn't hide.

"Callie, they're not gonna get you again. We're ready for the bastards this time."

"Where's Sebastian?"

"With Ray. Said he'll find out what the administrator is up to."

She wrapped her arms around his waist and hugged him. He couldn't pull away when she needed the comfort and security.

"Okay, Nate. Let's do this. I'm ready."

"Good." He was proud of her facing this head on and with chin high. "Remember, regarding Ray and anyone from the institution, neither of us have met the colonel yet. Okay?"

"Got it."

"Hold up a sec, my phone's vibrating." After snagging his cell from its holder, he puzzled over the number of the incoming call.

"Afternoon, Colonel Kenson. Pleasure to meet you." Nate recognized a few pictures of uniformed officers lining the hallway where they stood.

In a few minutes, Callie would enter the meeting room and greet those Kenson wanted to assign to her protection. Considering what she'd survived to date, no wonder her fingers trembled slightly in his hand.

Several muffled voices on the other side of the closed door held a mixture of grumble and frustration. Babysitting ranked low on the totem pole of assignments.

Boy are they in for a surprise if things go south.

"Hello, Mr. Crofton. After getting almost nothing from Conner, I wondered if you were the mysterious protector. Wish I could say I've heard a lot about you, but it seems your records remain sealed even to the likes of me." Extending his hand to Callie, the colonel maintained a cool façade, the opposite of his earlier demeanor.

"Hello, young lady. It's an honor to meet you. I've been hearing quite a bit of interesting things." Kenson slipped Nate a small envelope, who tucked it in his jacket pocket.

"Hello. Thank you for meeting with us." Callie's voice lost the edge of confidence she'd displayed earlier at the cabin.

Considering the covert nature of Nate's prior experience, he'd spent little time in public military venues. "More vehicles than I expected to see out there. Big turnout for a small meet-and-greet. What's up?"

"As I understand from the administrator of the institution where she *worked*, there are many who would like to have her talents under their direction, willingly or otherwise. Hence, increased security."

An undercurrent of steel lined the colonel's sarcasm. "I've called in a team to see to her safety, at least until we have this situation sorted out."

"Ahh, so you've met Ray. As I was walking in, I received a phone call concerning him—shady character at best." At least Kenson had caught on to the situation without them having to reveal Callie's secrets.

"Yes, and he'll be here shortly, so I'd like to take this opportunity for you to meet the squad before he arrives." The colonel's tilted head and frown betrayed curiosity as to the specific nature of Nate's recent information and informant.

"I assume you've handpicked these men?" Nate asked and drew Callie close as the older man's penetrating gaze locked onto her.

The colonel's half-smile and chuckle reminded him of the old days. Choosing men for particular ops had been a strategy wherein he excelled. "Of course. I prefer to be thorough. And like most commanders, I like to have *all* the information I can."

Hmm, still not subtle. You'll not get the full scoop on her just yet.

"Shall we go in?" When the older man opened the door for them, Callie retreated a step.

"It's okay, hon. They're just like the guys we train with." With Nate's uncensored utterance, the colonel's body stiffened.

Hell.

Kenson just gathered more fodder for friendly interrogation to top his list, including, *Why train an asset?*

Callie had accused him of distracting her during drills, yet she proved the biggest diversion of his life.

* * * *

As soon as the door opened, grumbling diminished to low murmurs. When Callie stepped through, all conversation stopped.

This was a simple meeting, no show-and-tell. Still, anxiety forced her hands deep into the pockets of her jacket. Nate's hand rubbing her back helped spread the warmth of his courage.

Kenson maintained a friendly demeanor, his lieutenant echoing his posture and smile.

Each of the five men seated frowned at her before glancing back toward the door, waiting expectantly. Nate's chuckle brought her gaze to him.

Her step faltered. *Who are they looking for?*

"Back in the old days, a gentleman rose from his chair when a lady walked into the room." Kenson's berating and frown brought an instant response.

Chairs scraped the smooth concrete floor as each man scrambled to stand.

Kenson smiled at Callie when addressing Nate. "Mr. Crofton, why don't you introduce your friend?"

"That's her?"

The whispered comment brought heat to her face.

She couldn't discern whether the disbelief stemmed from her age or gender. Perhaps they were expecting a mid-fifties woman with glasses and a cane. Continued glances at the door as if expecting someone else to enter.

The sudden clearing of their superior's throat wiped the confusion from their faces.

Indicating one of the two chairs by the desk toward the front of the room, Kenson suggested, "Have a seat, Ms. McKellen. I'd like you to get to know these men, even if they have lost their manners for the moment." Shaking his head, he scowled at the team.

"Men, this is Callie McKellen," Nate began. His voice rang strong and clear in offering introductions. "Pull your chairs up in a semi-circle, boys. This is gonna be informal, at least until our unwanted visitors arrive."

"Ma'am, sorry if we seem a little unfriendly. Most of these Neanderthals aren't used to polite company." The speaker rose and nodded his head toward the others as he grabbed his chair. With an eagerness that strummed her nerves, the others followed suit.

Though dressed in jeans and casual shirts, each man reminded her of Nate's team, layers of nonchalance covering intelligent, alert minds, and well-muscled bodies.

To receive a speculative, visual examination was nothing new. This felt much different from the observations received at the institution, more *intense*.

The semi-circle arrangement put her on display, a fish-bowl effect. Nate saw her seated but remained standing at her side.

Light spilling from the outside wall's bank of windows stopped halfway across the floor with each roller shade pulled three-quarters down. Two of the overhead florescent lights flickered softly. The atmosphere was nothing like the Think Tank, but it still reminded her of where she came from. Men assigned to *protect.*

With all seated, Kenson leaned against the edge of his desk, reaching for a thick folder. “Let me take a minute to hit the high points of why we’re gathered.”

The next half hour flew by as Callie explained her previous work. When unsure of how much to say and her voice faltered, Nate intuitively stepped in to give her a break, allowing her time to choose her words with care.

Chapter Twenty-Three

Escalating volume of voices in the hall signaled the confrontation to come. Nate welcomed the colonel posting a guard, but didn't appreciate the visitor's derogatory comment regarding Callie.

Her shoulder stiffened under his palm while the grating nasal voice of Sebastian forced his jaw to clench.

No doubt, Sebastian would take time later to gloat over what he'd gleaned from Ray.

Each man in the new team bristled with the grumbled derogatory insult directed at Callie. It hadn't taken five minutes into their conference for them to see the gravity of her situation.

Following orders was a given. The extra assurance from their nonverbal support was a bonus. Fierce expressions revealed they had as much interest in ferreting out the traitor as the colonel. Two of the men present had worked with Jake and Franklin.

Possibilities existed where either Ray or someone unknown wanted to sell her to foreign agents. Background checks found nothing definitive in their investigation. Still, he'd love to end them both. Ray for holding her prisoner, Sebastian for making his skin crawl.

"Move aside, mister, my missing ward is in there, and I'll be damned if you'll stand in my way. Do you know who I am?"

The door remained closed. Apparently, Ray's arrogance didn't impress the guard.

"Until I see and clear your identification, neither of you pass." The insolent, if calm reply held the patience of one use to dealing with spoiled children.

Several minutes and more grumbled threats later, the door opened.

Callie's quick intake of breath brought both visitors' gazes to her. As if seeking his warmth, she slid her hand up to cover Nate's. Turning his wrist, he entwined their fingers and gave a light squeeze.

"Here you are, Callie. I've been searching everywhere for you. Where have you been, and who's this with you?" Ray strode to within three feet of Callie then stopped when she stood.

Her rigid stance, shoulders straight, and head held high radiated more than confidence. She was pissed off.

"Hi, Ray. You're a long way from home." The smile never reached her narrowed eyes. "Get tired of clearing stained Minnesota snow?"

From her previous account of escape, the statement referenced Franklin's bloody body hunched against a fence.

Her poke hit its mark as Ray's mouth tightened.

"That's not an appropriate response, young lady."

"First, I've not been treated like a lady before meeting my new friends. Second, I'll respond however I damn well choose. Deal with it."

Nate and Kenson's men chuckled, not bothering to hide their amusement.

"You'll get half an answer, Ray. She's with me, and she'll only reply to questions *she* deems appropriate. Begin any time." Anger over her long-term imprisonment surged through Nate's thoughts, but to bring Ray to justice meant exposing Callie to the general public. Something he wouldn't do.

Life presented workarounds to every problem if the time was taken to search.

"As a matter of fact, the night she left work, wasn't there some type of trouble at your institution?" Nate frowned, not pausing before continuing. "Hope everybody's okay. I've been meaning to look into that, but don't worry. I'll get to it."

"Callie..." The way Ray drew her name out equaled a threat they all understood,

The colonel's men each took a step closer.

The administrator's flushed face and clenched fists would've amused Nate if not for the clusterfuck of her escape. Lack of news coverage indicated the level and significance of the administrator's connections.

A small click directed Ray's attention to his shirt pocket where an ink pen leaked blue in a widening arc down the front of his crisp white shirt.

Nate smothered a grin in remembering his own pen exploding during his first meeting with Callie.

"What the hell?" Ray sopped at the sloppy mess with a handkerchief and tossed it into the wastebasket by the desk.

Puzzled frowns and confusion crept across the men's expressions, except for Nate, who coughed into his fist to disguise the shake in his shoulders.

"I've never known you to be so careless with your things, Ray." A Cheshire's grin spread across Callie's face with the covert dig.

The administrator took a step forward then stumbled, catching himself using the desk. Hands fisted at his sides when Kenson's men each took another protective step forward.

Callie hid her giggle behind the fingers covering her mouth.

Enough of this crap. "Ray? Word to the wise here. She no longer works for or with you. Matter of fact, *my* girl here will have nothing else to do with you whatsoever. And make no mistake, I protect what's mine."

"She's not had time to meet anyone and form a relationship. I doubt she's even capable."

Grumbled threats arose from the tallest of Kenson's men.

"Oh? She's legally an adult, and competent. I have a copy of her birth certificate in my jacket." Nate tweezed the envelope from his jacket and waved it back and forth.

Several snickers around the room emphasized the administrator's lack of support.

Ray's subdued rage radiated from every pore and promised the issue not settled. "She needs protection. If the wrong people get hold of her, it could spell disaster for us all."

"And just who would the wrong people be, I wonder? A warden type?" Nate doubted the man's control would slip. He was wound tight but understood how to play the politics game.

"There's talk of terrorists trying to kidnap her. Have any info on that?" Ray's sneer directed at Callie was the last straw.

Stepping forward, Nate's intent on instructing the prick on how to speak to a lady took priority. "Here's the thing, the bastards knew where she was and who she was with. How do you suppose that happened, Ray?"

Colonel Kenson stepped between them, holding his hand up to halt Nate's stalk.

"I have no idea but intend to find out." With a frown at Sebastian, the administrator added, "Maybe some of Jake's friends would know. Where is Jake, by the way? I'd like to fire him personally."

Nate had handled Jake's funeral privately through back channels, but was still surprised at Ray's obvious lack of knowledge.

"Haven't seen him recently." Tightening around Sebastian's mouth and eyes indicated secrets bound within, at a cost.

Nate's direct stare at Sebastian resulted in a weaker version reflected back.

"I was off the evening she left the institution. Perhaps we should review the video footage to see what we can pick up. You all can't think I had anything to do with this. Ray informed *me* she was with Jake." The response slipped from Sebastian's lips as casual as a snake slithering down a blacktop road.

Ray doesn't suspect Sebastian's involvement with Callie's escape.

Callie wrapped her arms about her shoulders and held tight.

Kenson directed his next statement to the administrator and left no doubt of his authority, or that he was taking charge. "This meeting is now concluded. The only reason you gained entry, Ray, was to attest to Callie's wellbeing. You've done so. You will now leave." With a nod to several of his men, Ray was dismissed, with animosity.

The ensuing blustering response silenced when two team members faced off with the visitors, effectively cutting off their line of sight to Callie.

Ray took a step back. Even Nate would think twice on how to engage them considering their stiff stances radiating menace.

"This isn't over, Kenson. I have connections. A mind like hers is too dangerous to run loose. She needs direction." Even as the older man spoke, his retreating steps in the face of the approaching men echoed off the pitted block walls.

"Until she's back with me, keep her safe from those Korean bastards." A stumble-step necessitated throwing his arms out to catch his balance.

Nate bit the inside of his cheek when seeing the administrator's shoelaces flop against the cement floor.

With the pseudo-dignity of a naked man in front of a large audience, Ray pivoted and stormed out. His low growl echoed in the hall before the slamming door reverberated in the large room.

A glance at Callie revealed the same impish expression she'd worn after dumping a pile of snow on Nerd's head earlier in the week. Squaring off with her enemy gave her strength in the face of a very real and current threat.

"So, where to from here?" Sebastian looked to Nate as if they were heading out for a day of fun. The carefree demeanor lacked malice.

"No, Sebastian, sorry. It's just Callie and me." Even after knowing her for only a few weeks, his tolerance for trusting other men in her close proximity bordered on nil. His team members were the lone exception. Most of the time. Whisper tested his resolve of late, if only to instigate a response.

"What about the rest of the team?"

"Do you see them here? These men are assigned to her protection." Nate indicated Kenson's men in a sweeping gesture.

"That's preposterous. Your arrogance will get her killed. Look, I just want to speak with her. Jake and I were tight. He'd want me to talk to her. After all, he gave me instructions, too."

"It's all right, Nate. I'll hear him out." Callie's faltering voice gave him pause.

Sidestepping the men, Sebastian padded over to stand before her.

Nate backing up to stand by her other side resulted in Sebastian's glare, but sudden shouting in the hall drew everyone's attention as Ray's strident voice grated their nerves.

"I have sensitive information Kenson will want to hear! Let me in."

The guard's monotone answer remained muffled and unflappable. *"No, sir. However, if you'd like, you can have a seat outside the colonel's office. When he comes out, I'll let him know you're waiting."*

Another muffled string of expletives ensued.

Callie's sudden stiffening precluded Nate exiting and addressing Ray face-to-face. Sebastian had taken her hand in his and kneaded her forearm.

A slight tremble accompanied the bleaching of color from her rosy cheeks.

"Callie, you know Jake wanted me to look after you. He said so in the office at Ambrosia. Come with me."

Callie's instant cringe brought a surge of testosterone-filled soldiers crowding Sebastian before Nate's light shove sent him backward. Sebastian continued backing toward the door under the angry glares from each man present.

"You're making a mistake, Callie. You'll see that in time. If you're not careful, they'll have you building bombs and destroying millions of lives. Jake couldn't see what a danger you are, and you're responsible for his absence." Sebastian's calculative glare declared the subject unfinished and his retreat temporary.

A slight squeak preceded the quiet click of the door as he left.

"You okay?" She collapsed in her chair, her descent softened by Nate gripping her upper arms.

"I'm good. Glad that's over."

"Men, you mind entertaining Ms. McKellen for a sec while I borrow Mr. Crofton? We'll be just outside the door, back in a moment." Kenson's order brought grins to their faces.

Callie's flash of uncertainty gave Nate pause. When a team member sat on his haunches before her and extended his hand, Nate wanted to punch him square in the jaw.

"Ma'am, friends call me Lightning. It really is a pleasure to meet you." The prior grumbling tone now softened with reverence.

His moniker best be related to his mind.

The fact they resorted to call names indicated acceptance, not just an assignment.

Nate's step toward him halted with the colonel's hand on his shoulder. "Mr. Crofton? A word, please? She'll be fine."

Clamping his teeth together to keep from growling helped—a little. The greater the distance from Callie, the more Nate's stomach churned. Separation anxiety had never been an issue for him.

When the door closed and blocked Callie from Nate's sight, frustration spread throughout his system like wildfire.

"Hey, snap out of it, soldier. Are you certain you're the right one for this job? You can't protect her if you can't focus."

The colonel knew him well.

"Yeah, I got this. What's up that you didn't want Callie to hear? And for the record, she will ask, and I won't lie to her."

Shaking his head, Kenson replied, "Our intel says the North Koreans want her at any cost. They're not going to stop."

"I figured as much. On top of that, we have a traitor in our midst, but it's not my team. Somehow, they found us after we left Ambrosia."

"She okay?"

"They did a number on her, but she's healing. I'll let you know when I figure out my next target."

"Hopefully with a low body count?"

"Always my goal, sir. And by the way, I appreciate the offer for the second team but, for now, not needed. When this is sorted out, we'll revisit the subject."

"Taking her to your lair, then? I wondered where you all holed up. Mind sharing?"

"All in due time."

"I'll respect that—for now. Keep her safe until we figure this out. We'll take her off your hands when it's over."

"Ah, no. No, you won't. I meant what I said. She's mine."

"So, it's like that, is it? Okay. Makes one less headache for me. Just keep her under wraps until we find our traitor."

Chapter Twenty-Four

"I don't know how to thank you, Nate, for all you've done." The memory of Ray's fierce determination and Sebastian's backhanded accusation kept her quiet for the ride back despite his repeated attempts to draw her into a conversation.

"Let's get inside, we have things to discuss."

Ushered through the doorway, she let peace and serenity enfold her. "Where is everybody?"

"Perimeter checks. They'll be in shortly. They've already cleared the cabin." When he took her jacket to hang in the closet, a metallic clinking sound snapped his attention to the ring bouncing on the hardwood floor, startling them both.

Nate bent to pick up and examine the intricate coat of arms engraved in silver. "Callie, you didn't tell me you had—"

"Jake's military signet ring. I didn't. He always wore it." The realization brought tears to her eyes.

"Someone must've slipped it into your pocket today. The question is—who?" Closer visual inspection ended with an explosive string of curses.

"I haven't seen it since the night Jake left Ambrosia. I wasn't close enough to the other team today for anyone to slip it to me, except for Lightning. Then Sebastian held my forearm. I did shake hands with the colonel and his lieutenant, Jackson. At one time or another, each walked behind me and could've slipped it into my pocket."

"This ring's been modified. Look at the thickness of the band."

"It's not like yours."

"Or any other member of our team. Very clever work, I must say."

"They added a tracker? Would the colonel do that to pinpoint our location?"

"Definitely, but only for your security. The man doesn't like to be on the outs when it comes to secrets. The problem arises from how he acquired it."

"Should we leave?"

"No, but we might need backup. I'll make a few calls. Otherwise, this changes nothing. Go up and change your clothes. Be ready in five."

"We're still going to train? What if Ray comes?"

"Now, Callie. Follow orders."

"Okay."

Today was her first day wearing linen slacks since leaving the institution. A certain comfort had accompanied the tactical BDUs associated with her new life, and she looked forward to putting them back on.

Time would expose their traitor. If Nate was right, it would be unexpected and unique. She wasn't prepared to face any of them. With her TK skills still rudimentary, her concentration went to shit whenever doubt entered the equation.

Taking the steps two at a time then shucking her clothes, she prayed her team remained safe.

In descending to the first floor again, she saw Blade, Spirit, and Nate turn to watch her. Their tense postures and businesslike expressions belied slight smiles.

Over the prior weeks, she'd come to recognize the slide and click of Nate checking his Glock. This felt different. A murky foreboding radiated within the walls and sheathed the confidence of her developing talent. The darkness felt akin to that experienced at the truck stop.

A low buzz from the alarm on the kitchen wall sounded simultaneously with the vibrations from each of the team's phones.

Nate snagged his cell and checked the screen. "Breach on the northwest corner. This isn't Kenson's men. Let's go. Looks like the pricks didn't waste time. Multiple targets on the ground approaching low and fast."

"Breach? We're under attack? Now?"

"Yes, which is why we're going outside. Moving targets are harder to hit. This house has too much glass to secure any room." Confidence etched Nate's expression and tone as he handed her the heavy jacket she'd worn during training.

Callie turned toward Faith in the crate.

"Callie—" Nate began.

"I won't leave her behind. She'll be quiet as long as I hold her. She always is."

"All right." Nate tilted his head back and blew out a sigh.

"Where's Virus, Whisper, and Nerd?" From training drills to a real threat, Spirit's tone and demeanor never wavered. "Virus is on north,

Whisper and Nerd are on west and east perimeters."

"You think we're ready for this?" She didn't feel ready.

"Of course we're ready. Why else would fate throw it at us?" Spirit's logic didn't always make sense to her.

"Callie, you stay glued to my side unless I tell you otherwise. Understood? No telekinesis unless I direct it. Spirit, circle from the west and provide backup for Whisper. Blade, you back up Nerd on the east. I'll take Callie to the cave. We'll take stock of the situation then."

After handing her an ear mic and inserting his own, Nate tapped several times. "Okay, Whisper, Virus, and Nerd are online with us." Without hesitation, he took her hand and pulled her toward the back door. "Virus will signal when they've passed him. We'll take these bastards down from behind."

"Backup on the way?" Blade's casual question veiled the turmoil evidenced in the stiff set of his shoulders.

"Yeah, my brothers. Three men, three dogs. I know you guys haven't spent much time with them, but we all know and use the same codes and signals. They'll be coming from the north. ETA—forty-five minutes."

* * * *

Forty yards of clear space around the cabin had left each person vulnerable until reaching the comparative safety offered by white cedars, holly trees, and thick, snow-covered briars. With his gun in one hand and Callie in tow, Nate hustled forward while scanning the perimeter. At the tree line, he stopped to let her catch her breath.

"Callie, fill in our tracks leaving the cabin. If these dirtballs do make it this far, they won't know where to search for us." His fear for her closed the distance between them as she stood gazing at the snow filling in their path.

"I can do this and keep moving now that I've got a lock on it. I can also erase the tracks around the front since I've been doing it all week. Everything will look untouched, well, except for the where the vehicles are parked." With Faith snuggled in her arms, she concentrated on the task and kept pace with Nate.

"Good. We'll hold up in the grotto until they pass. Then, we'll take them down before they reach the cabin."

An eerie calm pervaded the quiet late-morning woods. Guerrilla fighting entailed nothing new for him. On the other hand, listening to the tremor in Callie's voice shook him to the core.

"Remember, stay with me unless directed otherwise and follow orders." He'd never been one to rail at fate, but feeling Callie's uncertainty renewed his determination to kill anything threatening them.

As they headed west toward the cave, he realized she'd probably never forgive him for what he intended to do. Keeping her safe wasn't just protecting national security. It meant protecting his heart as well. He felt no guilt for actions toward that end.

If they survived this threat, he'd one day tell her how he felt, giving her time in between to catch her breath and experience more of life.

Patches of sunlight filtering through branches crusted the melting snow, forming a blinding reflective sheen. Deer trails crisscrossing at odd angles delineated well-used paths through the thick underbrush and helped disguise their journey.

Precious minutes passed as they slipped and skidded down a deep ravine and climbed the opposite side. A glance over his shoulder revealed a smooth blanket of white. Whereas Callie's talent could fill in the tracks, only sunlight could form the glossy skin on top to erase the obscure evidence of their passing. Unless the pricks knew what to look for, they wouldn't notice the difference.

At the entrance to the small cave, he hesitated. "In you go, Callie. Just like in drill. I'll head northeast. Cover my tracks till I get to the top of that ridge. As soon as I'm there and my path is erased, cover your entrance with snow and ice. Make it look like part of the mountain like we practiced, okay?"

"No, Nate. You can't leave me here alone. I can help."

The panic in her tone fired all his protective instincts. "Callie, you and Faith wait here till I call for you. Keep your mic in. This won't take long."

Time was precious, yet when she clutched his shoulder, he could do naught but embrace her before kissing the top of her head. Anything more, and he wouldn't have the strength to leave.

Both hurt and fear encompassed her expression as she shuddered without another word. She'd already been set adrift from men promising her protection. Tears tracked her cheeks when he turned to go.

Various clicks from his ear bud informed him when their intruders passed Virus' position on the north front. Since the bastards must've used the GPS in the ring to pinpoint her general location, maybe they hadn't relayed the coordinates to reinforcements. If so, the cabin could remain a secure location.

If Kenson had sent the team for backup, they wouldn't be entering in stealth mode. This was a planned attack.

With the aggressor unit approaching the cabin, his team would close the loop behind them.

Another tapped message, this time from Whisper, relayed his sighting and number of targets passing his position. Soon after, Nerd relayed his sightings from the east.

Without benefit of Callie's telekinesis to continue erasing his trail, his best option entailed backtracking to create false paths and sticking to deer passages as much as possible. At least it would buy time if the intruders suspected his presence.

Thick underbrush slowed Nate's progress as he angled farther west. The foreigners at the cabin had proven themselves well-organized, which made them difficult targets. If the current attack consisted of domestic muscle, chances were good they lacked the same level of training and experience.

Sporadic gusts of wind shook branches and dumped clouds of wet flakes to reduce visibility. A

snapping twig ahead and to his right announced the first of their unwanted visitors. Several large cedars blocked the line of sight with clumsy commotion depicting the new arrivals' lack of skill.

He smiled. *Local boys.*

Fate gave him the geographical advantage as the intruders climbed a steep section of the mountain in their approach. He caught glimpses of three targets in white camouflage. Each carried an assault rifle. A silent message tapped on his mic let his team know he'd hunkered down until they passed his position.

Chapter Twenty-Five

Callie huddled on a large rock and wrapped her blanket tighter around her and Faith to retain heat. As ordered, she'd covered the cave's entrance with enough snow to disguise its presence.

"How dare he relegate us to hiding?" Faith licked Callie's face and whined.

Unable to sit still, she stood and paced back and forth in the dark. Counting steps prevented collision with obstacles and led to calculating various formulae before they dissolved into a mental snapshot of each team member in turn.

Weeks prior, they'd hauled small trunks to the shelter including blankets, food in plastic containers, candles, dog food, and water. She could last several days and had thought it romantic at the time. Current circumstances reversed her thinking.

Flashbacks of Nate sitting beside her on the granite slab felt like a dream now. Would they be cracking jokes again tomorrow?

Oddly enough, she minded the wait more than the dark. The urge to help and not cower rose to a crescendo in her chest. Flashbacks of gunfire returned her thoughts to Franklin sliding to sit at the base of a fence. She couldn't stop anything traveling at the speed of a bullet.

Her training hadn't progressed to anticipate Nate's approach to neutralizing this type of threat. Everything so far consisted of defense.

"*Only you can decide what kind of person you want to be.*"

Nate's words came back to remind her of her inner strength.

She had enough control of her talent to assist, but an ill-timed or inappropriate approach would forfeit all their lives. Just the same, to sit and do nothing while others risked their necks wasn't acceptable.

Jake had said he'd return. He hadn't.

Franklin died in front of her.

No one person was worth so many lives.

Time resisted signs of marked increments in the dark while her worst fears took flight to fill her mind with doubt and regret. She had no clue how much time had passed.

Too much.

Feeling for the supply chest, she removed a flashlight and flicked it on. The well-worn footpath from the entrance to her resting place underwent another trudging ramble.

“Oh, hell.” A sudden bilious sensation filled her. Something felt wrong in a way she couldn’t define. In her mind’s eye, Franklin lay gasping for breath, bleeding and in pain.

The same queasy awareness that had plagued her then, filled her now. Her abilities hadn’t extended beyond telekinesis, but her imagination supplied enough horror to galvanize her into action

Not wanting to distract the team, she refrained from tapping out a signal on her mic. If they were all right, Nate would go ballistic. If not, she could make a difference.

A flick of her thumb plunged the makeshift haven into darkness once again. The cold wafting from the wall of snow reminded her of how Nerd had burrowed in a large drift during one of their drills. Perhaps she could use the same tactic to help her team.

Anxiety flourished with the compulsion to test her skill at exiting without bringing down the entire wall of snow. Smashing it would necessitate precious minutes to rebuild, time she couldn’t waste.

Faith would have to come, too. Whether the others liked it or not, her pup was a part of the team she wouldn’t leave behind.

The deconstructing process was different, the level of difficulty paralleled cleaning up milk when Virus tossed the mug in the kitchen. That learning experience now helped as she replicated the picture of encompassing the icy circle she wanted to pull inward.

Minutes passed as she strained to hear anything indicating movement outside. Nate’s training favored patience and information gathering before action. She’d paid attention to everything said.

With the lightest mental touch, she imagined pulling the small cylinder of snow toward her to make a peephole. Seconds later, the concentrated effort resulted in a ray of knee-high light the size of a quarter cutting through the dark.

Loose dirt and rocks bit into her flesh in kneeling to peer through the small channel of the foot-thick barrier. Again, no sound indicated presence of life on the other side.

Faith squirmed to get down but didn’t vocally protest when Callie maintained her hold. “Not now, girl. We’ll play later, I promise.”

Checking her watch in the beam of light revealed eighteen minutes had passed since Nate deposited her there to wait out the confrontation. The perception of wrongness continued to permeate her spirit.

For Nate to be mad, he'd have to survive.

It took a little more effort to carve a tunnel large enough through which to crawl. Cold flakes melted on her neck in passing.

After filling it in behind her, she prayed a return trip would be unnecessary. The large mound of snow she'd fashioned appeared to be an outcropping of rocks, covered by the recent storm.

With each step toward the cabin, apprehension overrode guilt until the blood roaring in her ears drowned out the sounds of wind soughing overhead. Nate's plan included flanking the targets before they reached the cabin. The sound of shots firing hadn't reached her ears.

* * * *

"Last target down. Checking for ID. Still has a pulse—and now cuffs. Smashed his tracking receiver." Whisper's quiet words were the first spoken since they'd left the cabin.

"Virus, Nerd, check the cabin before we interrogate the survivor." Nate approached from the west side of the lodge. It'd been an adjustment not to take point, but securing Callie had taken precedence.

Adrenaline surge showed in each of his men's faces with Virus and Nerd's return. Not surprising, lack of recent experience hadn't slowed them down. Each remained highly motivated.

"Where're your brothers? Don't hear any ridiculous noises announcing their presence." Blade and the rest of the team strode forward to form a loose circle around the downed target dressed in snow camouflage.

The assailant's harsh breath sucked intermittently at the gauzy material covering his face. Blood oozed through the gloved fingers as he held pressure to his left shoulder.

"Be here soon with their dogs. They'll check the perimeter for stragglers and new arrivals. Let's get this one inside and see what he knows."

"Think Callie's gonna stay put? I'm thinking she won't." Spirit's gaze swept the surrounding forest. His nonchalant attitude didn't fool Nate. The Native American had incredible instincts.

“She’d better damn sight keep her ass in the cave.”

“Remember, Nate, she’s dealt with death but not extreme anger. They are two different things.” Virus’s softer side seldom made an appearance. The fact any one of these men would take his place where she was concerned continued to eat away at his patience.

“I think we have other things to deal with right now.” “Jeez, what’s this guy been eating? Whisper, give me a hand.” Several grunts indicated the target’s pain as the two men half-carried him toward the front steps.

The injured thug was all to eager to sit in the straight back kitchen chair.

Vibration of his cell alerted Nate to a text. “My brothers are here but not in place to stop the company who’s just arrived. One SUV, two occupants. Let’s get this party started and not waste time. Conner thinks it might be the colonel plus one.”

“*He* slipped Callie a tracker? I’d expect him to try and locate her, but not turning traitor.” Nate grimaced at the realization of being sandbagged.

The target’s sudden frantic fighting earned him a kidney punch from Nerd as they secured him to the chair.

“ETA sixty seconds. Make ready.” Tapping out a message for Callie to sit tight, Nate followed the team inside.

She’d better stay put.

As the large black SUV skidded to a stop in the drive, Nate puzzled over the occupants. He’d never suspect the colonel of a double cross.

From the first meeting in Ambrosia, Nate’s world had turned upside down. Only a fraction of his body provided a target in standing just inside the doorway.

“What’s up, sir? How’d you find us?” He kept his Glock by his side, visible to the new arrivals. His ex-boss understood the message and kept both hands away from his body.

“I didn’t. My lieutenant here intercepted a message from Sebastian detailing these coordinates. I wanted to come out and check on you all personally. You didn’t want Lightning’s help, and you know how I hate secrets.”

“Yeah, only the ones you’re not holding.”

So it was Sebastian, all along. The man had set Callie’s nerves on end since their encounter at the club. Her instincts were far better tuned than suspected.

Kenson's half-smile reminded Nate of the old days. Times missed on occasion.

"Mind if we come in?" And just like old times, Kenson's request was rhetorical. Keeping his hands out to his sides and away from the gun on his hip, he climbed the steps and nudged the door wide before striding inside. Jackson, his clone and lieutenant, followed.

"Do come in, gentlemen. We were just preparing a small party." Nate watched as Kenson and Jackson strode through the great room to the kitchen, and silently cursed the extra time Callie would have to wait. He shouldered his weapon.

Each of his team surrounded their intruder, tied securely to a ladder-back chair. Blood oozed from his broken nose and wounded shoulder to spatter his snow gear.

"Where is she?" Kenson's quiet monotone was more command than question.

"Safe. She'll be here when I call."

"Good." Kenson nodded his approval.

Jackson, his second-in-command frowned. "You left her somewhere alone?"

"And how would you know she's alone, Jackson? How do you know the number of our team?" Spirit's quiet words stilled all motion.

In the next heartbeat, Jackson back stepped toward the great room after drawing the Sig Sauer from his holster. "Oops. Ear mics out, everyone."

All gazes turned to the soft-spoken lieutenant. Unassuming is how Nate had thought of him. Always squared away, always ready to help.

"Jackson?" Kenson shook his head. "Damn. I never pegged you for a turncoat. How'd I miss that?"

"Recent occurrence." Light streaming through floor-to-ceiling windows from behind kept half the lieutenant's face in shadow.

"Well, now's as good a time as ever. Where is the little bitch?" From his pocket, Jackson pulled another handgun. "Helps to be prepared. So, one at a time, put your weapons on the floor. Let's not make this any harder than it has to be."

Nate's gaze flicked over his shoulder to Spirit, then the rest of his men. They weren't prepared for this. All had relaxed their guard. When Blade's hand inched toward his waistband, the shot Jackson fired reverberated within the confines of the cabin.

Blade wasn't the recipient of the lead projectile.

Their camouflaged intruder sagged in his bonds as Jackson warned, "Next one goes between *your* eyes, Blade." Determination radiated from Jackson's gaze.

Nate preferred sending intruders to Black Site seclusion over death. He wouldn't kill in cold blood unless circumstances demanded it. Obviously, Jackson subscribed to a different character. Crimson flowed from the camouflaged hood as the man sat slumped in the chair.

"Jackson, you've served under me for nine years."

"And you're wondering how I could take you by surprise. It's because I'm better than you, Kenson. Now, once again, where's the little bitch I came to collect? Sebastian couldn't get the job done..."

"You worked with Sebastian?" Kenson asked with disbelief.

"After the attempt at the cabin failed, he was afraid of retaliation by his foreign contacts. Speaking of which, they won't be happy with your performance in killing their agents." Sebastian snorted, his grimace suggesting unpleasant thoughts. "You should be glad I came and not them. I might let the rest of you live, providing she's here in the next ten minutes. Otherwise, I'll kill one of you every five minutes thereafter."

"She won't come in until she gets the signal. And none of us will give it," Nate advised.

Too much space existed between Jackson and his team to mount any kind of offense. The man would know his distance-to-target ratios and reaction times.

"*Hm*, have her that well-trained, do you? I think not. I saw the way she watched you at the office, Nate." Jackson snorted. "And once I contact these damned North Koreans and deliver the whore, I'll be a rich man."

Chapter Twenty-Six

From the cover of the wood line, Callie stared at the red patches of snow beside Nate's SUV. She didn't know how many bodies lay scattered through the woods, dead or dying. Fear congealed in the pit of her belly when no one answered the message tapped out on her mic.

Unlike the team, she couldn't move through the woods in stealth mode. It was a blessing Faith remained silent as she watched Kenson arrive and precede Jackson into the cabin.

From her vantage point, she studied the visitor's SUV in front of the porch.

Nate's brothers were advancing from the periphery with distance and timing unknown. Intuition urged her to move closer to see what transpired.

Nate always encouraged her to trust her instincts.

If all seemed right, she could backtrack and cover her footprints. Nate would notice the difference in the lack of reflection and smoothness of the skim, but it was the best she could do.

Faith yipped and squirmed to get down. A deeper understanding of Nate's warning about distractions focused her attention on the pup. The shiver originated from equal parts emotional and physical parentage. No way could she leave her pup alone in the forest.

Callie closed her eyes for a moment and rubbed her forehead against Faith's neck, willing her into submission with soft murmurs and gentle stroking. The pup groaned softly.

If everything was all right inside, they wouldn't have removed their ear mics.

A deep breath and it was time to move. Bolting across the open ground left them both vulnerable, yet no shout of alarm reached her ears, and no bullet punched her chest.

At the corner of the cabin, she ducked low to sidle under the den's window and gain access to the porch. Her heart hammered in her chest.

She had no offensive training, no weapon, and no plan. Her mind was the one defense available.

Except for the snow.

Exposing her talent would endanger her team. Kenson would hound them to hell and back, yet be alive to do it.

From the bay window's corner, she peeked inside and welcomed the thought of Nate talking with the visitor and all were safe. The alternative wasn't acceptable.

The scene inside froze the breath in her lungs and generated roots to hold her feet to the floorboards. Her team surrounded a man in white coveralls, his slumped body tied to a kitchen chair. Chin on chest position might've suggested an unconscious state if blood hadn't marked the whole in his forehead.

Nate wouldn't shoot a bound and helpless man.

The sight of two uniformed men rekindled earlier conversations from the morning's assembly. From the back, she recognized Colonel Kenson. His second-in-command held two guns pointed at her team.

Jackson couldn't have informed the foreigners she'd been with Nate. They'd only met hours prior. However, the lieutenant could have slipped the ring into her pocket. The picture finally came into focus. Sebastian and Jackson worked in tandem.

Pure disgust transformed into uncertainty as she studied their circumstances. A momentary blink and Nate locked gazes with Callie. The split-second pained expression crossing his face encompassed more emotion than she'd ever felt.

She saw the rhythm of the rise and fall of his chest increase in increments and she knew. He intended to rush the shooter.

Seen in profile, Jackson's half-smile reminded her of a demonic robot. Stiff movements alerted her to the tension bound within. It wouldn't take much to push him into action.

Blade started to kneel. Instinct advised he'd be next to die.

She couldn't wait for death. Not again.

Equations including speed of projectiles, angle of trajectory, and force needed to break the glass while remaining true to target flitted through her thoughts. With a prayer and calculations adjusted for her position, she took a deep breath.

* * * *

Views from the massive bay windows had always provided Nate a sense of oneness with nature.

Now, seeing Callie outside filled every corner of his soul with terror. Regardless of what happened to him in the coming moments, his team would protect her to their last breath.

Flashes of white flitting across the yard snatched his attention back to the porch. Callie stood with Faith clutched to her chest, a combination of horror and concentration etching her face. On the edge of the steps, dozens of snowballs rested in several piles, the stash growing with each heartbeat.

Oh, hell. She'd better not.

She'd blow her cover in front of the colonel. Since he wasn't certain how his ex-boss would react to that revelation at this point, it wasn't worth the risk.

Kenson wasn't a fool. Regardless of the end result, even his brothers couldn't throw ice balls through a plate-glass window and nail a target with precision. He wondered if Callie had warned his siblings and if they were now preparing for a tactical entry.

If not, she wouldn't wait for backup.

Before Nate could signal his team, Callie's answer came in the form of breaking glass and dozens of projectiles. Each icy grenade flew true to target to pelt Jackson's head and shoulders, knocking him to his knees.

Ice and blood mixed as it ran down the side of his face and neck. His shocked expression echoed in the colonel's face even as the reflexive action resulted in Jackson firing off two shots.

Sudden pain engulfed Nate's thigh and roared down his leg. Immediate spurting of blood from the wound soaked his jeans. A heartbeat later, his own gun bucked after he'd scooped it off the floor. The first round hit the traitor's chest.

Jackson stumbled back then turned to look through the window's jagged opening. His gasping breath turned wheezy as foamy blood dribbled from his mouth. He crumpled to the floor.

In close confines, the cacophony of each team member firing should've been deafening.

Instead, it sounded like a far-off popping.

Before blackness engulfed him, the last thing Nate saw was Callie, outside the shattered window with Faith in her arms and blood dripping from each nostril.

She turned and fled.

Chapter Twenty-Seven

Colonel Kenson paced at the foot of Nate's hospital bed with hands clasped behind his back. He'd complained all morning, posing one ridiculous scenario after another before gritting his teeth and shaking his head.

"Damn it, man, ice balls don't break plate-glass windows *and* fly true to target. There was nothing inside them. Not to mention the fact that they *remained* intact *until* hitting Jackson. Every damn one of them, like they were laser guided missiles."

"The ones that broke the glass probably melted down the wall, sir."

"No. The wall under the window, just like the floor there, was dry as a bone. Glass fragments yes, water and ice, no."

"Maybe he shot the window out first?"

"Who? Damn it, Nate. I was facing the window and *saw*... damn if I'm sure what I saw. A freaking lot of snowballs flying through the window, making *holes. As. They. Went*."

"Have you spoken to my brothers?"

Kenson snorted. "Like they're gonna give me anything to work with. I've spent mornings with you and afternoons drilling them. You know what? I got nothing."

"They must've said something, sir."

Kenson shook his head. "I didn't hear a shot preceding those snowballs. I also didn't find any bullets embedded in the ceiling or walls. Hell, I checked the cabin myself and the only bullet holes were the ones in Jackson and his crony. *On top of that,* they all came from your team's guns. I've double-checked ballistics myself."

Kenson huffed a heavy breath before continuing, "I've never seen the likes of it. Nor have I seen Callie since."

"She's safe. Trust me."

"Obviously more than you trust me."

Nate had never heard his ex-commander rant. It was difficult withholding a smile.

"Don't tell me it was your brothers' doing. They weren't even close. I went outside right away to see who our mystery savior was. Guess what I found—more ice balls in neat little piles. Piles that were *not* there when I first arrived! Oh, and no tracks in the snow."

"Obviously neither the team nor I had anything to do with it. Callie was tucked out of harm's way."

"Yeah, let's address the fact there were *no* tracks in the snow. Jackson and I had arrived less than fifteen minutes prior, there should have at least been our prints leading to the cabin. But no, not a damned one. Would you explain *that* to me?"

"How would I know what happened? I was standing with you before I was shot." Constant and extended hounding didn't shake Nate's resolve. Eventually, the colonel would give up. Or not.

"Four days. You've been in this hospital four damn days and I've visited each morning. Haven't I earned a little trust over the years?"

Nate chuckled as he answered the man whose tenacity should hold a world record. "Sir, you know I trust you. Hell, you're the only outsider who knows the location of my cabin."

"Only because Jackson took me there. If he hadn't been in cahoots with Sebastian, I still wouldn't know." Kenson pulled a chair closer to Nate's hospital bed and sat.

"Look, with Sebastian dead—and by the way, who in the hell cuts off a man's nuts unless there's a shit storm of hate fueling the fire? I can't see any reason for Jackson to have done that." A heart-felt cringe accompanied his words.

"I don't know, sir."

"Wait. Time of death for Sebastian's mutilation and demise was *after* Jackson and I arrived at your cabin. There's another player involved, who may or may not be on Callie's side."

"And you found no evidence at Sebastian's place?"

"We walked into Sebastian's apartment and found blood all over the kitchen floor. Someone wanted the bastard to suffer, which I'm sure he did."

"If Sebastian gave Jackson the coordinates to find Callie after slipping Jake's modified ring in her pocket, do you think he told the foreigners, too?"

"No. The mercenaries who attacked you were all local trash. Apparently, Jake's second was closed-mouthed. I don't think the foreigners got him. They wouldn't have done *that* to him."

"So, who killed the weasel?"

Kenson shrugged a shoulder. "We did find a note with Sebastian's body, but it made no sense. A tranq gun with spare darts in a case by Sebastian's desk matched the chemical we found carried by Jackson's camouflaged mercs as spares." From his side pocket, Kenson pulled out a baggie holding a small piece of paper. "This is what we found on his body. Looks like Callie has some type of guardian angel on her side."

Callie suspected there were others like her. Maybe not all remained in captivity. Not for the first time since meeting his enigma, Nate pondered the situation while reading the note.

Callie, you're safe from this bastard now. I don't think the North Koreans know how to find you. Sebastian was the only contact I've found. His lover is also out of the picture. Keep a low profile till we know for sure. I know you need to make sense of this nightmare. I think you'll find what you're looking for in Sebastian's wall safe. I hope we can meet some day.

Take care,
Your friend,
Penny.

Nate's half-remembered conversation with Jake at Ambrosia filtered through his thoughts but failed to form a complete picture. "Before you ask, I don't know who Penny is or how she's involved. I do have reason to suspect there are other prodigies being held captive, however."

"I don't think any woman is capable of the carnage I saw. It wouldn't have been romantically instigated. Sebastian was gay."

"As I said, Sir. I've never met anyone named Penny associated with Callie."

"You said Jake set the time and place for their meeting, so Penny might not have had a hand in his murder. Jake gets ambushed. And now this Penny eliminates a threat to Callie? Who *is* she?"

"I'm assuming you've checked for fingerprints?"

"Nate, I handpicked our best forensic specialists to go over that scene with a fine-tooth comb. We did find a gift-wrapped box inside a wall safe with Jake's name on it. Inside was a leather collar with a tag that read ***Jake's slave***. What the hell is that all about?"

"I guess Sebastian hoped Jake had plans for him."

"We also found two airline tickets, one in his name and one in Jake's. Sebastian was planning on them leaving together. Hell, I didn't know they'd maintained contact after military discharge. Guess I'm losing my touch. So, tell me, where is Callie? I checked the cabin. She's not there."

"She's safe and will remain so. Trust. Me."

"Obviously, I do. Your damn brothers are as tight-lipped as your team," he reiterated once again. "Just keep her safe. To have her in any spotlight would leave her vulnerable to threats from scientific groups, government splinter groups, and any depraved wacko out there."

"She'll stay safe, sir."

"So, you're getting out today?"

"She's not going to be with them when they pick me up. You'll not get access to her yet. She needs a little time. Did you find out why Sebastian picked Jackson?"

"Yeah. Jackson was in debt up to his eyeballs. That took me by surprise, too. We hacked his personal accounts and found a bunch of coded emails to an intermediary with terrorist ties. The last one stated he'd re-establish contact after acquiring the package, written the day he shot you. We also found a few messages written to Sebastian, demanding more money."

"Looks like this Penny ferreted out Callie's stalker and your traitorous lieutenant."

"Yeah, I want Penny found at all costs. She may hold valuable information pertaining to another group. Ray's not saying a word about anything, not that I'd tip my hand. Says he doesn't have a clue. He also has the connections to keep his files sealed, the bastard."

"This other group. Who are they?"

"Nothing for you to worry about, young man. It relates to a failed mission several years ago."

"Sorry your second-in-command turned rogue. Trust is an invaluable commodity."

"Guess Sebastian figured Jake would come to me eventually. Being under my protection must've been Jake's fail safe. Sebastian joined Jake's group during their last tour." With apparent great reluctance, the colonel rose from his chair, his expression a mask of defeat.

"Glad you came out of this without permanent damage. I assume you'll accept some type of protective custody for her."

"Yes. If you could see the team put on active duty, but off-limits, we'll keep her safe. She needs a few weeks to decompress and get her bearings before starting work. I'll be in touch by the end of the month."

"Work?"

"Yeah, she wants to work with plant genetics."

"Good, as long as she stays away from explosives and the like. Oh, and I'd put you all on the payroll since the night she escaped, retroactive. Any chance on getting some background on our little genius?"

"Planning to work on that. The only thing she's ever known is the institution. Jake didn't have time to go into more detail."

"I'd be more than happy to help with digging for her origins."

"I'll get back to you after we've talked. We all want to know about her parents."

"I can have a few friends take a sneak and peek at Ray's files. Bothers the hell out of me legal access is restricted."

"We'll talk in another few weeks about that, Colonel, but I'd appreciate it if you'd hold off. I'll explain why then."

"All right. Take care. Tell your crazy brothers I said hi."

Each jolt of Conner's truck sent a shaft of pain down Nate's thigh. The closer he got to the cabin, the less it registered.

"Thanks for the ride and fixing the windows. Looks like we'll be staying here awhile, at least until Callie and I decide where she wants to live and is settled."

"Little bro, she's become thick as thieves with the team. I don't think there's too much she doesn't understand." Conner's dark chuckle boded ill.

"Great."

"You're gonna have your hands full with that one. Listening to them, I don't think they're gonna let her get too far. They've all adopted her."

"Wonderful. Just how close have they gotten?" Tendrils of jealousy rose in Nate's chest. Again, something he didn't appreciate.

"Don't worry. Her thoughts have stayed with you. I believe she's a keeper, that one."

"Yeah. She inside now?"

Conner's grin widened with a waggle of his eyebrows. "Yep, and she's directed the men to perimeter checks."

Each afternoon, they'd talked on the phone for hours, discussing anything from continued drills with the team to supplies needed to study botany.

Odd that she wanted nothing to do with computers except in relation to finding others like herself. Neither had any idea how many prodigies were held prisoner, where they were located, or if there existed some type of blood tie between them.

Every minute in the hospital had amounted to an unrivaled torture as thoughts of what could've happened played out in his mind. Anticipation moistened his palms as he got out of the truck and climbed the steps.

"Callie?" Nudging the door open, he noted a new scent, sweet yet sensuous.

Damn, exactly what has she learned?

A look around the great room revealed she'd been busy. Swags of fresh garland draped the banister and fireplace mantle. Small Santa and reindeer figurines he'd never seen decorated side tables and countertops. Dozens of wrapped presents spilled out from under the Christmas tree.

Clearly, she'd embraced the holiday spirit.

From the kitchen, the aroma of rich stew wafted out and made his stomach growl. It seemed she'd also embraced the concept of home.

"Hey. I just turned this down. It'll need several hours of simmering before its ready."

His heart kept beating only out of habit. Thoughts of angels drifted through his mind as she approached. Her glossy locks brushed to a shine curled over her chest to caress her hips. A form-fitting long-sleeve tee showed off her curves yet embraced her new self-image.

Somebody's been shopping.

"Callie?"

"I've missed you. Tomorrow's Christmas Eve, but I have *one* present you can unwrap now..."

"My brothers—"

"Will be here tomorrow afternoon. Whisper and I have the meal planned, and your brothers are each bringing a dish."

When she placed her hands on either side of his chest and leaned in to kiss his cheek, the southern hardening was immediate.

"Any more nose bleeds, headaches?" As much as he wanted to crush her to his chest, they had other business to attend to first.

His intentions evaporated with her first touch.

"No. None at all."

No force between heaven and hell could prevent him from tasting her, regardless of what might happen later. Her gaze lowered from his, centered on his mouth as her tongue slipped out to moisten her lips.

To reach out and mold her hips seemed the most natural response in the world. In the back of his mind, doubts surfaced. She had so little experience with the world at large.

"You've not had a romantic relationship, sweetheart..." Words trailed off with the butterfly touch of her mouth. The first caress would remain in his memory until his thoughts, along with his body, turned to dust.

With a subtle exploration, he demanded entrance to the seductive sanctuary of her mouth, knowing she'd taste of temptation and paradise with a whole lot of spice thrown in.

Fantasies from his hospital stay rose in his mind as he pulled her closer. Even the smallest space between them was too much.

The soft fabric under his fingertips didn't negate the firmness of her hips. The natural progression to caressing her back augmented his stark hunger. Tilting his head for better access, he needed more, so much more.

Her breath quickened while her touch roamed over his shoulders, her need just as great. The feel of her twining her other hand in his hair to bring him closer instigated a low growl from his throat.

He hadn't entertained the idea of marriage before Callie. Yet the feel of her firm breasts pressing against him separated by two thin pieces of material brought reality home with the hardening of his body. They'd found common ground.

A doubt lingered in the back of his mind. *Will she want, can she handle, all that I'd give... and take?*

Even if she rejected him after life settled, he would always watch over her. Setting her free would be the hardest thing he'd ever do, but her happiness would always come first.

"We need to talk."

"I know what I want. I can tell you want me, too. I've done a lot of reading."

"I'm not sure you're ready."

"I've made up my mind, and I've learned how to drive you crazy. You see, what I couldn't get through the internet, well, the guys helped. Shall we see how it works?"

Dear God, she's gonna be the death of me.

If he lost control now, he'd never get it back. "I believe you." The gravelly nature of his voice echoed in the room.

"I can see you're not convinced."

You do remember the last order I gave you?" Changing the subject provided a last-ditch effort to keep his will in check. "

"Yes. To stay in the cave and not use my telekinesis. I'm never to use it in front of anyone outside of our team or your brothers."

"Correct." Frustration should have resulted in loose powder in place of teeth.

"I'm also an equal member of this team. As such, I have responsibilities." After taking a step back, she slid her arm down his shoulder to link their fingers.

Nate couldn't be angry in regards to her disobedience. Hell, he couldn't even think beyond the softness of her touch.

He let her tug him up the stairs.

"How do you know you're ready, sweetheart?"

"Because when I saw Jackson point a gun at you, I thought I'd die. I can't lose you. I won't. We're in this together."

Without another sound, she led him into the bedroom. Instead of laying her on the bed, he settled on his lap.

"We really need to have a conversation first," he started, knowing she'd feel the evidence of his desire through the layer of denim.

"I want you, Nate."

Her wide grin acknowledged awareness when he squirmed.

Stunned didn't come close to what he felt. His breath hitched as a lump formed in his throat.

"You haven't known me long."

When she glanced up to see his face, her mouth formed an O as her brow furrowed in confusion.

"I know what I feel."

"Understand this, your safety means everything to me. Everything. If at any time you're feelings interfere with my protection detail—"

"They won't. And I promise to follow orders from now on."

"We're not finished talking."
Her look said otherwise.

Chapter Twenty-Eight

"I'm sorry I worried you, Nate." In his bedroom, she let her lead him to the couch, sitting beside her after she sat. "But we're free and clear now. With Sebastian and Jackson dead, the North Koreans won't have a link to me."

When he placed his fingertips over her lips, she understood he couldn't think about that yet, he had more on his mind, something he wanted to tell her.

"As long as we keep a low profile, we'll be fine. I'm sure they'll keep beating the bushes for a while."

"Who killed Jake?" She couldn't stop the tears from spilling, but she had to know.

"Forensics matched a bullet from one of the intruder's weapons to the slug in Jake's chest. I believe Sebastian was the one who inserted the belly ring. We found a bottle of the sedative in his apartment that we think he used on you. That, and information on piercings in his computer's browser history."

Closing that chapter of her life left her free to grieve for Jake, who'd given his life for her freedom and wanted her to experience *normal*.

"Which leaves us with another loose end. Do you know a girl named Penny? She called Jake at the club and then contacted me before we met with Colonel Kenson. Said Ray was taking steps to get you back."

"Penny? No, I don't know anyone by that name. If she worked or lived at the institution, I haven't met her."

"We'll find her eventually. I've got quite a few questions I'd like to ask, not to mention wanting to thank her."

"Do you think we can find proof Ray had people at the institution killed for helping me escape? Franklin died that night."

"Eventually, yes, we'll tie him to Franklin and the rest of it. Not sure if whoever's funding his operation condones murder. Enough of this ordeal for now. Let's talk about your future. I've spoken at length to my brothers and the guys. We can stay here, add a lab for studying biotechnology, plant genetics, whatever you need."

"I've always wanted a simple life and to study what I choose without someone looking over my shoulder. But first, I want to find the other captives."

"We'll find them. And we'll have help from Kenson."

"Since this woman, Penny, helped me, I'd like to find her before we take on the Think Tank. If she's special like me, or in any capacity, she'd be a good fit for our team."

"Agreed. Let's take today and rest. We'll start researching the institution and begin planning our first op in the morning. Sound okay?"

"Fine, Nate, but all this is procrastination. Do you *not* want me?"

A harsh noise ended that debate.

Nate rose from the couch and led her to sit on the bed. His touch was so soft, treating her like a fragile vase, so contrary to the heat in his gaze.

"Are you sure your leg is healed enough for this?"

He smiled. "I'll let you be the judge of that. Feels like I've waited forever for you. The last four days in the hospital were torture." His wide stance and arched brow as he laid her down declared the matter settled. "Wait there, just like that."

She understood his need to soak in the moment. It was the same feeling engulfing her body and soul.

Tension became a sinuous prowl through her chest while anticipation tightened her belly.

Striking a long matchstick, he lit the candles covering every surface of the room. It'd been one of her tips picked up on the art of seduction.

"I haven't thanked you for saving our lives." The smile overtaking his mouth spoke of devious calculation and endless carnal pleasure. "How're you feeling? Any irritation around the piercing?"

"No, none."

"How many times in the past week have I dreamed of this?"

"Something we've shared."

"Callie..." His pupils dilated with his stalk forward.

Maybe his countenance and voice softened because he thought her inexperience would bring uncertainty, or perhaps the sexual hunger looming between them cautioned him to move slowly. For weeks, he'd used mutual attraction for diversions to further her training. Now, he would unleash every skill in his romantic arsenal to shatter her world.

She gulped as he nudged her to slide over.

She'd laid the top cover back that morning, exposing cool, crisp sheets now adding new and contrasting sensations.

There was possession both in his voice and in his gaze, one declaring he'd cherish and protect her with his last breath. She'd never get enough of him.

Her ability to reason dissipated when he cocked his head to the side and smiled. A fathomless hunger rolled through her soul to curl around her heart. Excitement overwhelmed the tension trickling down her spine.

The bed gave under the weight of his knee as he leaned over and placed his hands on either side of her head.

His arched brow stopped the words she thought to utter while a sensuous flame unfurling in her abdomen kept her in a state of craving.

Thankful he hadn't asked her to speak, she tried to swallow the lump in her throat. With no sign of moisture in her mouth, it was a moot point.

Nothing could stop the groan from escaping her throat.

"I'm gonna make you come till you're exhausted, then—I'll fill you and drive you even farther."

When his words cut through the haze of her confusion, all she could do was stare, dumbfounded.

The way he always saw to her needs doubled her anticipation as much as the simmering heat in his gaze.

The lightest of strokes evoked panting breaths that allowed only her broken whimpers to fill the air. Conscious thought failed to form coherent concepts in light of their combined passion.

The unspoken need revealed in his possessive gaze arose from their connection first formed at his club, nurtured and expanded until it filled her soul. He would always need her, want her, and protect her.

Never in her life had she dreamed of such an experience. His ability to make her feel, to soar to new heights, surpassed anything she'd ever known.

Afterward, when Nate readjusted their positions so she cuddled against his chest, she was where she belonged.

In his eyes shone everything she'd ever need, passion, protectiveness, and love. The connection they shared was a force beyond imagination. From first contact, they'd formed a spiritual link.

Now, their union was complete.

Still, he held her gaze, bonded by passion.

Never in her existence had she seen such emotion in another human being, a timeless unspoken promise to love for eternity. She hadn't thought anything would compare to the feeling of laying curled against him, his heart beating under her palm.

"This completes me in a way I've never imagined. I love you, Nate." The soft hair under her touch felt so at odds with the corded muscles of his chest. The aftermath of their loving would always be one of her favorite times.

"*Mmm*, I never thought listening to you snore would be on my to-do list, but I think it'll be keeping me awake at night, just to take it all in. I love you, too, Callie."

"I don't snore."

"*Uh-huh*. You're worse than Faith."

She wasn't aware she'd fallen asleep until he woke her by lightly stroking his fingers down her neck and upper chest. Everything about him instilled peace in her world.

"You're thinking too hard. Let's have it."

"You asked me once if I loved Jake. I understand better now, what I felt."

A quiet intake of breath and he stilled.

"I cared for Jake and Franklin very much. We'd grown close, kind of what I feel toward Blade and the rest of the team."

"The bond of family."

"In addition, I could never imagine sharing with them what we have."

"Well, not if you want your hide to remain intact." The grazing of his hand down her back took the sting out of his words. A sigh of satisfaction reverberated against her cheek.

"Nate, I love it here."

"We'll stay, add an office, lab, whatever you need."

"There's something about this place I never thought I'd find. Peace."

"Are you sore, sweetheart?"

"Just a little."

"Are we going to continue training?" The lazy circles she created on his chest advanced lower. His quick intake of breath signaled her effectiveness.

"Yes. I want you prepared for whatever some bastard might throw at us. We'll take another two or three days off, and then resume our drills and exercises. I think Spirit has some new challenges for you."

"Ugh. I was wondering if we'd go to the club again. Also—I would love to sing. There's such a freedom with letting go..."

"Count on it, sweetheart. Count on it."

After a kiss that stole her breath, he once again settled his body over hers.

Sitting in Nate's lap at dinner offered a sense of contentment she'd come to crave. A lifetime of it wouldn't be enough. "I don't know how to thank you guys. I've never felt like I fit in anywhere before."

"Your peace of mind stems from finding where you belong." Spirit's words usually hit the heart of the matter. For all his wisdom and calm demeanor, there now existed a certain restlessness about him that spread to the others. Apparently, they all had something to say.

"Yes, I do feel like I belong. What about you guys? Now that I'm free, what will you do?"

"Darlin', we're not going anywhere. We've been put back on selective active duty and each given relocation funds. We all want to bring Ray down." Blade's determined smile replicated in each man present.

"Speaking of Ray. During my imprisonment, I never got access to the information leading to the other prisoners..."

"Is next on our to-do list after we locate Penny and Nate is healed. You also need a little more training under your belt first." Virus opened the laptop beside him and powered it up. "I've been doing research, but ran into firewalls I can't breech."

Callie smiled. "More than happy to help. But I think his standalone is where we'll hit the jackpot."

"I've got ideas for training drills." Spirit smiled and gazed at the melting snow. "How do you feel about mud?"

Groans filled the kitchen, along with smiles and mumbled complaints. Each man would already be contriving scenarios to outdo the other.

Together, they'd find and free other captives, maybe expanding her makeshift family. "What do we know about Penny?"

"She may have saved us all by cutting the connection between Sebastian and the foreign bastards." Nate raised his cup of coffee in salute. "To finding Penny."

Each man raised his drink in a toast.

Blade pointed to the backyard. "I'll be living just west of you guys."

"I've always fancied a cabin in the woods. Virus and I are gonna build a cabin to the south. He's afraid to live alone." Nerd's smirk was rewarded with a muffin tossed at his head.

Callie halted its motion and floated it down to Nerd's plate.

"Whisper and I will build on the north side. The government won't know it, but they're also funding short interconnecting underground tunnels, along with a small room, a private space, should you ever need it." Spirit arched a brow in Nate's direction.

"I don't know what to say. You all have done so much for me. I will be forever grateful."

"Sweetheart, just say thank you and that you accept. Otherwise, I think the guys might lynch me." Nate's caress along her shoulders distracted her from his words.

"Not a bad idea. I've got plenty of rope." Blade pushed back his chair to stand.

Before he'd taken two steps around the table, Spirit stood then stepped before her. When he knelt to one knee, she had no idea what to do.

"What the hell?" Nate's low growl didn't faze Spirit's determination.

"Callie. You saved our lives last week. There's no way Jackson would've allowed us to live. I will be forever grateful. If you need anything, just ask." The sincerity in Spirit's gaze matched the tone of his voice.

She swallowed hard as the Native American stood and started clearing the table. Within the next few minutes, each man came to stand before her, thanking her, accepting her for who and what she'd become.

The End

Thank you for reading SILENT DEPTHS.

Callie McKellen has gained her freedom. Can she find Penny before Ray captures them both? Accepting her talent and honing her skills, she vows to find others held prisoner and set them free. Follow her journey in Shadow Guard as the Crofton men band together and hunt the predators preying on prodigies.

Shadow Guard

Light reflecting off something shiny flashed across his face, the blip startling him even as it disappeared. Seventy-five yards west, a small movement among the pine trees caught his eye. Last time he'd trekked through the woods, squirrels weren't using light-reflecting materials to spy on neighbors.

Even if Daniele were so inclined to teach woodland creatures the wonders of high-tech equipment, she'd instill proper manners. Considering her way with animals, she probably could.

Why is someone spying on the clinic?

A multitude of possibilities ranged from the normal drugs a vet would stock to catching a young woman leaving the office alone.

Darius alerted to Marc's reaction and the stranger's presence, sniffing the air to catch the voyeur's scent. Crouched and ready to spring, the shepherd's tight posture balanced aggression and self-discipline that could uncoil in a second's notice.

"Darius, *sook*! Find him, boy."

Various scenarios warped previous fantasies until his anger's slow burn urged him faster toward the woods. The previous night's snow continued to melt, making his passage slick.

With such a strong lead, the intruder would make it to the highway before Darius brought him down. Of all the Schutzhund dogs he'd trained, this shepherd held the most promise, but was still limited by the force with which his paws could strike the ground. His air-scenting ability had dazzled judges and trainers alike during his first trial. At least, now, they had the bastard's scent.

If the slick operator who just hit on Dani doubled as a stalker, Marc would take great pleasure in *educating* the man. If they couldn't catch him, he'd escort Dani home and ensure she had a good security system, then return Monday for a cozy little chat with Hutson.

"Darius, *gib laut*!"

After the dog's initial flash through thick underbrush, Marc followed the trail of moving briars and brambles until the shepherd advanced out of sight.

Come on, boy. Tell me where you are.

A deep-throated growl directed Marc's course adjustment down a small gorge through thick briars and tangles of viney undergrowth, over fallen trees, and the small, slow-moving stream.

Marshy water splashed his jeans at the water's edge, the soft, muddy ground sucking at his booted heel. Balance became a precious commodity after stepping on a black snake.

Ahead, the slam of a vehicle's door acknowledged his prey finding safety as the steep incline slowed Marc's progress. Squealing tires coincided with an engine's roar.

Yelling the command, "Darius, *platz,*" didn't guarantee his dog would obey and lay down instead of chasing the vehicle.

By the time Marc crested the hill at the wood's edge, Darius sat quietly by the road, huffing and whining his frustration.

"Damn it. Didn't even get a look at the truck. At least you got the bastard's scent. We'll find him." Bending down, he rubbed his canine's head. "Let's get back and see Dani home. I'll let Dr. Carari know something here has peaked a dirtball's interest."

Darius reluctantly circled to heel on command, continued fleeting glances down the one-lane dirt road holding his attention. Intermittent rumbles from his chest declared the battle unfinished.

"Wonder if that was Hutson? He didn't strike me as stupid or incompetent. I think I'll do some digging this afternoon and see if I can find him. Damn thing is, he came in after us and left before we did, so I didn't get a look at his ride. I've little to go on. Shame the vet's office doesn't have security cameras." Something he intended to mention during his talk with the good doctor.

When he'd returned to the office, Dani's car was pulling off the lot. Considering her cornered and spooked demeanor, he wondered if she'd show at the dog trial.

Reily's Books

Romantic Thrillers

McAllister Justice Series

Tender Echoes
Digital Velocity
Bound By Shadows
Inconclusive Evidence
Carbon Replacements
Shattered Reflections
Remnants of Evil

Moonlight and Murder Series

Shifting Targets
A Critical Tangent
Pivotal Decisions
Seeds of Murder
An Unlikely Grave
Deadly Interception
Love You To Death

Bayou Murders Series

Perfect In Death

Psychic Thrillers

Mind Stalkers

Bending Fate
Silent Depths
Shadow Guard
Whispers Beyond Death
Mind Hunters

Paranormal Romance

Immortal Lovers Series

Unholy Alliance

Blood Union

Standalone paranormal romance
Tiago

About Reily

Reily Garrett is a writer, mother, and companion to three long coat German shepherds. When not working with her dogs, she's sitting at her desk with her fur kids by her side.

Author of chilling suspense and snarky romance, her stories span the distance of romantic thrillers, paranormal romance, and erotic romance. Regardless of genre, each book delves into a dark and twisted imagination yet is tempered with romance and a touch of humor.

Reviews by Kirkus Reviews, San Francisco Bay Review, and BestThrillers.com best describe her work:

"This could be James Patterson, Lee Child, and Tess Gerritsen rolled into one, but the dark, twisted methods used by the serial killer could surprise even those readers..." - San Francisco Bay Review

"...steamy, seductive police procedural..." - BestThrillers.com

"...well-researched thriller that remains romantically genuine throughout." - Kirkus Review

Prior experience in the Military Police, private investigations, and as an ICU nurse gives her fiction a real-world flavor. Find Reily below.

Made in the USA
Coppell, TX
24 July 2024